Because I
Said
So

Praise for the works of Karin Kallmaker

My Lady Lipstick

Kallmaker fans and newcomers, both, will delight in this new tale. It has a well-written plot with innovative character drama and a love story that doesn't disappoint. The romance sparkles, the characters are enchanting, and their struggles are fascinating. Don't miss the distinctive pink cover, likely a tongue-in-cheek reference to "Anita's" grumble about her own covers! *My Lady Lipstick* is an intelligent and charming work that's sure to please.

- Lambda Literary Review

My Lady Lipstick is one heck of a ride and I loved every page. There were so many lovely touches that added layers to the story. I especially loved the gaming references, the baking and cooking and the depth of the characters. Both characters are expertly drawn and easy to love. I appreciated that Kallmaker made one a wonderfully complex and relatable butch. We need more butch women who are more than just one-dimensional characters. There is also something particularly special about this book. I can't quite put my finger on what it is, but there is no doubt that this going to be one of my favourites.

- The Lesbian Review

Karin Kallmaker writes exceedingly good romances, and this one is a masterful mixture of a fun tale, delightful characters and her wicked sense of humour. It isn't full of laugh out loud moments, but the more subtle wit that raises a smile at the play on words and the sarcastic banter. Add in Shakespearean character flaws along with the essential growth of our leading ladies and we have a classic. The whole is a perfectly wrapped bundle of enjoyment for anyone who likes a good romance.

- Lesbian Reading Room

With this two likable characters, some great secondary characters and her usual mature writing style, Kallmaker told us a very interesting story of deception, loneliness, vulnerability, broken dreams (and bones), family... and, of course, love. ... *My Lady Lipstick* is a well-written story that I really liked and can easily recommend. If you have never read any of Karin Kallmaker's books (she has written nearly thirty novels; what are you waiting for!?), this one can be a good start.

- Pin's Reviews, *goodreads*

I was also really happy with the pace of the book. I would say the book is slightly longer than average, but it never really lagged for me. I never felt bored, and really enjoyed the actual concept of the book. When it came to the romance, at first I thought maybe the characters had jumped into bed a little fast. But with how the rest of the story unfolded, I was okay with it. There was no rushing to say "I love you." I actually really appreciate that as it seems to happen too often lately in lesfic romances. The romance instead felt like it progressed really organically. Not including the one angsty part, I actually felt the romance was one of the more realistic romances I have read in a while.

This was absolutely the right romance at the right time for me. I enjoyed this read and I hope others do as much as I did. If you are a Kallmaker fan, I believe you will be happy with this read.

- Lex Kent's Reviews, *goodreads*

The Kiss That Counted

For years CJ Roshe has lived with the fear that "The Gathering" would find her and make her pay for turning against them. Constantly looking over her shoulder she has meticulously created a new life with no room for close friends or lovers who might ask too many questions. But her carefully constructed life begins to unravel when she falls in love with the beautiful

Karita... Full of suspense and mystery, award-winning Karin Kallmaker pens another page-turner that draws the reader in with her deeply moving characters and storytelling.

- Cecilia Martin, *Lambda Book Report*

The Kiss That Counted is Kallmaker at her finest—a not to be missed romance. She offers us characters with depth and dimension, along with a rich plot, peppered with an air of mystery to keep the reader turning pages long into the night. Read it to see if CJ will be able to take control of her past and if Karita will ever be able to let down her defenses to allow someone in again. Finally, read it to see if the kiss really counted.

- Anna Furtado, *Just About Write*

Kallmaker has used the darkness of Roshe and the glow of Hanssen to tell a story filled with mystery, excitement and danger. *The Kiss That Counted* is a gripping story that will delight Kallmaker fans, and win her many more.

- R. Lynne, *Just About Write*

There is a romance here, but there is also a bit of a mystery as the reader begins to wonder what CJ's secret is and how she will resolve the problem once it is revealed. In the end, *The Kiss That Counted* is also a testimony to friendship and the changes it can cause in a person's life. Kallmaker shows with the skill in this book why she deserves such a large fan following.

- Lynne Pierce, *Just About Write*

Love by the Numbers

First class rom-com! A wonderful witty romance and a great tale of character development and growth... The romance is sweet and the sex is hot, all in all this had my dopamine, seratonin and oxytocin levels creeping higher and higher.

- *The Lesbian Reading Room*

The love story is engaging and is filled with just the right amount of tension to make the nerve endings buzz as Nicole and Lily learn to adapt to the inevitable result of their growing passion for one another. The characters are appealing in spite of—or perhaps because of—the secrets each one holds, preventing them from opening their hearts. The story line is appealing and draws the reader in. It's also filled with that tongue-in-cheek, ever-so-sassy humor that Kallmaker does so well... Another win!

- Lambda Literary Review

Engrossing, Romantic and Sexy... Kallmaker's writing is so vivid—she paints the picture so wonderfully it's as if I'm right there with the characters, seeing what they are seeing, smelling the same aromas, tasting the same food. It's wonderful! I've never been to the places Nicole and Lily visit, but that doesn't matter. They are brought to life so beautifully I feel as if I have a scrapbook of my own... *Love by the Numbers* is another of Kallmaker's books that has been added to my "re-read" pile.

- Frivolous Views

Maybe Next Time

No "formula" romance, *Maybe Next Time* is an engrossing, compelling story of redemption, healing and surviving. Kallmaker has explored complicated themes and done so with heart and a touch of humor. In this reader's opinion, it is one of her best novels.

- Midwest Book Review

Maybe Next Time, winner of a Lambda Literary Award for Romance, has everything readers expect from a love story, but with an edge... Filled with angst, sensitivity, intimacy, and joy, *Maybe Next Time* delivers a memorable tale. With flawed but likeable main characters, an intriguing plot with many surprises, award-winning prose and flawless editing, this five-star novel epitomizes great romantic fiction. And in this reader's opinion, Karin Kallmaker tells it beautifully.

- Just About Write

Painted Moon

Painted Moon is a classic that could very well become the next *Curious Wine*.

- Lesbian Review of Books

Painted Moon has what this reader considers classic Kallmaker elements with interesting characters, wry wit and steamy love scenes. (Some of the images of Jackie and Leah have lingered in my mind for years.) If you missed this title the first time around, or if you are new to Kallmaker's novels, pick up a copy of *Painted Moon* and bask its glow.

- Midwest Book Review

Warming Trend

Kallmaker has given us insight into human emotion along with beautiful descriptions of the Alaskan glacial terrain. *Warming Trend* will teach as well as entertain, and the broken relationship between Eve and Ani will have the reader on tenterhooks until the end.

- Anna Furtado, Just About Write

Kallmaker has given her fans a beautifully written novel, complete with breathtaking descriptions of Alaska. Hers is not the Alaska of the cruise lines, but the heart of Alaska, with particular attention to its glaciers, ice, and northern lights... She has told her story with great language, wit, and warmth. She's even included a very large, very lovable dog. If you're a

Kallmaker fan, or if you're new to her work, *Warming Trend* is not to be missed.

- R. Lynne Watson, *Just About Write*

Substitute for Love

Kallmaker is a genius. I loved the angst, the drama and the passion... The story construction is fantastic. You get a really personal point of view from both characters. This takes a gifted storyteller, but never fear Kallmaker is here.

- *The Lesbian Review*

What would you do for someone you loved? It's easy to say you'd climb mountains and swim oceans, but when faced with a desperate choice, what would you do? That's the dilemma facing Reyna in Karin Kallmaker's newest, and I think, darkest novel... Kallmaker does a fine job exploring the anguish of Reyna's life, and the second plot, concerning a mathematician, is equally well-developed. Her major and minor characters are credible and spirited, a pleasure to meet and, sometimes, to hate. *Substitute for Love* may just be the best Kallmaker I've read in a long time, and given her extraordinary talent, that's saying something.

- Deborah Pffeifer, *Bay Area Reporter*

I've never been big on reading romance novels, which is why I'm so surprised to come to the revelation that I'm hooked on Karin Kallmaker's books... *Substitute for Love* is no exception. It doesn't seem likely for Holly, who is in a long-term straight relationship, to get involved with Reyna, who writes press releases and articles for a conservative, anti-gay Christian group, but it happens. As the story unfolds, Holly finds out some secrets about her past, while we find out the reason why Reyna has the job she has. This may be one of Karin Kallmaker's best and most engrossing books yet.

- Deborah DiRusso, *Womyn's Words*

Her plots are textured, her characters are engaging, her sex scenes are intense, and her prose style is better than workmanlike—she's the lesbian hybrid of Joyce Carol Oates (if Oates wrote briefer, less bleak books) and Danielle Steele (if Steele wrote well). *Substitute for Love* continues Kallmaker's string of darn good reads... That Kallmaker renders the tortuous travails of Holly and Reyna quite plausible is one of her novel's many charms.

- Richard LaBonte, *Book Marks*

In Karin Kallmaker's *Substitute for Love*, the undisputed Mistress of Romance skillfully weaves a tale of longing, need, and desire, creating a story complete with mystery, good guys, bad guys, tender moments, humor, and raw sexuality. Kallmaker continues her tradition of painstaking research in her latest work. Unlike some romance writers, she again creates new backgrounds and occupations for her heroines, while interweaving this information with their characters, interactions, and the storyline itself.

- Therese Szymanski, *Lambda Book Report*

When you purchase from the publisher more of your dollars reach the women who write and produce the books you love. Karin thanks you for your support of books for and about women who love women!

Other Bella Books by Karin Kallmaker

18th & Castro
Above Temptation
All the Wrong Places
Captain of Industry
Car Pool
Christabel
The Dawning
Embrace in Motion
Finders Keepers
Frosting on the Cake: The Original
Frosting on the Cake: Second Helpings
In Every Port
Just Like That
The Kiss that Counted
Love by the Numbers
Making Up for Lost Time
Maybe Next Time
My Lady Lipstick
Night Vision
One Degree of Separation
Painted Moon
Paperback Romance
Roller Coaster
Stepping Stone
Substitute for Love
Sugar
Touchwood
Unforgettable
Warming Trend
Watermark
Wild Things

About the Author

Karin Kallmaker has been exclusively devoted to lesbian fiction since the publication of her first novel in 1989. As an author published by the storied Naiad Press, she worked with Barbara Grier and Donna McBride and has been fortunate to be mentored by a number of editors, including Katherine V. Forrest.

In addition to multiple Lambda Literary Awards, she has been featured as a Stonewall Library and Archives Distinguished Author. Other accolades include the Ann Bannon Popular Choice and other awards for her writing, as well as the selection as a Trailblazer by the Golden Crown Literary Society. She is best known for novels such as *Painted Moon, Substitute for Love, Captain of Industry, Maybe Next Time,* and *The Kiss that Counted.*

The California native is the mother of two and blogs at kallmaker.com. Write to her at karin@kallmaker.com, visit her website https://kallmaker.com, or search for "Kallmaker" on social media—there's only one.

Because I Said So

Karin Kallmaker

BELLA
BOOKS
2019

Bella Books, Inc.
P.O. Box 10543
Tallahassee, FL 32302

Printed in the United States of America on acid-free paper.

First Bella Books Edition 2019

Editor: Medora MacDougall
Cover Designer: LJ Hill
Cover photo: Sweet Coffee Morning ID 67534379 © Nikolay Litov | Dreamstime.com

ISBN: 978-1-64247-073-4

Dedication

To the readers, who are with me when I write every word. I just can't quit you, but then, I'm not trying to.

To my all-grown-up kids, Kelson and Lee, who inspired pieces of this story. My son I'm sure would wish me to point out that UCLA is not the best University of California school, UC San Diego is. Physics is going to save the world, Mom. My daughter passionately pursues the ideal that the arts save people, one at a time. They are, of course, both right.

Twenty-Nine, a prime number and a good omen.

References to Characters from Other Novels

Jennifer Lamont-*Stepping Stone, Captain of Industry*
Suzanne Mason-*Captain of Industry*

CHAPTER ONE

"You can't get married!" Kesa Sapiro knew she was shouting and the neighbors would bang on the wall, but sometimes it was the only way Josie could hear her.

Her sister stomped one booted foot. "I knew you'd be against it. You never want me to have anything of my own."

The accusation was unfair and Josie even looked shamefaced as she said it. Or Kesa wanted to believe she did. "You don't even know this boy. Date him. But why get married?"

The truculent expression mutated instantly to one of besotted dreaminess, the same face Josie had displayed for years over pop stars and hunky actors. "Because we're in love, Key. We're meant for each other. We knew it the moment we met."

"That's absurd. You're not a kid anymore. Are you pregnant?" Kesa's blood raced in panic at the thought. They couldn't afford a child, and she was sure this boy had as much money as Josie did, which was none.

Josie's eyes widened in outrage. "As if! I met him three weeks ago. Besides, we're very, *very* careful. Paz and I both agree that we want to be parents, but not now."

"Then what's the hurry? Lots of people live together."

The dreamy expression was back. "I want a ring on him—he's gorgeous and thoughtful and kind and smart."

Kesa forced herself to take a calmer tone. She sat back down on the couch, instinctively avoiding the one spot where the cushions dipped precipitously. "If it takes a ring to keep him, you won't keep him."

"What do you know about it? Your last date was at least two years ago. Just because you can't find anyone doesn't mean love isn't real."

"I work, remember?" So much for calm. "My own business, and every single day. I don't have time to date."

Josie crossed her arms and lifted her chin. "I'm making time."

"Plenty of time for it when I pay all the bills—"

Josie rolled her eyes at a nonexistent audience. "Here we go."

They'd had this argument before, but Josie never seemed to get it. "You're only nineteen. You can't get married."

"Yes, I can. It's legal. I do not need your permission and I wouldn't even if you were my mother. Which you are not."

Kesa bit back a furious assertion that she'd done every last damn thing mothers were supposed to do for the last twelve years. "But you want me to help arrange this wedding and pay for it, right?"

Josie's gaze narrowed to angry slits. "I want you there because you're my sister."

First time that was the reason for anything, Kesa thought bitterly. If they kept at this, she was going to say that aloud, and she'd regret it. "This is absurd. I'm going to be late to the fitting in West Hollywood."

"Fine, you don't want to talk about it. But I'm still getting married."

"When I was nineteen I wasn't thinking about love and romance." Why bring up that having a love life—especially a lesbian one—would have heightened the scrutiny from Child Services? Her position had been precarious enough as it was. "I had to work, and I'm still working."

"Don't remind me what a burden I have always been to you."

"That's not what I meant, Jo-Jo." But sometimes, Lord help her, that was exactly what Kesa meant. Twelve years of being big-sister-turned-mother hadn't been easy. Their heads were finally above water, and now that Josie might be able to stand on her own two feet just a little more, go to college, have control over her own life, she wanted to give that all up for a boy. "We will talk about this later, but I can't be late. The fitting is for a big star—"

Josie waved a hand in dismissal. "I know, and she might say your name to the right people and we'll be rich, like Mom and Dad were."

"Word of mouth is the only thing that keeps new clients calling. It is everything in my business. I might finally be able to afford a workshop and we can finally have a living room without all this stuff." She gestured at the two sewing machines, the dressmaker dummies and the huge stack of fabric bolts, and coiled trim, thread, and glue supplies. It had been months since they'd opened the curtains. Half the living room and hallway of their tiny two-bedroom apartment was filled with the tools and supplies of her trade. She longed for a bedroom that didn't have the folding table she used to cut cloth leaning against the far side of her narrow, cold bed.

"You've been saying that for years." Josie's shrug was infuriating.

"No, I've been working for it for years. That's how you get what you want, not with dreams and wishes." Kesa pressed her lips together. Josie was already turning away and pulling her phone out of her pocket. "We'll talk about this when I get back."

"Whatever." The door to Josie's bedroom closed a little too loudly.

Kesa carefully transported the garment bag to her battered hatchback. After hanging it on the rung mounted across the cargo area, she said a little prayer and was rewarded by the car starting up without its usual histrionics.

At least today she didn't look like a junkyard on wheels. Usually, with the backseats folded down and master Tetris skills fully deployed, the car held a short folding table, portable sewing machine, fabric bolts, and two dressmaker dummies—enough for fitting out a bridal party. Her lack of a workshop meant she always went to her clients. Her flexibility had brought her to the notice of higher profile clients, like the one she was fitting today, on a sunny spring Sunday afternoon when other people were walking at the beach or having a coffee and eating muffins while they talked about books and movies and flirted with their perfect blond hair and perfect teeth smiles and enjoyed their perfect electronics and perfect lives.

That was life in La-La Land, according to commercials and TV. It had never been her life.

The traffic from Echo Park on 101 was slow in all directions, but no worse than usual for a weekend afternoon. She opted for the longer but less brutal surface route that skirted the Silver Lake neighborhood as she wended her way toward Hollywood. Her destination was where the storied Sunset and Santa Monica boulevards met and a condominium tower she had never thought she'd visit. Filipino daughters of once-wealthy parents didn't keep up with Kardashians.

Josie didn't really remember what it had been like to be rich, but Kesa did. Nor did Josie seem to understand—or really want to—that their parents had abandoned the Philippines ahead of the mob that was after anyone who had enjoyed the largess of a despot. They'd grabbed the money and jewelry they could and headed for the American Dream to have babies and live large. Their one precious gift to their daughters was their birthplace of Los Angeles. Josie knew kids at school who'd lived in LA almost all of their lives, but had no immigration status. On top of everything else, at least Kesa hadn't been terrified of being deported.

A decade in Los Angeles had left their parents broke. Josie had only been a bit of a bump in her mother's stomach on the February day her father, without warning, had driven Kesa to a new school, a public one that was free. She never spoke to any of her private school friends after that. No more ski trips, no more shopping at the bookstore, no more allowance for school clubs and field trips. Just when Kesa had finally adapted to the new school, they'd moved. Moved again, and again, one bewildering step after another. She was fifteen and Josie still a toddler before she realized that their moves were prompted by bill collectors. If her parents had practiced even the tiniest amount of prudence there might have been something for their daughters to live on when they and their latest BMW skidded on a wet road into a wall of concrete. There hadn't even been insurance to help with a funeral. She and Josie had had eight days to leave the house that was four months behind on rent.

That had been the first hard, bitter decision of Kesa's new life as a nineteen-year-old adult with a seven-year-old dependent. No money for a funeral, so there hadn't been one. She'd spent the time in government offices full of people like her, applying for assistance to get through a really rough patch. She and Josie had been on the verge of being homeless, and the Child Services people wanted to take Josie away the moment Kesa failed at any test.

She'd put the living over the dead. Every last dollar she had and anything she could sell had found them a studio apartment she could rent by the week. She'd turned to the only skill she had, sewing, and bitterly thanked a mother who had decided there was no point paying for fashion up-touches to her outfits, not when she had a child who could learn to do it for free. Kesa had been so good at it that she'd brought home projects for her to do as "favors" for friends. Halfway through high school Kesa had figured out that her mother was collecting gifts and tips from the friends. Nevertheless, her ability to quickly hem silk by hand had kept her and Josie in rent and basic food.

Josie didn't remember—or didn't want to remember—that Child Services had visited regularly. Kesa had finally given up trying to pay off the debts she'd inherited and declared bankruptcy, losing access to credit for years. Living on cash had garnered plenty of suspicion as to its source from landlords and social workers. Kesa had been tasked dozens of times to verify that she could make ends meet working from home, that Josie had regular meals and rarely missed school. Keeping them together had been priority number one. They'd eaten a lot of noodles, beans, generic peanut butter, and vegetables from dented cans.

The plain containers with her parents' ashes had sat gathering dust in a corner until one bleak night during a rare rainstorm she'd driven to a park she didn't know and poured them into a hole she dug with a plastic cup and her bare hands.

She'd been so angry. She was still angry. And afraid every day of losing everything she'd worked for through the caprice of other people.

Fear had already cost her a promising relationship—she'd clung so fast, and so hard, that the other woman had slipped through her fingers. Since then she'd decided she didn't have time to date. She hardly cared that she knew she was lying. It got her through lonely nights. Their lives were still precarious and the dynamic of a third person would have risked the delicate balance she worked so hard to maintain.

And now, she reminded herself with a shock, Josie wanted to do precisely that. She could not get married. She just couldn't.

Offshore fog had cooled the afternoon and sitting at a stoplight with the windows down was no hardship, especially since her favorite radio station tuned in well in this part of LA. The tinny speakers didn't do justice to Prince and the sports car next to her was pulsating with the thump of its own bass speakers. Didn't matter. The fight with Josie had left her shaken, but no elevator was going to bring her down from enjoying the fresh air.

She'd been extra stressed lately and knew that was part of her anxious, hostile reaction to Josie's big news. With the dream of having an actual workshop space almost realized, her gut told her that someone or something would snatch it away, like everything else. Lucky Josie lived like a butterfly when Kesa had to keep both eyes on potential predators.

She had hoped to leave thirty minutes earlier, but when Josie said she needed to talk, it was always some kind of bombshell. Two months ago it had been finding the meaning of life through watercolors and now there were stacks of portfolio sheets alongside Kesa's fabric bolts. Six months ago it had been joining a traveling musical group to master her passion for guitar. A year ago the passion had been filmmaking.

And now it was a boy.

As she turned onto Sunset and began the hunt for a parking space, she put Josie out of her mind to focus on the work. The actress she was working for was a huge name. The dress was for a charity awards gala, the kind of event where a Wang or Chanel gown would be ostentatiously out of place. Instead, the guest of honor wanted a gown designed and made locally, simpler in the details and fabric, and fitted perfectly. And increasingly, for exactly the right dress for the right occasion, a number of A-listers were calling on Kesa Sapiro.

She'd learned over the years that celebrities were people— kind, rude, dismissive, appreciative. The gamut. But none of them had a minute to waste. Being late was taken as disrespectful and wasn't tolerated more than once. Some of them liked to gossip and expected Kesa to Tweet about the wonder of working with them, but most didn't. She'd signed plenty of non-disclosure agreements—nobody wanted their measurements on Instagram. She stayed completely focused on the work, watched carefully, and listened hard. A flick of an eyebrow could be the difference between a one hundred percent-satisfied customer and utter disaster.

She circled the block again, hoping against hope someone would leave. Parking was the worst part of the gig. The best part was Lamont herself. You always knew where you stood with Jennifer Lamont. She was one of the ruling stateswomen of Hollywood and a plum to have as a client. This was her third gown for Lamont and she'd landed two other clients from direct referral, and that was why a workshop was finally a possible dream. Celebrities paid well, and gladly, for personal service and quality.

Lamont was friendly, but distant, and Kesa respected those boundaries. The star didn't need to know that Kesa had seen all of her movies and every episode of every TV show she'd been on and been thrilled to the absolute moon to discover her idol was also a lesbian.

"There's one!" The best thing about driving a cramped hatchback was winning at the parking wars. She slammed on the brakes, U-turned and parallel parked it into a space, leaving a double-wide Hummer to search elsewhere. She was only five minutes early instead of her preferred fifteen for Lamont.

The doorman in the exclusive building knew her, and had been instructed to let her up to the penthouse foyer where she could wait in privacy. Directly opposite the elevator was a clothing rack to hang her garment bag. A little bar-height table and chair were in full view of the security camera. There was already a dry cleaner's bag waiting—it looked like a tuxedo for Lamont's wife, unless Lamont was going full Marlene Dietrich somewhere.

A delicious and distracting thought she would mull over later.

Glad to have a moment to compose herself, she took advantage of the electrical outlet next to the chair to add some juice to her phone. Service providers like her waited on the celebrity, not the other way around, but at least Lamont made it comfortable. She checked her hair and smoothed the velvet collar on her oxford blouse, glad she hadn't been so frazzled she'd forgotten to change. Nobody wanted to buy *haute couture* from a disheveled designer.

Josie had resumed churning in her thoughts when the elevator dinged and Jennifer Lamont strode out. As usual, Kesa had a moment of vertigo being in her presence. Lamont was *vivid*, that was always the word Kesa thought of in response. The first impression was the deep blue eyes and full crimson lips, then the smoky dark hair, flawless ecru skin, and the kind of perfectly molded female curves that made Kesa doubt they were the same species. She reeled in her tongue and hopped down from the barstool.

Hard on Jennifer's heels was her wife, Suzanne Mason. She was even taller than Lamont and lanky. She was involved in tech and financing, which made her oodles of money. She seemed nice, was attractive in her own way, Kesa supposed. Her best feature was her smile, and she did plenty of that around Lamont.

Their palpable affection for each other made Kesa all the more aware of her own empty bed and empty prospects.

After greetings, Kesa ignored the stunning view and went directly to the bedroom that Lamont used as a wardrobe and dressing area. She set her tailoring kit on the small worktable and unzipped the garment bag.

Lamont breezed in, yelling over her shoulder, "Don't you dare put the last wall on without me." To Kesa she said, "Crazy woman thinks the Legos are all hers."

Kesa laughed. "This won't take long."

"I'd appreciate a few minutes to relax before the event," Lamont said as she unceremoniously stripped down to her undergarments. Kesa supposed in another setting she'd be having a heart attack, but her appreciation for Lamont's curves was purely professional at the moment. The last thing she wanted was for a client to get a skeevy vibe from her.

She shook the dress out of its bag and was pleased when Lamont exclaimed, "That's even more gorgeous than I expected—and I expected it to be beautiful. You're a genius."

The rich, blue silk was supple and enhanced with over-threading in the same shade that caught the light with a subtle glow. The color was what Kesa called "Lamont Sapphire" in her mind, and having made three dresses for Lamont now, she was always on the lookout for it in shops and catalogs. Retro cuts suited Lamont perfectly, and the gown was based on a 1930s Butterick cocktail dress pattern that featured a demure high collar in the front with a not-so-demure keyhole opening across the shoulder blades. Lamont had plenty of jewelry to suit the look, and the wall behind Kesa was lined with shoes that Kesa lusted after every time she saw them.

With the dress slipped over her head and hair adjusted, Kesa tsk'd at how the opening on the back fell and marked two places with pins. "Your bra is showing, but I can gather the top and bottom so it won't."

Lamont was looking at her silhouette over one shoulder. "Where will you hem it to?"

Kesa folded up the back over one calf and clipped it. "I was thinking about here. There's so much fabric that it will flatter at a slightly longer cut. The drape is better."

"That seems perfect. I was thinking mid-height heel. Those vintage Saks on the end there."

Kesa looked where Lamont was pointing and tried not to drool. "The silver lamé and gold satin T-straps? Those would be killer."

"Add a long string of pearls and I'm done. You've made this very easy."

Relief washed over Kesa. "I should have this ready in about twenty minutes," she said as she helped Lamont avoid the pins as she maneuvered out of the dress.

"I appreciate the time you take to put in these hidden zippers. I hate being sewn into clothes. Makes me feel trapped."

"And you never know when the zombies will be after you." Kesa hoped her reference to one of Lamont's most famous television roles wasn't over a boundary of some kind.

But Lamont laughed appreciatively as she wrapped herself in a white French terry robe. "I know, right? We can't fight with just our principles. I'll be down the hall. Call out when you want me back."

Kesa got down to work. Nobody liked hemming anything by hand, but delicate fabrics were easily ruined by machines. It was a meditative exercise, punctuated by the silver flash of the needle and the *shush* of the thread as she pulled it gently through the silk.

Twenty minutes later the hem and sleeves were done, and the dress looked smashing on Lamont, especially after she stepped into the gorgeous vintage shoes. Lamont's wife approved the dress, declaring that it made the nape of Lamont's neck the most sensuous two inches of skin on the planet.

Kesa was still smiling when she got back into her car, and her smile redoubled as she thought of the invoice she'd forward to Lamont's accountant tomorrow. They paid promptly—the deposit and three month's rent on the workshop space were nearly hers.

As she left the rising glitter of Santa Monica Boulevard behind, her thoughts of course returned to Josie. What was she going to do?

Josie was the age now Kesa had been that horrible day their parents had died. She had completely different choices than Kesa had faced with a grade school sister to feed and care for. She was on track for a degree from UCLA, courtesy of a hard-won mathematics scholarship. She could be anything, go anywhere, be almost anyone she chose to be. All horizons were open to her. Why on earth would she say no to all of them for a boy she'd met only weeks ago?

True love, picket fences, and the American Dream—how could Josie think they were gifts that fell from the sky instead of something you earned?

"Twoo wuv," Kesa muttered, "and mawiage." Josie was no Princess Buttercup and she was sure this boy was no knight in shining armor.

CHAPTER TWO

"You can't get married!" Shannon Dealan abruptly realized that Paz hadn't joined her laughter at the very idea. "Oh. You're serious."

"Very serious." Paz wasn't quite meeting her gaze, which meant he was anticipating a bad reaction.

Shannon set her mug on the marble breakfast bar that separated their small, efficient kitchen from the more generously sized living room. She'd suspected something was up with him for the past week. Phoenix Lopez had always shown his feelings on his sleeve, and he'd been acting almost secretive. Given their history, it had of course caught her attention. She'd worried that someone from his past had turned up or that he'd run afoul of some kind of Big Bad on campus or decided to champion a cause that led to dangerous people bringing their guns to the party.

It had never occurred to her that the issue might be romantic in nature. He'd shown little interest in dating, but then the last few years hadn't held lots of opportunities. "So tell me about this person."

His big brown baby deer eyes became liquid with emotion. "Her name is Josie and she's amazing."

"She must be. Tell me more."

He visibly relaxed. "She's really smart and interested in the same issues I am. That's how we met, at school, during the rally for *Nuestras Voces*. She's incredibly articulate, and very cute."

"When was this?"

"Three weeks ago." He said it with an odd mix of sheepishness and defiance.

"Is she...I mean, are you—"

"She isn't pregnant. We know perfectly well how that happens and we're not taking any chances. Yet."

"I'm glad you're careful." He was ready for her to protest that it was too soon to take such a big step, so she didn't. "Have you met her family?"

"Not yet. She lives with her big sister, who I gather is a bit of a hard-ass."

"The same could be said of me." Shannon kept her expression mild and interested while a voice inside her wailed, "After everything he's been through, he can't derail his life, he *can't*."

"That's true. You are a great big hard-ass."

They sipped their coffee in mutual silence. Shannon didn't know which particular memory of their shared journey Paz was recalling, but her mind went right back to the beginning when she'd seen a skinny, ragged teen in the yard next door who wanted to shoot hoops with kids a lot bigger than he was and they wouldn't let him. He'd persisted, day after day, tearful, sometimes angry. They said no and he came back. The older boys in their group home weren't exactly mean, but they weren't kind either.

The evening he'd been outside by himself, staring at the hoop with no basketball, had ended up magical for them both. Maybe it had been the emptiness of the house after her aunt's death or the realization that all of her aunt's warnings to keep a good distance from all those boys had robbed her of a simple pleasure neighbors could share. She had nothing to fear from a kid who just wanted to shoot hoops.

She'd hurriedly blown up the ancient basketball in the garage and they'd played one-on-one until the big kids had joined them. Their surprise had been palpable. She was one of the unnamed white lady neighbors, and they had awkwardly expressed sympathy when she told them the old lady who'd barked at them for years about their balls coming over the fence had passed away. They'd let the two of them finish their game, and after that, they'd let Paz play with them—if, they officiously fussed, he'd done his homework. They even asked her to fill out sides a couple of times. They'd all lived on the edge of Boyle Heights then. That was before The Incident.

"I want to hear all about Josie, I really do, but work is calling. Happy Monday." She finished the last of her coffee and began her ritual of making sure she had her credentials in her pocket and daypack with lunch, book, and declassified case reading she'd brought home Friday night. "Marriage is a huge step. You just got your application in for your master's program, and there's a lot of hard work in front of you. Marriage takes time and energy. It's not like dating."

He cocked an eyebrow and let silence convey his skepticism.

"Yes, I know. Never-married person giving you advice. I've never even been tempted," she lied. "You know I want what's best for you."

"I'm plenty old enough now to know what that is."

She didn't say that at thirty-nine she knew exactly how clueless she'd been when she was twenty. She'd always known she was a lesbian, but that didn't mean she'd known anything about love or sex or what could motivate people. He wouldn't be twenty-one until this summer. He wasn't even fully grown into his body yet. Some days, when he came into the kitchen in his ratty robe, yawning and eating cereal out of the box, he was every bit that skinny kid she'd just met.

As she slung her bag over her shoulder, he said, like he usually did when she went to work, "Be safe out there, *wey*."

She answered with her usual rejoinder of, "You too, dude," and added, "Campuses are scary places these days."

"You're telling me shit I already know."

"Language," she chided.

"Sorry," he said without any sign that he was.

She wanted to pat his cheek as she'd done when he was eleven, but his dignity no longer allowed endearments like that. "Leftover ravioli for dinner. It's your turn to shop. If you get spinach or arugula I'll make a salad to go with."

"Um, I was going to have dinner with Josie."

"Oh." It was a jolt. "More ravioli for me. Dinner or not, you still have to do the grocery shopping this week."

"Sure, I know." He waved as she closed the door and headed down the short, cobbled walk from the bungalow to the street.

It was a cool Southern California morning with yellow-orange sunshine pouring out of soft blue air. It was no hardship to walk the three blocks to the bus stop. Hill Street service was brisk and frequent, and she'd be downtown in fifteen minutes or so. She could drive, but she had better uses for the twenty-five dollars a day it cost to park near the Federal Courthouse.

The plum tree on the corner she used to benchmark the subtle change of seasons was snowing delicate white-pink blossoms across the sidewalk. Her footsteps puffed them back into the air in a delightful dance that felt like a touch of magic to start the day. The branches were covered with tight green sprigs of future leaves, which meant plenty of shade when the morning temperature was 90, not 65. Aunt Ryanne's house in Boyle Heights had had plum trees in the front yard too, and she was pleased that the new house she and Paz shared had reminders of the old neighborhood.

She leaned against the bus stop shelter, but instead of reaching for her book she tried to sort out Paz's surprising news. What on earth was she going to do? He couldn't get married. Love at first sight was so…so…impossible. She knew how it felt, but it wasn't real. They'd unpacked the final moving box only last weekend. After working so hard to get into UCLA's engineering program he couldn't afford the distraction of a wife.

Good lord, what about kids? He was not ready to be a parent. He still drank milk out of the carton and thought toasting Pop Tarts took too much time.

The bus arrived in a cloud of diesel fumes. There were no seats left, which happened on Mondays more often than not. She clung to the overhead bar after making sure the zips on her bag were turned against her body. As usual one of the business-suited guys wanted to make eye contact. She knew what he saw: a stick figure with shoulder-length dusty blond hair, thin lips without a trace of gloss, and breasts scarcely noticeable under the clearly off-the-rack jacket. All of which scarcely qualified as average by LA standards. Nevertheless, female and employed counted for something.

Wrong tree, your dudeship. She turned aside and pushed her sunglasses more firmly into place.

It wasn't years on the calendar that made Paz too young for marriage, either. He was old in some ways. The world had made him intimately aware of its dark side. He'd had little experience of the bright sides of life either. It seemed as if he was drunk on his first taste, and she did remember what that felt like. The first woman she'd dated had changed over the course of that year of self-discovery in college. Shannon had changed too. They hadn't so much broken up as stopped making dates. This girl could change, or Paz could change—it happened. "Dreams are like pie crust, they always crumble," her aunt had often said.

A hard lurch to the right made Shannon realize she'd mulled away most of the ride, thinking about lost loves—mostly the one that had hurt like hell. She didn't want that for Paz. But an experience like heartbreak wasn't one you could warn another person about. They had to feel it for themselves, like a hot stove, before they'd think about keeping their distance.

The bus lumbered to a halt in the downtown transit center. Two gates and a flight of stairs later she was buying an iced can of Diet Mountain Dew. The dollar she dropped into the street vendor's basket for her daily indulgence completed her morning rituals.

Heat reflected off the adobe, brick, and marble facades of the mid-rise office buildings that lined the streets of the upper downtown district. In spite of the concrete canyons and thick traffic, the air was morning fresh with a spring ocean breeze she'd hunger for by June. The breeze was strong enough to make the palm trees creak overhead. Los Angeles in spring— love it while you can, she thought.

The soda was drained by the time she had made her way across First Street and into the restored art deco building she'd called her workplace home for much of her adult life. Not for the first time she wished they had two security screening lines. There ought to be one for people who were regularly screened and knew how to do it quickly and one for newbies who were digging in their pockets for forgotten keys and loose change. The suggestion always fell on deaf ears. She finally scooped her bag off the conveyor belt and picked up her pace to make the elevator currently loading. There was no penalty at her grade level for being late, but she always felt it got the day off to a skewed, anxious start.

The elevator emptied completely on the fifth floor, the twelve or so occupants streaming in all directions as they donned their credentials for their final destinations. She brushed her fingers over the bold lettering on her destination door before she swiped her credential through the reader and opened it.

Justice. Integrity. Service: United States Marshals Service. Even an investigative research analyst could be moved by those words, and she believed in them. She had never wanted to be a deputy. She was wholly content that what she did was vital. The people with badges did things she could not and vice versa.

The main office was full of people with badges. The persistent singsong trill of landline phones blended with clipped conversations at dozens of squat, industrial, tan desks, all relics of earlier days. The steel chairs were so heavy that anyone limping could be presumed to have walked into one. The floors were indestructible linoleum that looked exactly the same as it had the first day Shannon had walked in fifteen years ago.

The Office of Protective Services was quiet as usual. Conversations were muted, and the only persistent sound was the click of keyboards. Her own cubicle was a veteran of at least eight administrations. Cleverly placed personal photographs and service directives covered stains that were probably coffee, though there was always someone willing to tell the story about "a guy who was here when a detainee shot up the place." It was a much mythologized event that had likely happened at county lockup where detainees were lodged, courtesy of an interagency agreement between the USMS and the LAPD.

Tau, the keeper of the safe that held all the relevant keys used in their department, tossed Shannon's set to her as she walked by. "Happy Monday."

"Back at ya." Nothing she was working on was ever left out on her desk, and analysts, no matter what their grade, didn't rate offices. She stowed her bag and went in search of the workday's first cup of coffee before returning to unlock her cabinets, log into her computer, and pick up where she'd left off on Friday.

Classified raw intel from intelligence services that made any mention of courthouse security was always the first order of the day, especially anything flagged by the analyst who covered weekends. That was followed by standing search parameters for any new or updated info for fugitives in her case portfolio. As one of three analysts at her grade in the Central District of California, she studied fugitive backgrounds or proceedings that needed a top secret security clearance to read the case files and dossiers, which in turn allowed her to assess whether new intel had relevance to finding said fugitive.

As she told people when she glossed over the content of her job for the Marshals Service, she spent her day sifting through random puzzle pieces to find the ones that fit the puzzles assigned to her. She let the emerging puzzle picture tell her a story. Her conclusions then went to the deputies involved, suitably without reference to any of the classified material. She was the person who didn't let operational secrets get in the way of the Marshals Service's work. Her intuition and discretion were solid enough that the service had quickly found her a position in Portland when Paz had been relocated there.

"No news is good news," she muttered as the courthouse search turned up nothing to report onward. She cleared two more standing queries and then turned to her ongoing cases. "Come on, Seychelles. I know you've been somewhere."

She wrinkled her nose as the first file hits for her searches under all the aliases for "Seychelles" rolled up on the screen. She'd seen all of these results before. The fact that the fugitive was the younger brother of an Eastern European head of state kept his file "need-to-know." He had provided useful intelligence on mutual enemies in the past to handlers at other agencies. When his name had turned up in child trafficking contexts he'd dropped out of sight for several years, with chatter alluding to him by one alias or another but not the one linked to the arrest warrant held by the Marshals Service.

Because they didn't know who he really was the deputies trying to locate him thought he'd gone underground and stayed there. Ultimately, they didn't care: a fugitive was a fugitive. The problem for Shannon's peace of mind was that his USMS warrant for bank fraud and flight to avoid prosecution weren't the highest priority, which meant he might still be involved in trafficking—and she did care about that. There were bad guys, and then there were bad guys, and this was a bad, bad guy. His last rumored location was Toronto and that hadn't changed.

They'd catch him, eventually. Shannon had great faith in the service, and she loved the work she did.

After another cup of coffee she processed the second daily round of interagency updates and then turned her full attention to digging up reports for a new Most Wanted, a domestic felon with a thick firearms and explosives dossier courtesy of the ATF. After stumbling around with different identities she found the steady chain that linked across activities and names which made it vastly easier to request info. She was grinning into her monitor when Gustavo, her boss, leaned in.

"Got a moment—and why do you look so happy?"

"I deduced that two people are actually one and the same. I like pointing that sort of thing out to my counterparts at Justice. Score one for the Marshals Service."

"Good on you." They shared a fist bump.

"What's up? Or should I come to your office?"

His smile was relaxed, that is, relaxed for him. Former Army, he'd never lost the razor-sharp creases and perfect-just-so shirt and tie, and Shannon doubted his hair was longer now than it had been in boot camp. "Not that big a deal. It's about time for quarterly reviews and I was wondering how you were settling back in. I think I have my answer."

"The work is the same wherever I am. This building hasn't changed, but the coffee is even worse." She laughed at the last item, but it was absolutely true.

"We cleaned the coffeepot about five months ago and it hasn't been the same since." Gustavo seemed about to add something else when his desk phone chirped loudly. "Talk to you again later. We'll do the formal review next week."

She put her head back down and wrote up her evidence chain linking the two profiles in the interagency database, then submitted the recommendation to have them officially linked.

By the time the day ended she was eager to get outside again and stretch her legs. Maybe go for a run after dinner. Thoughts about Paz resurfaced on the bus ride home. Who was this girl? If she knew her full name Shannon could no doubt find out more and easily. It would be unethical to use her resources that way except, given Paz's status as a former protected witness, it would be prudent to make sure the girl was who she said she was. But if she asked him for Josie's last name, he'd know exactly why she wanted it. Paz was not dumb.

Deep down she knew she was also feeling hurt. Maybe that wasn't the right word. Supplanted? She wanted Paz to grow up, but did it have to be this fast? It was what happened in the natural order of things, though. She'd liked living in Portland. It was a huge change from Los Angeles. Aunt Ryanne would have hated it there—too many eejits with daft ideas.

Living there had done her a world of good. She'd taken cooking lessons, joined a hiking club, and socialized with people at work as she had in LA, but she had given it up to move back to help Paz settle into college. She probably should have stayed in Portland and let him find his own feet. He'd have been fine without her.

But what if this girl was dangerous? Perps had long memories and families on the outside. She'd encountered plenty of gruesome stories in her line of work to know that her aunt's perpetual paranoia about bogeymen weren't without foundation. She could easily imagine harm around every corner in Paz's life.

She struggled her way around the whole question through dinner. *Jeopardy!* diverted her for a while, as did a well-deserved bowl of Ben and Jerry's after she went for the run she'd been telling herself to do for several days. Who was this girl, and could she find out more about her without inciting any resentment or suspicion from Paz? He'd only known her for three weeks.

She heard the echo of Aunt Ryanne's reedy voice, heavy with warnings about "daft" ideas and reckless choices. She didn't want to turn into Aunt Ryanne, to be sure, but she did want to protect Paz from All Things Daft. Love at first sight counted.

CHAPTER THREE

For the next several days, Josie managed to avoid being at home when Kesa was. The one time Kesa attempted to bring it up, Josie immediately shut her down with "I have to go to the library." Kesa was sorry she'd not heard Josie through and probably spiked any chance of Josie listening to her.

Though, really, who was this boy? Couldn't they live together? Kesa was sure it would help if they found out what it took to keep a roof over their heads before they signed on the dotted line of what was supposed to be "forever."

Her worries receded into the background when she saw that she'd been tagged in a Tweet from a model's account, in which she was showing off the three-piece "suit-kini" Kesa had adapted for her. The woman wasn't an A-lister like Jennifer Lamont, but she was high enough in LA's celebrity strata to immediately generate three appointments over the next week for Kesa. The workshop was looking more and more a reality. The broker for a perfect space was calling her daily for a decision. Not only would she get all of the machines, dummies, and materials out of their apartment, it would allow her to work smarter.

Much as she tried to tell herself that this marriage madness with Josie wasn't jeopardizing all her plans, the anxiety was making her stomach do backflips. Every time she'd counted on something—or someone—they'd let her down.

It was a perfect spring afternoon, so she decided to walk to the weekly Mahjong game. Exercise, sunshine, fresh air—they would all help. At least that was the theory. During rush hour she could walk the three miles in about the same time it took to drive and park near the always-congested Koreatown Plaza. Plus, walking was free. She'd take the route through MacArthur Park and enjoy the garden and lake. Refreshing after a day hunched over patterns and bolts of grosgrain and jacquard.

Besides, if there was one thing that hadn't let her down, it was the Mahjong gang. She had met Auntie Ivy at the local high school almost three years ago when she'd volunteered to do simple costumes for the spring play. It promoted her business, and at the time steady orders for altered and enhanced formal dresses for proms and *quinceañeras* had been essential to her cash flow. Auntie Ivy had persistently asked Kesa to join "the gang" made up of her granddaughter and a neighbor. Four made it easier to play, and they would teach her, happily. Hah—they were cutthroats, all of them. Even so, the evenings were full of laughter, talk, and food. As Auntie Ivy proclaimed, four women playing Manila Mahjong could fix the world.

She allowed herself to be cautiously hopeful about the appointments she'd made today. One of the women was the *Real Housewives* type. If Kesa made her happy, she would tell a number of friends and they would also want a suit-kini, uniquely cut and modified to their personal taste. The jacket, fully buttoned, was tailored and sophisticated, reminiscent of Chanel. The neckline highlighted jewelry and a bit of cleavage. The skirt fell in a straight A-line to right above the knee. It went from business lunch to speaking engagement with ease.

Lots of people could sew that.

Her stroke of genius was the transformation of the shell worn under the jacket into a sleek, midriff-baring "bikini" top with built-in breast shields and support. That took the outfit from speaking engagement to after-dinner party with a wow factor.

You're not out here to think about work, she reminded herself. She hooked earbuds into place and cranked up Beyoncé. Her sneakers kept time with the "is y'all alright" beat, and she visualized the rest of her life disappearing into the dust behind her.

The construction on West Temple gave way to gridlocked intersections the length of South Alvarado, and it was a relief to leave the honking and endless roar of engines behind. She followed Wilshire into the park and chose the footpath that would let her out on Seventh.

The neighborhood quickly changed. Bars on windows disappeared, the streets widened, and gridlocked cars were mostly BMWs. Houses were replaced by generic apartment and office buildings that always struck her as drab compared to the rest of Koreatown. She relaxed when the white and gray structures gave way to goldenrod and paprika. A scarlet and lime mural paying tribute to the local music scene was almost finished, turning a concrete slab wall into a thing of beauty. That was the Los Angeles she knew. Her feet flew and she finally felt lighter than her worries.

She stopped in at Lee Kum's for their special baked lumpia. Inhaling the savory mist of garlic and black pepper brought her back to earth and in a good way. She turned down the sweet-and-sour dipping sauce as always. Auntie Ivy's homemade tamarind-orange marmalade was way better.

Bag swinging from one hand, she padded up the stairs to Auntie Ivy's apartment, not surprised to find the door open and the pungent scent of pinakbet permeating the air. Her stomach growled. At least she thought it was pinakbet—okra and eggplant, sweet tomatoes, and bitter squash all stewed together in a shrimp sauce that woke up every taste bud she had. She had grown up on American food, and Auntie Ivy was determined to expose her to Filipino delights. Pinakbet had become a personal favorite.

"Kesa!" Auntie Ivy's granddaughter, Cami, bear-hugged her and adroitly took the warm bag of lumpia out of Kesa's hand.

"You don't get those all to yourself," Kesa chided. "They're the baked kind, not your favorite anyway."

"But better for me. It means I can have twice as many."

"Sure, sure."

Cami tossed back her bright purple hair. The asymmetrical cut only allowed that on one side, but Cami made it work. Naturally theatrical, she had been the vivacious, eventually redeemed villain of the student-written play Kesa had made costumes for. Today she wore no makeup on her round face, which made her look fourteen, not seventeen. The small diamond stud in one nostril had caused no end of discussion. Auntie Ivy didn't approve, but she finally agreed to stop bringing it up because Cami was a good girl and had a job at the grocery. Cami's permissive parents, who spent ten months of the year observing primates in Tanzania, had said they were fine with it during one of their Skype calls. Kesa suspected that Cami had a few more surprises in store for all of them. Time would tell.

She kissed Auntie Ivy's cheek gently and assured her she was well. The hug she got in response was strong and heartfelt, belying the heart attack the old lady had had two months ago. Her short gray hair looked freshly cut and she smelled as always of roses and green tea. When Auntie Ivy's back was turned she sent a raised eyebrow look to Marisol, already pouring tiles out onto the card table.

Marisol, who lived in the apartment next door, shrugged and rolled her eyes. That meant Auntie Ivy was taking her medication, but probably not following any of the other recommendations the doctor had made.

Cami already had the lion's share of the lumpia on a plate and they all made a grateful pass at the assembled buffet. Marisol's delicate handiwork was wonderfully apparent in the small half-watermelon hollowed out and heaped with grapes and strawberries and ringed with fanciful honeydew and cantaloupe rabbits and owls. Kesa was saving that for dessert. Marisol carved fruit to relax after long, stressful days of nursing. Kesa could think of nothing more refreshing for a California spring evening.

She ladled out Auntie Ivy's pinakbet, grabbed a couple of the lumpia before Cami could take the rest, and threw spinach leaves alongside—because greens. She didn't have nearly enough of them, and the scare over Auntie Ivy's heart attack had brought her face-to-face with all the stats about Filipinos and too-common heart disease.

She hurried to the table where Marisol and Auntie Ivy were already seated as they rapidly stacked and lined up the tiles. When it was time to play, it was time to play.

The tiles dealt, Marisol stretched out her short, sturdy legs. One hand released the large orange hair clip that had held her long black hair back from her face, transforming her from a tidy, impassive professional woman into a smiling, relaxed friend. "Finally. It feels great to take a load off."

"What's new in your world?" Kesa frowned at her hand while she gobbled up the savory stew. She had drawn a pong, but the rest was disjointed and Cami hadn't discarded anything she could use. She had no winds, which never boded well.

"I got a raise and I'll get an extra week's vacation. If I keep saving, I can go home for a visit this fall." Marisol grinned as she declared chow with Auntie Ivy's discarded tile, making Auntie Ivy groan.

"That's great," Cami said, picking up the four-stick Marisol discarded. "Mahjong." She set out her tiles in front of her—four pongs and a pair of green dragons.

They all threw up their hands with a variety of G-rated invectives while Cami smiled gleefully.

"We'd only been around twice," Auntie Ivy grumbled as she wrote the score and swept up the tiles for the next deal.

"That explains why my hand was so horrible," Kesa said. "You got all the winds. I'll never catch up. Can I pay you in lumpia?"

"That's better than the pennies we bet," Cami said.

"Mari, if you visit Manila will you see that handsome Federico again?" Auntie Ivy had a teasing twinkle in her eye, though Kesa wasn't sure if it was caused by the query to Marisol or the pong of red dragons she played off Kesa's discard.

"Perhaps," Marisol said primly, her dark eyes giving away nothing behind her lashes. She had a way of making her expression blandly nonthreatening, which Kesa supposed was helpful in a nurse—and really helpful in a card player. She drew a fresh tile slowly, which Kesa had learned the hard way meant she was thinking carefully about strategies to go out. She probably already had two pongs.

Her discard made Kesa wince. "You have my bamboos."

"Perhaps," Marisol said, less primly.

"You are all card sharks," Kesa announced. It was true. "And you make good food. It's a fair trade."

Cami muttered something in Filipino that Kesa missed, but it made the other two women laugh. "Are you plotting?"

"You should learn your cultural language," Auntie Ivy said, not for the first time.

"I will, Auntie. I'm too busy now. I would have to give up losing my pennies to you all to make time."

"Why are you so busy?"

"Work. And more work."

"I thought it might be your love life."

"Hah." Kesa pounced on the discarded purple dragon and played her second pong. If she got a three-bamboo she had a shot at Mahjong. "No time for that, and women don't seem interested regardless."

"If you considered men you would have twice the chances."

"Double zero is still zero." Kesa rolled her eyes. "Besides, it doesn't work that way, Auntie Ivy…"

"I know, I know. I am teasing."

Kesa was aware that both of them were carefully not looking at Cami. Auntie Ivy didn't normally bring up Kesa's sexuality. It was possible she had begun to suspect what Kesa had the day she'd met Cami. She drew a North Wind and kept it for her pair. Just as she thought her chances of going out were good, Marisol claimed the seven-dot Kesa had discarded and played her third pong.

"It's not that the thought of men makes me ill so much as it doesn't raise my heart rate, not even a little bit. Whereas some women do." She finished her last lumpia and wiped her fingers carefully on her napkin before touching the tiles again. "I have a client, a really famous actress. You know her name, but I can't say. I could easily build up a nice fantasy. She's got all the assets in all the right places and she's super smart. But she's married."

"You watch out—her husband could come after you."

"Her wife, Auntie." Kesa saw Cami blink in surprise. "And I have no intention of arousing the anger of someone who could buy half the state, not when I want to sell her wife an Oscar dress some day." She picked up Cami's discarded three-bamboo with a triumphant shout. "Mahjong! Woohoo!"

Marisol laughed appreciatively as Auntie Ivy totaled the score. "So what kind of real women are you interested in?"

She admired the dance of four pairs of hands over the tiles, turning them face down, deftly sliding them over the felt. The *snick* as tile met tile was soothing. What had once been an incomprehensible process to her quickly led to four neat, long walls of stacked tiles and the resumption of play.

Noting Cami's apparent nonchalance at Marisol's question, Kesa said, "There haven't been enough to have an obvious preference. The last one I really went for was taller than me."

"Everybody is." Cami laughed when Kesa gave her the finger, prompting Auntie Ivy to swat Kesa's hand.

"Anyway, she looked like the kind of suntanned Southern California girl who gets to the beach but doesn't live there. Nice eyes, brown like sepia silk. Funny when she relaxed. A smartass when she wasn't relaxed." Kesa pushed the memory away. Saying "I love you" and getting silence as an answer had been the end of it all. "And a good job she really loved that came first."

"How long ago was that?"

"A couple of years, maybe."

"So you mean four or five then. Girl, you have got to get out more." Cami melded a pong of nine-bamboos before popping the last bite of her lumpia into her mouth.

"You are very pretty and a hard worker," Auntie Ivy said. These were stellar qualities to Auntie Ivy. "You don't look like you turned thirty last year, either. And your eyes are beautiful."

"Thank you, Auntie." It was the only right answer, even though the only true thing she'd said was that Kesa knew how to work hard. She didn't feel attractive most of the time, always lugging around sample books and garment bags and with needle pricks in her fingers. Sure, her blue eyes were uncommon for Filipinos, but the perpetual frown between her brows from poring over hems and embellishments detracted from their luster. She kept her hair long, but to her color-trained eye the once-rich black was fading. More time with conditioner and keratin treatments would help, no doubt. She had neither the time nor money for it.

"My big news—because of the actress client mostly, I can finally get a workshop."

There was a uniform cheer. Auntie Ivy played chow on the discard, putting her a pair away from Mahjong. "Then you will have time to date and find someone who appreciates you."

"I might. At the least I will be able to exercise, eat more home-cooked food, treat myself better, like we're supposed to."

"No heart attacks for you?" Cami shot her grandmother a sidelong look.

"That's the plan. I should set a better example for Josie too." She toyed with the idea of asking the group's advice about Josie's announcement. It was easy to talk to all of them, so much easier than talking to Josie. But perhaps waiting a week would allow her to share more details. It was possible Josie would have broken up with the boy by then. "Our parents didn't live long enough for me to know what they might have passed on to me genetically, so diet and exercise is all I've got."

"And regular checkups," Cami added, again with a sidelong glance at her grandmother.

"I see you, *bata*. I don't want to talk about the doctor. I don't need any of you to be my nanny."

"Auntie Ivy," Kesa finally said into the ensuing silence, "we don't think you need a nanny. We know you're a grown-ass— grownup woman. This is us saying we love you and want you around for lots of years."

Cami said in a rush, "You didn't go to your last checkup."

"I don't want to be a bother. Let's play."

"It isn't a bother, *lola*. Coming home and finding you on the floor again—that would be a bother."

"I will call tomorrow."

"Promise me." Cami put her hands over the draw stack of tiles, preventing Auntie Ivy from moving on.

The old lady said something in a burst of Filipino that made Marisol smother a smile, and then said, "Oh, all right."

Marisol nodded gravely. "That's very accommodating of you, Ivy. Would you like some fruit now?"

The word Auntie Ivy said in response sent Cami into a fit of laughter before explaining to Kesa, "If bee-yotch had a Filipino equivalent, that's what she said."

"I'm shocked, I tell you." Kesa drew a seven-dot and discarded it. "Teach me sometime."

Auntie Ivy picked up Kesa's seven-dot and laid it out with the rest of her hand. "Mahjong, bitches!"

CHAPTER FOUR

"So Josie and I were thinking…"

Shannon spooned another helping of spaghetti onto her plate and hoped her face didn't reflect her sinking heart at Paz's words. She got up from the dining room table to fetch the Parmesan cheese. So much for the hope that a week would change their minds. In terms of their relationship length, another week was a long time. "Yes?"

"Her sister kind of flipped out. Seriously. So we were thinking what if we all got together and talked?" His voice took on a touch of rehearsed script. "You have reason to be concerned for our future and welfare, and it's a good idea to talk about things before they fester."

She could hardly disagree. "That seems…Like a good idea. I would like to meet Josie's family."

"There's just her sister. I think you'll get along with her." Amusement flickered over his face, then he was serious again. "Josie doesn't know of any other family. Their folks died twelve, thirteen years ago. She was just a kid." He speared a meatball and popped it into his mouth whole.

"I'm sorry to hear that." The older sister had probably been *in loco parentis* ever since—she must be a lot older, then. She peeled back more foil to expose another slice of the warm sourdough bread Paz had buttered and seasoned while she'd boiled the noodles and doctored their favorite bottled marinara with hot sauce and more basil. "When do you want to do this?"

"There's a coffee shop near school, and they have really good desserts. Josie loves the lemon tarts, and the peanut butter fudge cake puts me in a coma."

He was talking her language with the cake, and he knew it, the little shit. "That sounds like good neutral ground."

"Friday night? Seven thirty?"

"Sure." She tapped the name of the coffee shop into her phone and set the calendar to remind her Friday morning. It would no doubt be a mature and measured discussion—if she could silence the voice still wailing inside that he was too young, that it put him at risk, and he had too much he wanted to do to invest in marriage.

She nearly took a picture of their full plates covered in red. The two of them could put away a lot of spaghetti. She ignored the pang that said the number of times they'd feast like this might be limited. "So, how much does Josie know about you?"

He hesitated, then admitted, "Everything."

He'd only known her a month. He cut off her reaction by adding, "I told her last week when I proposed. She already knew I was a foster kid. But she should know my real name. And everything that happened."

"She was okay about it all?"

He blinked. "She was not 'okay.'"

"I'm sorry. That was a bad word choice. How did she handle it?"

He shrugged. "She's never—nothing like that has ever happened to her. At first she thought I was pulling her leg."

"In spite of television, not many people see the kind of thing you did."

"She really wants to meet you. At first she was pissed at what you did—"

It was Shannon's turn to blink. "For getting you into witness protection?"

"I told it to her wrong. I mean, I didn't want to get graphic about..." After she nodded, he went on, "So she thought you overreacted, like some white savior for the poor brown kid. But after I explained more, she got it. She promised not to tell her sister either."

His nightmares had eased after their first year in Portland. She'd never stopped checking the streets when they left for school in the morning, even after a Los Angeles-based colleague had sent word that the suspect was now in federal lockup on drug trafficking charges under what turned out to be his real name. She'd kept tabs on his incarceration and now knew the perp wasn't ever getting out. Until she'd seen the picture and custody order with her own eyes, she'd worried every day that a guy capable of slaughtering his wife with a hunting knife would come looking for a witness, a helpless kid. She didn't regret for even a minute her pressure on the system to get Paz into WITSEC and fast.

Fortunately, he'd always gone by Paz, and that hadn't changed. It had made adapting to a new name easier. Juan Feliz Pulido, witness to a domestic violence murder, had become Phoenix William Lopez, of interest to no one except the UCLA School of Engineering. And a girl named Josie. "I was the nice white lady next door. With serious law enforcement connections."

"Lucky for me."

"It shouldn't be about luck."

"I know." They'd talked about it before. "Luck or the grace of God, whatever. Josie agrees..." His voice slowed with shyness. "I should pay it forward. Somehow. If I hadn't known you, that guy probably would have found me before anybody thought I was worth protecting. I couldn't have picked him out again. I didn't look at him. I wasn't even sure which house it was—they all look alike in that neighborhood. But he didn't know that. And there's the whole fact that he was a maniac."

Picking up pocket money by tucking flyers into doors for a local Chinese restaurant had landed Paz in the wrong place at the wrong time. He'd heard a noise, glanced through open curtains and seen blood, a figure on the floor, someone standing over it. She'd told him over and over that running had been the absolute right thing to do. And he had run, nearly two miles, right to her back door. She'd helped him call it in, rode along in the back of the police car while he narrowed down the houses it might have been, and then insisted he be taken away before the officers began their sweep. He had seen nothing but blood, and he didn't need to see it again.

LAPD had found the right house and the wife's body. No sign of the husband, but a car was missing. A suspect at large had meant risk to Paz, and she'd ruthlessly used her credentials and her connections to push jurisdictional boundaries. Fortunately, the suspect fled into Nevada, and crossing state lines meant it became a matter for the Marshals Service. So why not also protection of the witness who could testify about time, day, location? WITSEC had developed his new identity and moved him to Portland.

She'd quickly followed. Though memories of her aunt's Boyle Heights home were not bad, per se, she hadn't regretted selling the house and leaving the weight of Aunt Ryanne's negativity and bleak predictions of doom and gloom behind. It had been time for her to get some distance from LA anyway— and her own failings.

Plus, she knew that WITSEC payments wouldn't be enough to keep Paz college bound, and protection would end the moment the USMS deemed him no longer at risk. He'd be in a new city, with a new name and not yet twenty when the money that barely covered rent stopped arriving. It was every kind of wrong to her that his being a witness would cost him his goals and forever set him back in life.

She wanted to ask if talking about it to his girlfriend had brought back the nightmares, but she worried that if she did he'd have a nightmare. Three years was not that long ago. He'd been shaking so hard she could hardly keep hold of him, and it had gotten worse as he'd struggled to put what he'd seen into words. He'd desperately needed someone to make it safe for him to breathe. To promise him that a blood-covered bogeyman wouldn't find him in his sleep. A promise he believed when it came from Shannon.

Gia Pagan, who ran the group home next door, had had six boys under her roof, and she kept them fed and focused on school. Shannon had found herself with maternal feelings she had never suspected were inside her and had enjoyed helping Paz plan out community college with a hope of transferring to a four-year program. Over the years of casual basketball games on the weekend, day trips to the beach, and Lakers tickets for his birthday he'd gone from elbow height to being able to look her in the eye.

All his hopes and dreams—and hers for him—disappeared in the time it took to glance through a window.

Dreams resumed in Portland. Painful pasts and her regrets became distant. He'd thrived in college classes and she had learned not to borrow trouble in every situation. Aunt Ryanne's obsessive caution lingered, but she was getting much better at not anticipating worst-outcomes-possible during simple trips to the grocery store.

He looked unhappy and stressed now, and she worried it was because he'd had to recall that bloody night. A change of subject was due. "Did you get any notification yet about them accepting your birth certificate?"

His grin was quick as his shoulders relaxed. "Yes, finally. Form letter. Nobody acknowledged that they already had a copy. Copies."

Well, that was a relief, though the whole thing was upsetting. There were realities she couldn't change about Paz's world, and him being asked to prove he was a citizen, over and over, was a depressingly real part of it. Even though they would, of course, always pass muster, it made her anxious any time his official papers—courtesy of USMS witness protection—were examined. "The whole thing was annoying."

"Yes, but friends at other schools say it happens to them, especially when they're in programs that get grant money or federal money. Friends with last names like Morales and Isfahani."

"That doesn't make it any more acceptable. I can't believe it's entirely a bureaucratic mix-up, not since this is the third time a program has wanted confirmation." She rubbed her overfull stomach as if that would ease her distress. Spaghetti—she had no willpower over it. "And I know what bureaucracies are capable of. I spent two hours today on the phone confirming to four different people that two records should be combined to create one identity with aliases. I was thinking I'd need an act of Congress when I had all the supporting material."

Paz forked up the last of his spaghetti. The bite was too large and he ended up with sauce on his chin. How could she possibly think him grown-up enough to get married?

As he mopped at the mess, Paz said, "I'd rather live in a world with flawed people than perfect machines."

She couldn't disagree with that. Later, as she stared at the textured ceiling and wished for too elusive sleep, she acknowledged that Paz was so much more mature and self-aware than she'd ever felt at his age.

But he was not ready for marriage and she had no idea how to slow him down.

His nightmares had stopped. Hers had not. They weren't nightmares so much as waking with a start to wonder if that was a window breaking or merely the wind and immediately getting up to make sure Paz was sleeping and safe. When they'd first settled in Portland she had found herself using her lunch breaks to drive by the college to know he was safe. That there was no active shooter. No gang presence. No anything that would hurt him. He was a brown kid in a hostile world and her aunt had raised Shannon to be pessimistic. She had told herself it was impossible to protect him, but that didn't stop her from trying.

How could she tell him about her fear? That the skill of seeing connections and possibilities was great for work but had meant anxious nights all her life. She could picture so many ways for the worst imaginable tragedies to happen.

She closed her eyes, snuggled her feet to a slightly warmer place in the bed and tried to quiet her mind by counting backward from one thousand. No thinking about work. *999.* No thinking about politics. *998.* Or Paz getting married... Damn. *1000.* Yes, it would be good to meet Josie's older sister. *999.* Allies were always useful. *998...*

CHAPTER FIVE

Josie's crossed arms meant both sharp elbows were pointed at Kesa, which left her feeling in the line of fire. "So you'll come?"

"Yes. I'm free on Friday night. What else is new?"

"Thanks for the reminder of how hard you work."

"That remark was for me, not you." She held back a sigh Josie would no doubt take the wrong way too.

"If you dated, maybe you'd get what I'm feeling."

"Don't go down that road," Kesa said sharply. "How I feel about you getting married isn't about my love life."

Josie coughed "bullshit" into her hand and dodged the wadded napkin Kesa threw at her. "Paz's guardian isn't happy about it, just so you know. You two have a lot in common. Paz says she's also qu…" She took a deep breath as if looking for the right word. "Quite the hard worker. We think talking about it will convince you both that we're serious. That we've thought about the challenges."

"Why does he have a guardian? He's an adult, right?"

"Yes," Josie snapped. "He's an orphan. She's not like his official guardian or anything. She's always watched out for him. Through…stuff."

An orphan. No family. No support, nobody to help them get by when life inevitably turned hard. It always turned hard. "What kind of stuff?"

"He's a Latinx kid, living in foster care and group homes most of his life. There was stuff, and none of it was his fault."

"Criminal stuff?"

"He didn't do anything."

Kesa wanted to point out that all criminals said nothing was their fault. That would put the fight that was simmering into full boil. Great, just great. Josie had always loved lost causes. This boy sounded like another one, and Josie didn't want to see that it could steal away her entire future. "Is this rush to get married because…"

"I told you already, I'm not pregnant!" Josie scrambled to her feet, picked up her dinner plate, and carried it to the kitchen. "It's only been a month—besides, we're very careful. We want to get married. We want to have kids, but not now. See? If you were listening, you'd have heard me say all that."

"I am listening. I'm trying."

"Maybe you are. But you don't hear me."

Kesa blinked fast and hard to hold back tears. "I feel exactly the same way about your listening skills, so we agree on something."

Josie didn't answer as Kesa headed to her bedroom to resume cutting cloth for her second suit-kini order. Her breathing steadied as she worked. Josie wasn't old enough to get married, and that was a fact. It had nothing to do with Kesa's dating or their parents or anything else. She was simply too young. Too immature.

"Love at first sight. Love conquers all," she muttered. "Next she'll be saying 'He completes me' and I'll need a barf bag."

She comforted herself by hoping that Paz's guardian was sensible. If they presented a united front, maybe the lovebirds would agree to a long engagement. Trial cohabitation. Save the legal documents and "I do" pledges until they were more certain it would last.

The workshop lease paperwork was finished and the deposit check was written. Her plans would go into motion the moment she dropped off the thick envelope. She'd been hesitating all week, pleased that her financial history finally had not factored into the rates being offered and yet terrified of signing a lease. The thought of having to meet that payment every month even though her current cash flow and savings met all her targets gave her the shakes. She could tell herself it was okay, but she didn't feel it. Her caution had gotten her and Josie through the past twelve years. She'd only screwed it up once, and that had just been her stupid heart, which wasn't ever going to run her life again.

She idly rubbed the permanent scissor notch in the fleshy part of her thumb and studied her neatly cut pieces. Going after the upscale market had been a change from alterations and a good one. It had taken belief in herself, networking with strangers, and so much practice.

She rolled up the pieces and collapsed the table, making enough space to reach her tiny closet. Her favorite sweater, a patchwork of crimson cashmere and white wool, would keep the night air away.

"Errands to run," she told Josie, who had settled with her books in front of the TV. "Back in a while."

L.A. after sunset always soothed her. The lights from any high ground became magical. The whimsy of street art or the happenstance of turning a corner to find a dance party spilling out onto the sidewalk reminded her there was life without work.

I can do this.

By the time she reached the leasing office her heart was hammering in her ears so loud she almost couldn't hear Santana streaming from the car radio. The parking lot was deserted and there didn't seem to be anyone around, so she pulled up close to the doors. She left the engine running as she carried the flat envelope of papers to the door. As she'd hoped, there was a mail drop.

She couldn't make her fingers let go.

This is ridiculous, she scolded herself.

You're wasting gas standing here.

Just do it.

Don't do it.

You can't.

You can.

Everything you have and your entire future is at risk.

You're not a bankrupt, jumped-up, uneducated, unproven nobody anymore.

Make up your mind.

With a long shaky breath she let it go. The envelope containing all her hopes dropped out of sight, not making a sound.

CHAPTER SIX

With a never-seen-before shy pride, Paz said, "This is Josie."
Shannon shook hands with the young woman. "I'm Shannon.
Paz has told me a lot about you, but not nearly enough."

"Same here." Josie broke off as the coffee shop host waved
at them to follow him to a table.

Shannon trailed after the kids, noting Paz's hand at the small
of Josie's back. She probably ought to stop thinking about them
as kids. They were adults, and they were here to discuss an adult
situation.

Josie was not quite what Shannon had expected. Her plain
black leggings showed off powerful thighs and rock hard calves.
Her backpack and tennis shoes had both seen better days in the
scruffy student getting-the-most-out-of-it way. Her haircut was
simple, and where many of her peers in the diner had eyes with
black liner and rosy cheeks, Josie's face was free of makeup. Yet
her denim jacket fit perfectly and was embellished with a long
vee of copper studs on the back and shoulders, clearly designer
quality.

Once they were seated, leaving an empty seat across from her for Josie's sister, Shannon said, "One of the things he hasn't told me is where you live."

"With my sister. Near Echo Park, just off Temple." Josie glanced at her watch. "Looks like she's late."

"Is that rare?"

"Actually, yes. It makes her really cranky, because the world should run like clockwork for her." Josie craned her neck to check the front of the restaurant for new arrivals.

"I get that."

"You would," Paz said. "Punctuality is your superpower."

Feigning outrage, Shannon protested, "I have others. Spaghetti."

He winked at Josie. "Shannon's spaghetti is a superpower, it's true."

Josie sounded more forty-nine than nineteen as she said, "I hope someday to have the pleasure." The nineteen-year-old came back in a rush as she added, "But I'm not cadging for a free meal or anything! O-M-G, my sister would be all over me for sponging dinner off anyone."

Shannon caught the eye-roll that went along with the prediction of sisterly disapproval. "She sounds independent."

Paz flipped pages on his menu. "She's a lot older."

"Than me?"

He grinned. "No, she's younger than you, *vieja.*"

"Be careful how you say that, my young apprentice." Shannon looked down at the menu as well, though if there was peanut butter fudge cake her order was decided. She stole a quick glance at Josie. She had the feeling that she'd met her before somewhere. Or seen her in a photograph.

She quelled the sensation of ice water running down her back. She looked at a lot of photographs in her work, and most of the time the people in them weren't good. Be rational, she told herself. Mr. Knife-Wife Murderer is in prison for life.

Paz wasn't in danger from this vivacious sprite of a girl. At least not physically. She was lively and bright-eyed, talked fast, and was quick with a smile. His heart was the thing in danger. She got it—falling for a woman like this was like falling for the sun. When the clouds came in you felt it right away. A permanent sunset would be very painful.

Young love. Love at first sight. The concepts were nonsensical, so Shakespearian. Tragedy was around the corner, no doubt. Give me strength, she thought. Paz didn't even seem the least bit scared.

Scared—that's you, remember? Not him.

She pushed away the thought. "Peanut butter fudge cake—I was promised this. But I don't see it on the menu."

Josie gestured toward the front of the restaurant. "It's in the case—Friday special."

"So how many times have you two been here?"

"Every Friday night since we met," Paz admitted.

Josie quickly added, "I save up all week. Gave up lattes so I could afford cake with my guy."

It was so freaking adorable that Shannon was unwillingly charmed. There was no doubt the two of them felt something, but why marriage? A question she would ask when Josie's sister arrived. "The wallet and the waistline—dating takes a toll."

"We get exercise," Paz said.

Shannon shoved her fingers into her ears. "La-la-la, not listening to that."

His face predictably flamed and Josie laughed.

Shannon removed her fingers for a moment to look directly at Josie. "You're safe, right?"

Josie's eyes widened. "Every single time!"

It was Paz's turn to shove his fingers into his ears. "Girl talk! Cooties!"

Shannon swatted him affectionately. "It's not girl talk."

"I know. Responsibility rests on both people." He launched into his imitation of her. "This is important. Nobody should die from having sex."

Josie, still grinning, was shaking her head. "You sound just like Kesa."

Shannon blinked at Josie. "Who?"

"My sis—there she is." Josie's face lost its good humor as she stood up. "Let the games begin."

CHAPTER SEVEN

The evening was off to a great start. Kesa slammed the car door, cursing LA and everyone like her out looking for parking near UCLA on a Friday night. She was going to be late, and she had four blocks to cover and in heels.

She walked as fast as she could, wishing with every step for her black boots. She'd picked heels because they made her feel substantial, especially paired with the perfectly tailored bolero jacket and skirt she'd constructed from clearance bin remnants of turquoise raw silk. At the end of the first block she realized she hadn't taken her notebook out of her bag and it weighed more with every step. She stabbed at the pedestrian signal to cross Wilshire and glared at the unbroken stream of cars. So much for finding LA nightlife soothing.

The entire week had turned into a complete shitshow, she thought bitterly. A fitting that resulted in a customer rejecting her custom-made dress had capped a week that had included a broken bobbin assembly on one of her sewing machines.

What had she been thinking?

She had drained her cash cushions to nearly zero for the initial deposits on the workspace and, sure enough, business had gone downhill from there. Hadn't she learned that's how life worked? A customer who decided not to take her final outfit because "It's just not what I thought it would be—the drawing looked different" meant she had to use a credit card to pay for the machine repair. Picking up the keys to her new workshop earlier in the day had been terrifying instead of exhilarating.

It didn't help that there was a grain of truth to the client's complaint. Drawing wasn't her strong suit, and she'd never found time to take the classes that would help her present her ideas more accurately and persuasively on paper. The part of her brain that wasn't panicking over the state of her cash flow tried to calm the waters by reviewing the sound business sense of her decision. Having a place that allowed her to work more quickly meant she wouldn't be devastated by the loss of a single sale. If she had the space, she could slowly invest in additional machines and specialty equipment and even hire helpers for the basic work while she drummed up more lucrative contracts.

The facts, repeated over the next two blocks, helped with her worries—a little. Mahjong had helped her mood, like it always did, though she still hadn't told anyone at this week's game about Josie's madness. Auntie Ivy and Marisol were having a difference of opinion about healthy food. Cami and she had spent most of the night smoothing over huffy silences. There had been moments of laughter and ease, but not nearly as much as usual.

The streets near UCLA were always crowded with cars and people. Being small, even in heels, meant dodging backpacks and shoulders, which slowed her down even more. The coffee shop was right on the edge of the sprawling campus's medical center, and its heritage as a boulevard diner was obvious in the chrome-framed marquee proclaiming "World's Best Pie." The tinted windows were papered with posters promising locally sourced food, fair-trade purchased coffee, ethically paid workers, and an all-are-welcome philosophy.

She paused in the foyer to take a deep breath. Her gaze was caught by the luscious caramel drizzled over chocolate blackout cake in the display case. No matter how this conversation went, she was having a slice of that and she was going to eat it all.

This really couldn't be happening—Josie could not get married. They could wait a year, why not? If the boy's guardian was the least bit sensible they might be able to get the young people to agree to slow down.

She stepped into the dining area and saw Josie before Josie saw her. Across from Josie was a very attractive young man. He seemed to be half a foot taller than Josie, still not all that tall for the male of the species, but the compact triangular set of his shoulders, over which stretched a blue UCLA Engineering T-shirt, was the result of weights or swimming or both. His smooth umber skin was a pleasing result of genetics and LA sunshine.

The infatuation made sense now. Even she would turn her head to admire him. Josie was gazing at him in nothing short of adoration.

For a moment, she could see Josie as a stranger would. Her jaw-length hair was a glossy black that hinted at indigo in certain lights, and it was a perfect foil for her sienna skin. The outside corners of her eyes curved slightly upward when she smiled the way she was doing now, a charming trait their father had had, but only Josie had inherited. Kesa had gotten their mother's blue eyes instead. The wide-mouthed smile that Kesa rarely saw was lively and genuine. At that moment her boyfriend had his fingers in his ears and they were both laughing.

They would, Kesa realized, make beautiful babies.

Marriage. Babies. Her chest ached at the very idea.

She could only make out the outline of the woman sitting on the other side of Josie's boyfriend. That must be the guardian, Kesa thought. The window reflected a blur of shoulder-length dark blond hair, and the arm on the table was ivory in the artificial light.

They were all so relaxed, as if this was an ordinary family event.

The boyfriend leaned back in his chair and Kesa could suddenly see the other woman's profile: a long nose and wide smile as she teased the young man about something. Her laugh was slightly husky and seemed to come to her easily.

Josie saw her then and the animation drained from her face. She rose to awkwardly hug Kesa, saying, "You're late."

This can't be happening, Kesa thought. She let go of Josie when she realized Josie might feel her shaking. "Traffic and parking. I thought I allowed enough time."

The young man had risen as well and extended his hand. "You must be Kesa. I'm Paz." His grip was firm, confident. Not a boy. A man.

This can't be happening.

He gestured at the woman seated next to him. She began to rise, and Kesa managed to say, "Don't get up on my account."

Words failed her at that point. After a moment the other woman extended her hand across the table. "Shannon."

The brush of Shannon's fingers against her palm sent an electrical charge through Kesa's body so searing that her skin seemed on fire while her brain stopped working entirely. With the tiny amount of air she could pull into her lungs, Kesa responded with her name. She dove for the empty chair next to Josie, which put her across from Shannon. She jerked back as she trod on what was probably Shannon's foot under the table. Her heavy purse bumped the edge of the table hard enough to rattle the water glasses. "Oh my gosh, let me stash this thing."

At least that's what Kesa thought she said. She felt as if she'd slipped into another dimension where she could hear only babble.

Josie shot her a "What is wrong with you?" glance.

A frazzled server with a coffee-stained apron promptly arrived. "Ready to order?" She didn't say "finally," but Kesa heard it plainly.

Desperate for a moment that felt normal, Kesa said, "There's a chocolate cake in the window that has caramel on it. I want that."

"The whole cake?"

Kesa nearly said yes. "Just a slice."

Josie asked for a lemon tart, her favorite thing in the world, while Paz and Shannon ordered peanut butter fudge cake.

"So you're only having dessert?" The server didn't hide her disappointment.

"Coffee," Shannon said abruptly. The warmth and laughter were gone, replaced by a mask of polite detachment. "Whatever you have that has twice the normal amount of caffeine."

"Americano with an espresso shot?"

"Sure." Shannon's hands fluttered over the cutlery and water glass, minutely shifting them into perfect alignment.

Kesa focused on Paz, who was looking at his guardian with a puzzled line between his brows.

"Coming right up." The server departed with an understated flounce.

"So…" Josie said.

"So…Paz." Kesa was only partially successful at clearing her tight, dry throat. "Josie tells me you're going to UCLA."

"I transferred in as a junior this year, into the engineering undergrad program."

"Will you stay on for a master's degree?"

"I've already applied because there are some extra hoops to go through when you're a transfer student. And I'm looking for a corporate sponsor."

So he meant to stay in school. How would the two of them possibly live?

"And Josie, you're studying mathematics?" Shannon's question came out abruptly.

"Yes, my scholarship requires it. I'd rather be taking art and music history and political science, but math pays the tuition, so math it is."

"The curriculum is fairly general for a freshman, though, isn't it?"

Josie nodded as she sipped her water, and Paz filled in, "It still crowds her schedule. But I can help her with study guides for some of the classes because I had to take them too. Integration and Infinite Series—major brain hurt. She's way better at it than I am, though."

Josie gave him an approving smile. "You're a very good teacher."

Pass the insulin, Kesa thought. "It's not like I can help her with it. I can solve for X, end of story."

Shannon waved a graceful hand in surrender. "Don't look at me. I need fancy math done, I ask him."

Paz filled in as Shannon's voice faded away. "So how do we talk about this?"

"What is there to talk about?" Kesa eased her tone but knew she sounded harsh anyway. It was hard to hear over clanging of alarms bells and hammering of her heart. "I feel Josie is too young to make the commitment that marriage requires. Not just young in actual years," she hastened to add. "But the choices and opportunities of life in the next few years will be greatly reduced if she is planning for two, or three, instead of just herself."

Josie's chin took on the stubborn jut that Kesa saw every day. "Life isn't about just yourself."

"Marriage is all or nothing. In another few years, you can be more certain... Certain that it will work out."

"There are no guarantees in love." Shannon worried a blue packet of sugar substitute between her long fingers as she spoke. "There's only time and commitment."

"The more life throws at it the harder it is to maintain." Kesa tried to steady her voice as she evaded Shannon's gaze. "Job offers, and health, and...things."

"I'm very adaptable," Paz said. "There have been...things." His smile was genuine, relaxed even. "I want to be an engineer, and I want to see Josie's smile every day."

"What will you live on?"

"It's always money with you," Josie muttered.

"It's always money with the landlord and the grocery store. And the university and the Metro."

Shannon came to Kesa's support with, "Love doesn't pay the bills."

Paz answered with, "The bills don't diminish the love."

They can, Kesa thought. It was the wrong time to think of her irresponsible parents. They'd loved each other plenty, she supposed. But there was little evidence that she and Josie had been anything other than accessories to their merry, precarious lives.

The server delivered Shannon's coffee and Josie's tart and hurried away again. Shannon tore open the blue packet of sweetener and dumped it in the coffee, then stirred with a fast, decisive swirl of the spoon. "For me, this is the crux of the issue. I don't want to seem unsympathetic, but I would feel much better about the speed you want to do this with if I saw that you had a plan to get by financially. That's tough these days."

Paz watched his guardian sip at the coffee. When she set the cup down he said, "We both will get part-time jobs to pay rent and food, and I was hoping you would be our landlord."

Shannon choked, then gasped out, "You might have waited until I swallowed."

Paz laughed—he was entirely too casual for Kesa's peace of mind. "I waited until you put the cup down. I am serious. You're right. It would be hard to get into a place of our own. But we could rent from you. A business arrangement."

"Working will cut into your studies."

"Happiness will help them along."

Kesa's gaze went back and forth between the two of them, wondering how they had come to know each other. There was a lot of genuine affection, easily apparent in both sets of eyes. They seemed more like family than she and Josie did.

"Why is there such a hurry? Why not date for a while? Even live together?"

"The world sucks," Josie burst out. "How long are we going to be here? The planet is turning into a dust bowl of Mad Max Land. Some superbug or superwar could happen any day. Waiting for the perfect future that never comes would be super sad."

Kesa couldn't help but glance at Shannon. Shannon was staring into her coffee, quickly hiding a mirthless smile. Did she agree with Josie?

This can't be happening, she thought one more time. Her heart felt three times its normal size, making it hard to breathe. The cake arrived and she hesitated to take a bite, not at all sure she could swallow.

CHAPTER EIGHT

The caffeine was steadying Shannon's nerves—barely.
This can't be happening. But it was. Long, lustrous, dark hair,
a serious smile, and an unsettling, perceptive blue gaze Shannon
couldn't bring herself to meet, all sitting so close that Shannon
couldn't seem to catch her breath.

She tapped in a little more sweetener and busied herself
with her spoon. Her head was spinning, but she had spent so
much of her life surrounded by law enforcement types that she
knew how to school her expression. She didn't disagree with
Josie's passionate outburst, at least not entirely. But she'd only
been serious about someone once in her life, and the perfect
future had never arrived.

"I knew Josie was the one for me the moment I saw her," Paz
was saying to Kesa.

She had never seen this side of him, but it didn't surprise
her either. The traumatic experiences of his past had deepened
his enjoyment of life in ways she sometimes envied. When they
went to the beach, he would run right into the water while she

waited to test the temperature. Josie seemed to possess equal zest—she was halfway through her lemon tart already.

Kesa hadn't touched her cake yet. She glanced up then, her deep blue eyes catching Shannon in the act of staring. Look away, she told herself, but she couldn't make herself do it until Paz suddenly grabbed his phone from the table.

"Damn—I forgot to pick up my book from Lucio," he explained as he furiously tapped at his phone. "We share textbooks. I need it for tonight."

"Can you get it on the way home?"

"He has work." Paz furrowed his brow at the display. "He's about to leave his dorm, but I can intersect with him. I'll be right back, maybe ten minutes total." He grabbed his wallet off the table.

"I'll come with you," Josie announced and moments later they were both hurrying up the street. It seemed prearranged to Shannon, meant to give the older folks a chance to talk.

Kesa's gaze met Shannon's and they both stilled. The silence grew longer, heavier.

This *can't* be happening.

The nape of Shannon's neck was damp, then cold. The clatter of dishes and hum of voices seemed far away, and a rising siren from a passing ambulance reached the pitch of the alarm bells in her head telling her to run now, before it was too late.

Words. She thought of Paz and Josie, how strong they were and unafraid. She thought about possible futures and the immutable past. Risk, and love at first sight, and fear. She searched for the right words, came up with none, and all the while she felt caught in Kesa's burning sapphire eyes.

Finally all she could think to say was, "So, how have you been?"

CHAPTER NINE

As the going-away gathering had slowly broken up, Shannon had lifted her margarita one last time at Deputy Marshal Carnutt, who was proof that a deputy could make it to retirement. She had quite a lot left to her drink and was disinclined to leave it, so when the table emptied she carried it to the patio where the bar would be open all night. She liked Olvera Street, including the bright, continuous Latin music that encouraged dancing wherever you happened to be standing.

As she surveyed the available barstools her gaze was caught by a woman in the process of literally showing a cold shoulder to a scruffy-chic, Rolex-sporting "I could be a producer" dude. The woman's bare arms, amber in the neon lights over the bar, were taut with tension, and one foot was hooked on the barstool rung as if to keep her from kicking him with her this-will-hurt-and-I-mean-it Doc Marten boots. Long, heavy hair hung down her back in a black cape, and she was tiny enough to make Shannon feel gangly.

Rolex Dude was a type that filled bars everywhere in LA. The woman was not. Her sleeveless shell was silk in a flame orange that was translucent over her midriff. Simple black jeans with no sign of a designer label were set off with a braided fabric belt of purple and saffron. Long purple and pink earrings tangled in her dark hair, making her an explosion of color in a room full of business casual office types. Shannon was drab by comparison in her serviceable gray suit and white blouse.

It was the no-nonsense black boots, though, that pinged her gaydar and pinged it hard. If the likes of Rolex Dude were on her menu, the woman would probably be wearing CFM stilettos. All at once Shannon's intentions of finishing her margarita and catching the next Metro train toward home to rewatch a superhero movie were gone. LA was full of beautiful women, but this one wasn't wrapped in a plastic facade that sparkled for men to appreciate. An artist, maybe, and dressed to please her own vivid aesthetic.

How did Shannon approach her without being as obnoxious as Rolex Dude? It's not as if she had any practice at picking up women in bars. Or anywhere. Living with a very elderly aunt had acted as an all-purpose Libido Suppressant. Well, if she got a "go away" signal, she'd respect it and back off, for one thing.

Rolex Dude leaned over the rigid shoulder to say something in the woman's ear. She jerked away and snapped a few short words that made Rolex Dude laugh like they were oh-so-funny when Shannon was absolutely certain the woman had meant "fuck off" in every language women spoke.

Though there was room elsewhere, Shannon slid in between Rolex Dude and the woman and set her margarita glass on the coral-tinted bar. Rolex Dude had to take a step back. He was about to assert himself when Shannon turned completely to face him.

"Been in LA long?"

"Huh?"

So literate. "You seem new in town. Time is precious and you're wasting it here."

He puffed out his chest. "Was I talking to you?"

Shannon felt the woman shift on her barstool perch, as if she were going to take off now that Rolex Dude was distracted. "Sweetheart, you're not talking to anybody here."

He didn't know what to make of her. She wasn't his type, yet she was looking at him, which was the best response he'd had all night, she was willing to bet. He opened his mouth and probably closed it again, but Shannon was no longer facing him.

"So," she said to the woman, who was indeed about to slide off the barstool. "Come here often? What's your sign? Read any good books lately?"

She froze, looked Shannon up and down, and then relaxed back onto her seat. "First time. None of your business. And I haven't had time to read in years."

"Taking a break from work then?" She guessed she was eight or nine inches taller than the woman, who, from closer observation, was probably of Pacific Islander extraction.

"That was my plan. I'd forgotten how…" She sipped her Corona, adding to the mauve lipstick on the bottle's lip. "How this works."

"Me too." She shrugged a shoulder in the direction of Rolex Dude, who'd gone further down the bar to pout. "Except it doesn't work the way he thinks it does."

The shoulder was now noticeably less rigid. "Your turn. Come here often?"

"Not really. We had a retirement sendoff earlier. I was planning to finish my drink and head home."

"And now?"

"I'm a Virgo, so I'm analyzing the situation and revising my plan accordingly."

The woman's thin, soft lips were pressed together as if she was fighting a smile. "I see."

"Well, I've been reading this book on how to make friends and influence people so I thought I'd practice."

"Is it to make friends or to influence people you're after right now?" She finally looked up at Shannon, revealing unexpected, startling blue eyes.

Shannon surprised herself by saying, "Something else entirely."

The other woman had been about to respond lightly, but something arced between them, hot and palpable. They stared at each other, then sipped their drinks. The air seemed thin.

"He's gone, you know."

"Hmm?" Shannon blinked.

"Mr. God's Gift with the Armani knock-off suit and the fake Rolex. If you were just being gallant, then you can go off duty."

"I really wanted to finish my drink," Shannon said. "Then I saw the idiot and decided to finish it here. Not that you seemed to need rescuing. Solidarity."

"He was going to end up with a boot in his ass." She sipped her Corona and seemed to make a decision. "I'm Kesa."

"Shannon."

They ordered another round and when their drinks had been delivered, their fingers tangled around the glasses and bottles as if magnetized. Shannon's brain was on a seesaw between devising any way she could to touch Kesa and not wanting to be a skeevy pervert. She pushed away the voice of Aunt Ryanne reminding her that pubs weren't where quality people were to be found.

As the music rose they moved closer together, shouting names of movies and songs they liked into each other's ears. Kesa's cologne was working on her senses even more than the second margarita, filling her head with a dizzy desire to press her lips to the small circle of bare skin behind Kesa's earlobe. She didn't remember feeling like this before, but wasn't that how desire worked? Their chemistry clicked.

They were free associating favorite movies and swapping lines when they said in stereo, "By Grapthar's Hammer, you shall be avenged!" Shannon burst out laughing as Kesa ducked her head to dab the bar napkin at her eyes.

Shannon was so lost in the smell of Kesa's cologne that she didn't lean away in time. The crown of Kesa's head caught her full on the chin.

She staggered, seeing stars, and felt the barstool begin to slip out from under her.

Kesa was a lot stronger than she looked, because the arm that came around Shannon to steady her was like iron.

"I'm so sorry!"

"My fault," Shannon said. She loved the way Kesa's arm felt around her. "I was smelling your perfume. It's lovely."

Kesa didn't let go of her. In fact, she inched her barstool closer so that the most comfortable place for Shannon's leg was braced on one of Kesa's rungs. "Thank you. It's *Belle de Nuit*. Are you okay?"

"Yes. 'Pain don't hurt,'" she added, and loved that she could feel Kesa's giggle. Her chin would be tender for a day or two, but she didn't think the bruise would show. "I didn't bite my tongue."

"I am very glad of that," Kesa said, and then she kissed Shannon, hard and fast. Shannon had enough time to smile into the warm, soft lips, then Kesa leaned away. Shannon checked with a sidelong glance to make sure their display hadn't drawn unwelcome attention.

"I know a quieter place," Kesa said. "Friendlier than this for us, perhaps."

"If I may be so bold—so do I, and it's about ten minutes from here. I keep a very good supply of red wines." She saw Kesa hesitate and said, "I'm on foot, so if you have a car, you could drive me home and then leave whenever you want."

"Um, well. It's not that you're scary…" Kesa began.

"I understand," Shannon said quickly. What had she been thinking, asking for such a leap of trust? She didn't know this woman either. It wasn't smart, inviting strangers into her home. Aunt Ryanne was rolling over in her grave, no doubt. Besides, the house wasn't ready for a guest. Some player she was. "I shouldn't have suggested it. We can go wherever you like. But I am on foot. I take the bus to work and a co-worker gave me a lift here."

"If you don't like the place, I'll give you a lift home. It's called The Grog and Game—if you Google it, you'll see it on the map."

Kesa was right. The Googles said it wasn't far as distances in LA were measured. "It looks great."

They went out into the warm night, surrounded by a glitter of gold stars and bright music. At first Shannon thought there was someone sitting in the backseat of Kesa's well-used hatchback, but it turned out to be a dress form that Kesa explained was for a wedding dress fitting she'd done earlier in the day. The life of a seamstress/tailor sounded grueling.

"It's enough for rent and the necessities, until my sister is old enough to support herself. Our parents died when she was seven. She's fifteen now, so a couple more years."

"Then you've both been on your own for a while," Shannon said. "I was raised by my Aunt Ryanne. She was in her fifties when she adopted me as a baby. She passed away two years ago." She added carefully, because people reacted in all sorts of odd ways, "I work for the US Marshals Service."

"You're a deputy?" Kesa's surprise was obvious.

"No. And it's not all like in *The Fugitive*. The marshals make sure federal courthouses are safe and secure, and we track and apprehend fugitives. I'm an analyst. I gather and evaluate information from other agencies and services and pass it along to the deputies as they need it. A desk job." It wasn't the time to bring up her hopes of moving up her security clearance, which not only paid better but brought far more interesting cases. After several years, bank robbers were routine and drug runners tediously predictable. The scary part was that if she outed herself in the process as required there was no guarantee she wouldn't be not only denied a higher clearance but then eased out of the job she had because someone didn't like queers. Not that she'd seen that behavior around her so far, but the ghost of Aunt Ryanne often whispered that shite and malice were life's undoubted reward for getting noticed. In Aunt Ryanne's telling, leprechauns weren't cute little munchkins with pots o'gold, but tricksters who liked to lure folks off safe paths into sucking bogs.

Kesa's gaze never left the road as she spoke. "It sounds much more interesting than making clothes."

"It sounds like you're making art to order. I think working with people that way would make me crazy."

"It's frustrating sometimes," Kesa admitted. "I have to read the client very closely. I just did my first evening gown for a celebrity—not quite the A-list, but getting there. So I am hoping for referrals. It would be nice to move in that direction, instead of routine tailoring."

"Fashion by Kesa? Your own label?"

"I wish. For that I need lots of work to show or the patronage of a designer. Which isn't all that plentiful. And I'm not willing to do some of the things—" her tone made it clear these options were unpleasant "—that would garner a designer's favor."

"I get that." She found herself relaxing as Kesa drove, liking the competent way she moved through traffic. LA driving took both patience and aggression, and at the right times. Kesa drove the way Shannon did, leaving her to wonder if they were well matched in other ways. The dark windows provided plenty of blank space she could fill in with fevered, intimate images.

"This is it," Kesa said. "I've only read about it, but it sounds friendly and laid-back."

The brew pub wasn't overtly queer, but the decor featured flags from all over the world, including the rainbow one. Pinball machines interspersed with long, crowded tables dominated the first floor. "Looks like it's self-service at the bar."

"Not a problem," Kesa said.

"Want a snack?"

"Sure. Anything but onion rings. I like them, but they seriously don't like me."

As they carried their beers and a basket of fries upstairs, Shannon saw that tables below were filled by people hunched over cards, worksheets, and twenty-sided dice. The upstairs tables were for two and four, and some were inlaid with chess gameboards. They chose a plain table against the window with a view of the street.

"I like this place," Shannon said. The music was not too loud and given that the song had segued from "Help" to "Yellow Submarine" it was set to an all-Beatles channel. "And I don't even game."

"A client told me about it. She was super worried about her kid going here, and pot and gaming, and, you know." Her voice took on a nasal tone. "All sorts of the wrong people. So I made a note of it, being all sorts of the wrong people myself."

"I'm happy to be the wrong sort of person. She sounds swell."

Kesa shrugged. "She pays her bills and I can't afford to be picky."

A silence fell and they each sipped from their frosty pilsner glasses. They'd ordered the night's special local brew, which turned out to be closer to an IPA than Shannon liked, but she managed. She didn't want to come off fussy or hard to please. On the other hand, she didn't want to seem like she had no standards or cultivated tastes. Like any beer would do. Or any woman. "It's drinkable."

"A bit strong. The fries are great though."

She nodded. There suddenly didn't seem to be anything much to talk about. Shannon was mostly aware that her skin was tingling, as if she'd rubbed a balloon across it to make static electricity. She knew exactly what would complete the electrical connection, and the pull got stronger every time Kesa looked at her as if she felt the same dancing energy as well.

"So tell me more about working for the marshals."

"I love it," Shannon said honestly. "It's important work. I graduated after 9-11 and they seemed like the perfect place for me. There's more chatter than ever, and sorting out the inconsequential from the important is a skill I'm good at. Other people do the dangerous work."

"It's less dangerous if you do your work well, isn't it?"

"That's the goal. Movies and TV don't get much of anything right. No bomb threat every day. No terrorist threat minutes from wiping out a subway. Most of what we do is intervene long before there's a countdown. Look for the same person with five aliases. I draw lines between pieces of data and decide how connected they are, all from my safe little cubicle. I hope you weren't picturing me in one of those tight-fitting bulletproof vests and a sidearm set at the perfect, completely useless angle on my hip."

Kesa's throaty laugh made Shannon's toes curl. "I have wondered if bulletproof vests really came in women's size two."

"Not on a government budget. Deputies will wear thicker clothes under for a better fit, but looks really aren't the point."

"Is that kind of work something you went to school for?"

"Criminal justice studies and public administration at Cal State LA. I specialized in cyber threats and digital data gathering and decided the Marshals Service was a good use of those skills. It's worked out." She didn't see any reason to add that after 9-11 all the fears her Aunt Ryanne had drilled into her seemed to be coming true, and she had felt that working in intelligence for the USMS to keep them safe had been her duty. "Why did you take up making custom clothes?"

"After my parents died I had to make money fast and at home. Child Services would have put my sister in foster care otherwise. I went to all the dry cleaners in Beverly Hills and Hollywood that took in alterations and did the work by the piece. One day enough for groceries, another day to pay the rent for the week. No time for college." She gave Shannon a sidelong look as if she feared Shannon would judge her choices.

"You did what you had to do. No choice was a bad choice."

"We ate a lot of rice and beans, and my sister got breakfast and lunch at school. That saved our lives. After a couple of years I got more requests to make dresses and suits, and from better and better fabrics. I hope someday…"

Shannon waited for Kesa to sip her beer.

"Someday," she went on, her eyes soft with a cherished dream, "I will have my own workshop and hire helpers. And pay them better than I got paid."

"That's a good dream." It was exactly the kind of dream Aunt Ryanne had said would only lead to disappointment and despair, but Shannon believed Kesa could do it.

Kesa smiled wistfully, then touched a fingertip to the back of Shannon's hand. "Would you like to dance?"

Shannon had had no idea what song was playing or if there was even music. She had said yes.

CHAPTER TEN

Shannon picked another packet of sweetener to fidget with. Anything not to meet Kesa's gaze again. "This is quite a coincidence."

"I thought you had moved away."

"I did. Because of Paz. He needed…space." She didn't know what Josie might have told her.

Kesa's voice was tight and guarded. "I had wanted to say… wanted to say a lot of things."

"I didn't let you." Say you're sorry, she told herself. But then she would have to explain the inexplicable and what did any of that matter four years later?

"No, you didn't." Kesa finally took a bite of her cake, though she didn't seem to take any pleasure in it. "This is awkward."

Shannon took a deep breath. "I think we'll have to adult our way through this. I'd rather the kids didn't know."

"Me too," Kesa said quickly. "There's no reason for them to. It was just a…"

"Thing." A wild, crazy, three-day thing that Shannon could easily picture the moment she closed her eyes.

"A thing." Kesa's shoulders rose and fell from a long, deep breath. "Josie's too young. They're both too young, with too much ahead of them in the next couple of years to get married. Live together, okay, maybe."

"I don't disagree. But they are adults."

"I know. Look, Josie—I love her, but she can be mercurial with her passions. I don't mean relationships. This is a first. But in general, she gets into new things with a lot of enthusiasm and it fades quickly. I can tell her that, but she won't hear a word of it." Kesa frowned at her cake. "We have trouble talking about groceries, let alone important stuff. And there'd be four lives disrupted over something that could fade in a few more weeks."

Shannon remembered Paz saying Josie's older sister was a bit of a hard-ass. She saw that side of her now, a tough resilience that put herself between any threat and her nest. That hadn't been the Kesa she'd met, though they hadn't gotten to know each other beyond the general outline. They'd been too busy learning unspoken truths and intimate secrets to care about day-to-day reality.

At least she could take off her marshals' hat for the time being. The reason she thought she might have seen Josie before was her resemblance to Kesa. They shared cheekbones and jawlines, had the same narrow nose with a slight nostril flare, but different eyes. Josie was stockier and solid, while Kesa was all edges that had grown sharper in the last four years. And which could yet feel so yielding and soft.

Stop that, Shannon warned herself.

"I'm afraid," she finally said. "I'm afraid that if I push him too hard, he'll stop listening to me. I'm not his guardian even. He needed out of the group home next door. Do you remember from when we...?" At Kesa's nod she continued, "I was able to convince the right people he was safer with me. We moved."

"Where to?"

"Portland. We came back because he got into UCLA as a transfer. He had to take two classes over, but UCLA is UCLA. There are more promising internships here as well."

"Josie getting in was a godsend, with covered tuition. It's life-changing. No student loans and a degree from that kind of school? I don't want her to throw it away." Kesa had finished about half of the cake by now, and her lips had lost their straight, hard line.

Shannon smacked her brain for bringing up memories of those soft, red lips on her body. Kesa clearly remembered their time together—and how it had fizzled. Shannon had tried to forget it. It hadn't been her finest hour. "I think the two of them are feeling like some kind of magic arrow hit them and that means life will be perfect."

"And nothing we say will convince them that lust isn't love."

Kesa's words were like a gray fog to Shannon, settling over everything with finality. It was the truth, wasn't it? Their sensuality had been like a river at flood stage, sweeping away common sense. At first it had been an exhilarating ride, running ahead of the current with nothing but blue sky.

Kesa had cocked her head as if daring Shannon to say otherwise. If Shannon had had any doubts that Kesa remembered all the details of their "thing," they were gone. Those blue eyes that she'd once fancifully thought the color of a deep lake on a sunny day were as hard as sapphire and a lot colder.

Kesa remembered, all right.

CHAPTER ELEVEN

The first night Kesa had had to herself in years and she had been tempted to buy mint chip ice cream and surf TV channels. The impulse to snap up a surprisingly available parking space near Olvera Street had led to an aimless, pleasant hour of window-shopping. She pondered and then shrugged off the boxy new retro '80s styles aimed at women not old enough to have experienced shoulder pads and leg warmers the first time around. The trend wouldn't last.

She decided she could afford a beer, which also bought her lively music and a perch on a barstool at one of the open-air eateries. The shade from the bare, thick wisteria vines overhead made Olvera so inviting in autumn, when LA's sunshine felt like the inside of a microwave to her—crispy and smelling of old, burnt things. Which, she supposed, described her as well.

Ice cream had seemed a better choice when Lingering Annoying Dude had decided she was meat on his menu. But then Shannon had leaned in next to her and the bland evening had quickly turned memorable.

At first she hadn't known what to make of Shannon. She was tall, but then nearly everyone was tall to her. Her brown eyes were mischievous, and her pale lips curved easily into smiles, at odds with a staid workday suit that said, "Nothing to see here, move along." Behind all of that was an air of confidence and charm that Kesa found truly alluring. Her ivory skin suggested she would blush easily, while her frank flirtation said she wouldn't mind—for the right reasons.

Kesa was out of practice at flirting. She was out of practice at dancing. And *really* out of practice at what might happen later if neither of them got scared. She'd become a de facto parent before she'd ever thought of anyone as a "girlfriend." She'd become so used to her own company that her ease with Shannon was a welcome surprise. Scary, but in a wonderful kind of way.

Her head tucked perfectly under Shannon's chin. The slow rhythm and George Harrison's low voice in "Something" was perfect. The heat of Shannon's body felt as if it could melt her thin blouse. She wished she were dressed for a date. Though Shannon had said she liked her perfume, she probably smelled like sewing machine oil with notes of pickle and cheeseburger.

Those thoughts hardly registered as Shannon's hands worked magic on her back. Kesa's nerves relaxed and her muscles tightened, a contradiction that sent flash and sparkle down her spine. Her hips had never felt so languid while other nearby parts of her were increasing their throb for attention.

A disapproving inner voice demanded an explanation for what she thought she was doing, dancing with a stranger in a bar. Josie got home Sunday afternoon, it pointed out. Life would go back to the way it had been, with no time for continuing anything. There was no time in her life for anything but hustling for work and putting food on the table. It reminded her that Josie was smart enough for college and she could get scholarships, but that meant application fees, and that meant more clients, more sewing. She'd heard clients talking about hiring consultants to get their kids into the schools of their choice and there was no money—

Shannon kissed her and just like that, with a whisper-sparkle of light across her brain, Kesa's mind was finally clear. All the worry, distraction, and questioning evaporated in a flash of white, hot heat.

Be right now, she told herself. And melted into Shannon's arms.

More kisses followed, slow and lingering. Warmth she had never felt before, as if she'd opened the door of a winter room to let in a summer day, gave her hips a mind of their own. They fit well together, like two different fabrics that became interesting, stronger, and more luminous side-by-side. Her hands burned to feel their edges and test their resilience.

Shannon's little laugh was self-conscious when they finally separated and sat down again. "Octopus's Garden" wasn't conducive to making out, Kesa had to admit.

"Would you like another beer?"

"Not really," Kesa said. All at once the idea that a night with this woman could slip through her fingers made her say, "I'm not ready for the night to end, though."

"Me neither." Shannon touched the back of Kesa's hand with a pale fingertip.

Kesa turned her hand upright, feeling a river of desire as Shannon slowly traced a line across her palm. "So…"

"Okay, I'm going to say it. There was a motel—"

"Yes."

"Are you sure?"

"Yes." She was grateful not to have to worry about going to a stranger's house, though her heart told her that Shannon wasn't a scary ax murderer. She found a smile, feeling very nervous, and followed Shannon out of the bar.

The motel marquee still said "Vacancy" and there were a few parking spaces left. When Kesa turned off the engine and darkness settled on the car, she was aware all at once that she didn't know how to do this.

Shannon opened the passenger door and the dim light revealed a shy smile. "I'll get the room."

"Let me give you some cash."

"This is my treat. In every way. Oh good lord." Shannon groaned. "That sounded way cheesy, didn't it?"

"Yes," Kesa agreed. "But I was about to say it."

Shannon quickly leaned in to kiss her. "It's like I wished for you from a genie."

She was gone before Kesa caught her breath, and minutes later, letting Shannon direct her to the room, she was still trying to find something that seemed like calm. Desires she never let herself feel had become screaming demands so insistent that she thought Shannon would hear the *now now now* throbbing inside her.

This is reckless, a distant voice whispered. Sex with a stranger. A one-night stand. What kind of girl are you?

This kind of girl, she thought. This is the girl I might have been. It was someone she could be, for a few hours at least.

She slowly pulled her silk shell over her head, very aware that Shannon was watching her with lips slightly parted. "Why don't you turn on the air or the fan?"

"Yes, you're right. It's stuffy." In moments a cooling breeze helped clear Kesa's head, and she moved behind Shannon, who was still fiddling with the knobs.

Her hands stilled as Kesa reached around to undo the buttons on Shannon's shirt, then pull it out of her slacks. Shannon didn't protest as Kesa slipped the garment off her shoulders and tossed it on the chair. The sound Shannon made when Kesa's small, satin-covered breasts pressed into her bare back made Kesa's head spin. Her fingers went to the zipper on Shannon's slacks, deftly flicking open the hook at the top and loosening them enough so they slid down Shannon's slim hips.

"Is this okay?" She gathered her hair in one hand and brushed it over Shannon's back.

"God yes. I've been wondering what your hair would feel like." Shannon put her hands on the wall, and Kesa was relieved to see she wasn't the only one trembling.

Skin to skin. Lips pressed to shoulders. The supple underside of breasts and the soft swell of bellies and hips. Knees bumping as they moved toward the bed tangled in each other's arms. Kesa surrendered all her caution and spread like a swollen river across the sheets, her fingers wound in Shannon's hair as she begged *please please* and shivered at Shannon's low, easy laugh.

"There?"

"Yes."

"Are you sure?"

She pulled Shannon's mouth into her with a lust that changed all the light to red and held her there. With so many years of desire and fantasy twined in her body the first was fast.

The radiant heat would have sent Kesa to sleep had Shannon not purred with satisfaction and said, "Let's do that again, but slower."

"I might not survive." Kesa gulped for air. "But what a way to go."

Shannon nipped at Kesa's thigh. "I'm trained in CPR and other forms of first aid."

"Are you going to talk or—"

There was no talking for a while, except needful, short words to heighten the conversation their bodies were having. Frantic kisses and hurried sips of water, intimate laughter and so much skin.

So much skin.

Kesa savored the soft place behind Shannon's knee, the rough texture of her nipples, and the tender, wet, needy places that responded to her touch as if she were a magician of all sensual delights.

She stirred, in the early morning hours, not sure when they'd fallen asleep. In moments she succumbed to the shelter of Shannon's arms again. Safe, every part of her had relaxed as if she were floating outside of time, and that had been the rarest sensation of all.

CHAPTER TWELVE

The reappearance of Paz and Josie, with Paz conspicuously holding a hefty textbook, gave Kesa a chance to catch her breath. She couldn't close her ears to the replay of stifled gasps and heavy, hot words whispered between them that first night. Josie's excited recounting of Paz dodging traffic to grab the book out of his friend's car only partially drowned out the graphic visuals in her head.

Paz immediately had a bite of his cake. "You didn't eat it while I was gone."

Shannon feigned an arrow to the heart. "You wound me, sir."

Josie eyed her next bite of tart with an anticipatory gleam. "He says he doesn't care for lemon sweets, but I went to the restroom last week and when I came back he tried to claim a Redguard appeared out of nowhere and took a huge bite."

"A Redguard?" Kesa busied herself with sectioning off a bite of her cake with the right ratio of sponge-to-icing.

"Skyrim. I introduced her to it and now she kicks my butt." Paz wrinkled his nose in response to Josie blowing him a kiss.

They were so obvious about their affection. Kesa supposed it was adorkable, but at the moment it was making her queasy. That, or the audio loop in her head. She glanced at Shannon and found her looking back. Was she remembering how they'd been together? The mutual fire, the wet heat, the moans and short, sharp shouts? The scratch of motel sheets against their backs? Their mutual shudder of pleasure when Kesa had wound her long hair around Shannon's wrists? Shannon hadn't challenged the pretense at restraint—had, in fact, relaxed into it with a noise of satisfaction that had made Kesa lightheaded.

It was all too vivid in her memory now. Moments she had tried hard to forget because after them had come foolish words and naive expectations. Then the long, disbelieving fall into heartbreak.

It was hard to breathe.

"So how did you two get on?" Kesa didn't know what to make of Paz's expression or the sidelong look he gave Josie.

Shannon frowned at her coffee. "If you mean did we solve anything going forward, the answer is no."

On more than one level, Kesa thought. Then Josie's too bright-eyed glance at Paz connected the dots.

This simply, unequivocally, absolutely could not be happening.

Her gaze met Shannon's long enough to read bitter amusement before Shannon closed her eyes as if to acknowledge the cosmic jest the universe had just heaped on them.

Well, it wasn't funny. Not funny in the least. Josie and Paz were too smart for their own good. *Did they really think that if they introduced the two lesbians we'd become so distracted we'd forget all about this marriage madness?*

It wasn't going to work, Kesa vowed, even as she realized she was so distracted with Shannon she'd stopped listening.

"So what do you think?" Paz was looking at Shannon expectantly.

"I haven't come to any conclusions." Shannon shook her head. "I don't know how to make you both see that there's no hurry."

Josie sent a glare in Kesa's direction. "You've infected her."

"That's not fair—"

Shannon cut off Kesa's angry retort with, "This is about common sense. Which may not seem like it has anything to do with love, but it does. Love's not a magic wand that solves all the difficulties. Surviving life takes more than that."

Was Shannon describing four years ago? Kesa had believed in magic until Shannon stopped returning her calls.

She chose her words with all the care she could manage over the anguished twisting of her heart. "Anything worth building takes a blueprint, right? Can you make a timeline with the steps you want to take? You admit you need some support—"

"If we were both women you'd be totally leading the Get Married parade," Josie snapped.

Kesa told herself to count to ten but only made it to three. "I'd be saying what I'm saying now. Take your time. Why rush? Have fun. Enjoy this."

"Because it won't last." Josie stabbed at the remains of her lemon tart.

"I didn't say that."

"You don't have to. I know that's what you're thinking."

Kesa glanced at Paz because she still couldn't look at Shannon.

His voice low and gentle, he said to Josie, "I can't even afford to buy you a ring yet."

"Rings are ten bucks at Walmart. I'm not asking for more than that."

"But I do want to give you more."

"Being poor doesn't frighten me, Paz."

"I know. Me neither. That's not the point, *cariña* Jo-Jo."

Shannon was back to stirring her coffee as if her life depended on it. "I don't doubt your courage. I'm kind of awed by it, in fact."

Kesa noticed that Josie was listening to Shannon and not bristling to interrupt her. It stung. "Courage all by itself isn't enough."

Shannon's spoon clattered against the table. "I think the idea of making up a timeline, a list, is a good one. I can support something when I know what it is."

"It's love," Josie said, but without the snark she would have given Kesa. "That's what it is."

Shannon resumed stirring, making it the best stirred coffee on the planet. "That's not everything. It's only a beginning. It takes care and feeding. That's what we're trying to say."

Kesa was floored to see tears in Josie's eyes. "You don't understand."

Shannon's voice was very low. "I do, better than you know."

Paz was looking at Shannon with some surprise, but he didn't say anything.

"Fine," Josie muttered. "We'll make a stupid list. Whatever makes you happy. But it doesn't change anything."

Disaster averted—for now, Kesa thought. Shannon too brightly asked if Kesa had made the jacket Josie was wearing.

"Kind of." Josie touched the denim sleeve. "I got it at a thrift store and Kesa took in the shoulders and let the waist out a little. And added the design on the back. It's for when I'm fancy. How did you know Kesa made clothes?"

Shannon didn't even blink. "We shared bios while you were gone." She seemed oblivious to the speculative glance Paz and Josie shared. "It looks like it was made for you. Very attractive."

Josie glanced at Kesa. "So you know she's a marshal."

"Not a marshal," Kesa corrected. "An analyst for the marshals."

Paz cocked his head. "It took me years to realize there's a big difference."

Kesa gulped. She was not very good at the lying thing, obviously.

Shannon distracted the table by opening her jacket to reveal her blouse. "No sidearm. It's one of the ways you can tell."

Kesa stared at the silhouette of Shannon's torso and fought back the memory of her fingertips on Shannon's ribs.

The server dropped off the bill with a false, "Take your time, no hurry."

Shannon reached for it first. "Let me."

"Don't be silly," Kesa protested.

"We'll take turns."

Dear lord, Kesa thought. Of course we'll see each other again. And again. The universe was having a great big laugh, and it was so totally and completely not fair.

"Thank you, Shannon," Josie and Paz said in unison.

As they finished their desserts and then gathered their things to leave, Kesa went back and forth between a heated swoon and what felt like a more than justifiable outrage. To have been thrown back into Shannon's path again was one thing. But Josie clearly already had more respect for Shannon than Kesa had ever received, and it was hard not to be bitter about that.

The kids were quickly out of sight, but not before glancing over their shoulders then putting their heads together to share excited whispers. Kesa gazed after them to keep from looking at Shannon as they left the crowded area in front of the diner.

"I don't know what I expected," Shannon finally said, "but it wasn't this."

"None of this. Josie never said Paz's guardian was gay or your name."

"Same here. They seem to think they were giving us a nice surprise."

"It was a surprise all right." Kesa turned in the direction of her car and was both pleased and alarmed that Shannon turned in sync with her. Tendrils of awareness seemed to sparkle between them.

Shannon scuffed a piece of broken glass into the gutter. "You never answered my question. How have you been?"

How had she been in the four years since she'd gotten dressed on Sunday afternoon and left Shannon's house to pick up Josie? Not knowing Shannon would ghost her? She didn't bother to hide the bitterness. "Does it matter how I've been?"

"I don't know what to say."

Kesa could think of two words: "I'm" and "sorry." Though really, what was there to say about two nights and an afternoon? About false courage and the fools that love makes of us? "What matters is they can't get married. Josie is too young. Paz seems very nice, but he has a life that won't be made any easier with marriage."

"I certainly saw a side of him tonight that is brand new to me. I don't doubt they believe they're in love."

"We both know it doesn't work that way." Love at first sight is lust in a pretty package, she could have added. They'd proved that.

"I don't think," Shannon said quietly, "you understand the first thing about what I know."

Kesa would not be put off by Shannon's stony cop face. "I don't. You're right. I never did, clearly. Nevertheless, Josie is too young." Stay on target, she told herself. Part of her wanted to laugh hysterically—why was she thinking about Death Stars?

Focus was hard, because now the only thing she could picture in her mind was the first time she had been in Shannon's arms and how every care melted off her body the moment Shannon's arms were around her.

"Josie is too young," Kesa said again. It was the one immutable truth of this situation and she clung to it like a life preserver.

They had been slowly walking away from the diner, ostensibly looking in the windows of the UCLA Bruins Gear store. Shannon seemed greatly interested in a blue and gold stadium cushion. "What are we going to do about it?"

"I'm afraid if I squeeze her any harder she'll run. She's very independent. Very strong-willed." What Paz admires now he might find wearing in the long run, she thought. "They can live together. I would rather that, frankly."

"It works out quite nicely, if I become their landlord." Shannon's expression didn't let on whether she liked that idea.

"You could refuse. Let them discover that paying bills is harder than they think."

"It won't deter Paz." Shannon drifted to the next shop window.

Kesa kept pace with her, once again wishing she'd simply worn her boots. "When did you…? I mean, he wasn't in your life when we…"

"He was, actually. A kid I shot hoops with next door. We became very close over the last few years."

"Josie called you his guardian."

"It's the simplest word, but there's no legal tie between us. Just history."

She would not elaborate, Kesa decided. Whatever their history was, it had brought out a steely edge. Did Josie know this history?

They didn't have more to say to each other and Kesa reminded herself she had hoped for an early night so she could start moving into the workshop before most people were up and about on a Saturday. She had a lost commission to make up for and the sooner she settled in, the sooner she would create more cash flow. Inevitably there would be unexpected expenses. She couldn't afford the time this stroll down Unhappy Memory Lane was taking.

They'd paused again, this time jostled closer together by a sudden stream of chattering people emerging from what turned out to be an art house theater. Kesa glanced at the marquee but didn't recognize the film. She was lucky to have the time to stay caught up on the superhero movies when they were in theaters.

All at once she was aware that Shannon's scent—shampoo and laundry soap, salt and citrus—was in her head. She felt steeped in it, like a luxurious hot bath, and it left her ridiculously weak.

She managed to murmur the inanely obvious, "It's gotten crowded."

"Where are you parked?"

"Blocks from here on the other side of Wilshire. You?"

"That direction too."

They turned in unison and Kesa blamed the heat from the sidewalk for her flushed skin. It didn't improve when they finally escaped the worst of the crowded Friday night sidewalks, but the noise at least diminished. It would have been easier to talk if only Kesa could have thought of something to say.

"And you still haven't answered my question." Shannon was back to window-shopping, her steps slow and her gaze on mannequins showing off the latest in swimwear.

Stripes were in, Kesa noted. "How have I been? More of the same. Until lately, nothing really any different. You?"

"I got my security clearance. Did you get your workshop?"

"I'm moving into my brand-new space tomorrow."

"Good for you!" Shannon finally looked at Kesa, but her face was in shadow. "I'm sure it was a lot of hard work."

"It was." Were they really talking as if the past hadn't happened? As if there was merely a civilized "one of those things not meant to be" between them? And not scalding-hot memories that Kesa had worked hard to bury? She didn't know what might show in her face, but for the first time she met Shannon's gaze directly. In the low light the dark brown eyes she had never forgotten were gleaming black.

"Your hair is a little shorter," Shannon murmured. "It was past your waist before."

"I just trimmed it." She should go home. Excuse herself politely and run for her life. Her hair had been a curtain around them that sunny Sunday afternoon in Shannon's bed, as she'd straddled Shannon's waist and bent to kiss her. There had still been an hour before she had to pick up Josie. A final hour of joy and abandon.

"Kesa," Shannon said.

She wanted to say that Shannon's shoulders seemed broader, her legs longer, and that she liked the soft highlights in her hair. The buzz of traffic faded, and headlights from passing cars seemed to dim. She turned to face the street and thought, "This is your last chance to save yourself."

Shannon said her name again, and it didn't matter why. When she turned back, Shannon's face was bathed in the white light of the sign above them promising WiFi and HBO and a refrigerator in every room.

It could have been the same motel from four years ago. The pounding in her ears, the throb of her heart beating high in her throat—just like four years ago. This couldn't be happening. These feelings weren't real. She couldn't afford to get mixed up in her head again about lust and love and what was supposed to be.

She had no idea how long they kissed on the sidewalk, lips pressed in wordless, helpless abandon. Her memory of registering for the room was a blur, and all the opportunities where she could have said "stop" or "no" or "this is a bad idea" were past.

Her jacket and skirt were on the floor, Shannon's shirt was unbuttoned, and her body knew only that the years had been so empty. Anger and disillusionment hadn't lessened the longing for Shannon's touch, her voice, her skin. Shannon was wanted and impossible and dangerous. And finally their connection was complete again.

The pale rose of Shannon's nipples, the freckles that sprinkled across her back and thighs—Kesa remembered all of Shannon and had never thought she would touch her again. Or hear that low sound of arousal followed by a rising gasp of passion.

Gulping in air, stunned, dizzy, clinging to a pillow as if it could save her, Kesa remembered and felt again the knowing, possessive exploration of Shannon's mouth and fingers. She was open again, saying "yes" again, telling herself not to cry and not to say the words that had ruined everything, even though they seemed—against all understanding—to still be true. They couldn't be. She'd spent so many nights telling herself that she had not fallen in love with Shannon in a single night.

The sound of her name on Shannon's lips had blown away all of her tissue-paper lies. The tiny part of her that was capable of wondering how she could come so undone was too weak to be heard as Shannon whispered her name and said "yes" to the questions Kesa dared to ask.

"Is this okay?"

"Can you do that again?"

"Do you want...?"

Her entire life had taught her that gifts came with price tags. Shared kisses, breathless whispers, their mutual surprise and laughter—all of it was a gift.

For a few hours she could indulge every foolish feeling. Tomorrow the bill would come due.

CHAPTER THIRTEEN

The moment Shannon's eyes fluttered open she knew she was alone. Her back was cold. She glanced at the motel room hutch for confirmation. Kesa's purse was gone.

She rolled over with a groan. What had she been thinking? It was after four a.m. and she'd never not been home at this hour since Paz had lived under her roof. How would she explain it to him?

She hated lying, but that's what she was going to do. No way was she admitting to Paz that she'd jumped into bed with his girlfriend's sister. Not because they'd fallen into lust in an evening and certainly not because that was precisely what had happened four years ago.

No, she wasn't going to explain anything to him. There was such a thing as personal privacy, and there were choices that you didn't have to tell your kids about. Not that he was her kid, but it was the same great big *eww*. She'd gone for a drive to the beach and fallen asleep. There. That would work.

After a quick shower and a truly horrible cup of motel-room brewed coffee, she left the room key on the dresser and let herself out into the cool pre-dawn air. The stillness felt as if morning was holding its breath because night wasn't ready to go just yet. There was only the faintest hint of sunrise at the horizon as she walked to her car along an almost deserted Wilshire Boulevard. Maybe she would get home before Paz even realized she wasn't there.

In spite of the shower she could smell Kesa on her skin. And could taste her on her lips. They had been like liquid electricity, like that first night all over again. It was impossible. The past was an ugly blot in Shannon's memory. They weren't the same people and yet.

And yet.

After she parked the car, she stood on the front porch for a few minutes, trying not to relive the past few hours. But she couldn't stop. There it was, in vivid digital display across her mind, the moment when Kesa had pushed Shannon's legs open and trailed her sensitive, supple fingers over her inner thighs.

Kesa's gaze on her face had been knowing and heated with anticipation. "Slow or fast?"

Shannon had shuddered at the sensation of Kesa's fingertips so close to where she wanted them. "You decide."

"Well, then." Kesa's tongue was suddenly on her and it was fast, desperately fast, a spillway opening as all the feelings she'd dammed up seem to pour out of her all at once.

In that moment Shannon had felt exploded, all her bones and nerves spread from each other, and Kesa had flowed into those empty spaces, like she had that first night, their second night, and all of that last lazy Sunday afternoon four years ago. Kesa was wound all through her again.

She put the key in the door with a shaking hand. As hard as she'd worked to shake it, her aunt's voice was all at once in her ear. *Don't go down that road again. The situation is daft, reckless, dangerous. You haven't changed.*

They were two consenting adults who had obviously needed sex. Sex and closure.

She hadn't expected to ever see Kesa again, that was a certainty. The spackle she'd used to cover the hole inside her had crumbled to dust with a single glance.

She crept into the house and was relieved to see Paz's door closed and hear the reassuring sound of his snores. She stripped off her clothes, pulled on a sleep tee, and curled up in her cold bed.

1000. She'd driven out to the beach. *999.* Fallen asleep. *998.* Her hands on Kesa's breasts.

Damn.

1000. 999...

CHAPTER FOURTEEN

"I went for a drive," Kesa lied. "Trying to sort things out. I stopped at a drive-thru for coffee and fell asleep for a while in the parking lot."

Josie didn't seem concerned with the details, which was fortunate because Kesa was learning just how bad a liar she was.

"We went dancing at a friend's house party." Josie pushed at the textbooks scattered across the tiny dining room table, her face drooping with fatigue. "But he dropped me off early. We both have midterms on Monday."

"I thought he helped you study."

"He's distracting most of the time." Josie closed the book on top as she yawned. "His tests from this class are helpful, but I'm better at conceptual math than he is. So he can only help so much."

"That's a good thing to have figured out."

"I'm in love with who he is, not some fake made-up paragon."

What did Josie know about love? Kesa felt steeped in Shannon's scent. She wanted to take a shower and try to scrub it off because it was making it so hard to think. She'd run away like a thief in the night. How could she possibly think she knew more about love than Josie did? "I'm afraid for you, Jo-Jo."

"I know, Key." Josie seemed too tired to find her usual anger. "You don't have to be Mother anymore. I've grown up."

"I can't turn it off like a light switch."

"Are you even trying?" Josie's slippers scuffed across the kitchen linoleum as she went to rinse out her cereal bowl and set it in the drainer.

"Yes, actually. It's just not working."

Josie's mouth twisted, but a snarky retort seemed beyond her. "Do you still need help moving into your workshop? Paz could bring his car on Sunday afternoon. It's a hatchback too."

"You guys have to study. I can manage." It would take her a lot of trips, but hard labor might help her sort out the waves of longing and regret—why did she hurt? She ached, deeper than her bones. "Maybe I'll leave the machines until Monday night and you can help then. It'll take a while to move all the fabric and supplies as it is. Plus I have to do some cutting and assembly to stay on schedule. So it can be all moving all weekend."

Josie stifled a yawn. "Okay." She absentmindedly scratched her butt on her way to her room.

She's still a kid, Kesa thought. She doesn't know.

The shower wasn't hot enough to leave her feeling clean, even though she emerged steaming and ruddy. Wiping the fogged mirror clean, she regarded her tired eyes for a moment and had to look away. Josie didn't know how deep some hurts could go.

After a few scant hours of sleep she was up again, loading the handcart the building super had lent her and jamming as much as she could into her car for each trip. By the middle of the day Kesa found it easier to push away the memories of the previous night's hours in Shannon's arms. The weather had turned hot and sticky, and every ten-minute drive between home and her new workshop was sweltering. Multiple trips with bolt rolls left her sneezing from the dust. The boxes and bags of thread, trim, bias tape, buttons, and other accessories became heavier with every step.

Still, her spirit lifted every time she put the key in the lock of her new space. The three-story building was generic 1950s LA industrial, with the interior gutted and rewired sometime in the last decade for artist and crafts trade space. Her room was in a second-floor corner and looked out over a community garden and small park. A weaver was a neighbor on one side and a nutritionist on the other. The leasing agent had said that some of the other tenants worked all hours so there was usually someone in the building. She would be able to work in the evenings in relative safety. Her lease agreement included a numbered parking space in the gated basement.

It was a long way from LA's renowned Fashion District, but she thought it much smarter to be closer to the people she wanted to make clothes for: celebrities and wannabees. Beverly Hills, Laurel Canyon, and West Hollywood were all within a 25-minute radius. This location was smart and cheap at a third of the rent a Fashion District spot half the size would have cost.

She had one large, high-ceiling room, a kitchenette, and a water closet to herself. The built-in storage cabinets gave her more room for supplies than she'd ever had before. The old walls were freshly painted white, and the vinyl wood grain flooring was unmarred. When she could afford it she would add a TV and a DVD player so she could go on listening to movies, concerts, and documentaries from the library while she worked. Once she was organized, she would be able to set up decorative screens in a corner for measurements and fittings. Many clients would be willing to come to her, but only if they felt comfortable. It was worth the investment in mirrors and decor because of the hidden financial bonus of reducing wear and tear on her aged car. She really didn't want to replace it anytime soon.

When she opened the windows she discovered she was downwind of the Asian bakery on the corner. It wouldn't help her waistline to have such mouth-watering carbohydrates so close, but the aroma of baking bread chased away the dust and mustiness of the room and comforted her aching heart.

Her last trip of the day was the one she had looked forward to the most. The table that leaned on one side of her bed, that she used to cut cloth, was now set up and ready for work. Her bedroom had floor space for the first time since they'd moved in. She would even be able to reach the window and let in light. Which didn't make it any less lonely, she thought. Only less pathetic. She pushed away images of Shannon in her bed. Not helpful.

She tugged and pulled the table up the stairs after discovering it wouldn't fit in the old elevator. A very hot shower and large glass of wine was in order when she got home.

Even so, sleep was hard to find for a second night in a row. Toward dawn on Sunday, when the city was at its most quiet, she fancied that she could hear Shannon's heartbeat in the pillow under her ear.

CHAPTER FIFTEEN

"So what did you think of Josie?"

Shannon had been expecting Paz to ask that question all day Sunday, but he'd hurried off to his once-a-week gig washing dishes at the local chicken and waffles diner and had been buried in his books when he'd gotten home. Now he was eating Captain Crunch out of the box and watching Shannon pack up her shoulder bag with files to take back to work.

"I liked her. She seemed smart and articulate. Full of energy."

"She's way smarter than I am. It's like she can have three conversations at the same time, while reading. She remembers factorials and when I showed her Skyrim she understood all the battle advantages in a few minutes. It's awesome."

"Sounds like she has a great memory."

He bobbed his head enthusiastically. "She can reel off movie dialogue word for word, even a movie she's only seen once."

Shannon didn't volunteer that Josie's sister did that as well. "I do like her. And I get why you like her."

With a nonchalance so obvious it proved he would never have a career that involved subterfuge, Paz asked, "What did you think of her sister?"

There's no way he could know about the motel, Shannon told herself. "She's also very smart and articulate. Must run in the family."

"I was surprised how alike they are. Not on the surface," he added quickly.

They were both intense. And able to risk their hearts, she thought, but Paz didn't know that about Kesa. "It's probably not a good idea to tell Josie that."

"*Wey*, I am not stupid."

Shannon laughed and agreed. "I'm still worried about your future."

"I know. At some point, I'm on my own, though. *Es mi vida.* Mistakes and all."

Shannon slung her bag on her shoulder. "One of the fun aspects of adulthood is how mistakes latch on and don't let go."

"'Fun' is not the word I'd use."

"I chose it instead of another F-word," she said over her shoulder as she went out the front door.

The short spring season was clearly waning, and the morning heat slowed Shannon's pace toward the bus stop. The plum blossoms had all dropped, but the trees weren't fully leaved yet and the sun was almost more than her sunglasses could handle. She hadn't slept well for the third night in a row and was really hoping that immersing herself at work would push Kesa completely out of her mind, at least for a while.

They were going to meet again. They'd told the kids to make a plan and at some point they'd all get together to talk again. She dreaded it and hoped it was soon, creating a deeply annoying mental swirl she couldn't resolve.

Her morning ritual Diet Mountain Dew, security screening, and passage through the Marshals Service door did steady her mind somewhat, but she felt off her game. Let it go for a while, she told herself. You can only do your job if you are completely focused. She made herself read the weekend analyst's messages twice and reviewed the report of fugitives taken into custody twice as well, cross-referencing names into her classified database to make sure intelligence agencies didn't have first dibs.

Her morning got better when she saw that colleagues at the Justice Department had agreed with her assessment to consolidate several aliases into a single suspect. She forwarded the information to her supervisor, Gustavo, and got back an all caps "YOU ROCK!" from him. He'd given her a great review last week, which had eased her lingering anxiety about working with a new supervisor. Her security clearance had come up for renewal just after she'd arrived back in LA, and that meant he'd seen her background—including her tick of the box next to "homosexual." The high marks meant she probably didn't have to watch her back on that count. She hoped for a world someday where nobody had to worry about it.

In spite of that relief, as she sat looking at her lunch of homemade PB&J and a bag of pretzels, her mind treated her to a full-on replay of Friday night. If she and Kesa met up again—not if, she corrected, when—it would be even more awkward, especially if both kids were hoping she and Kesa would be distracted with each other. Didn't it make sense to get together in some neutral place and clear the air? Some place where there was no motel in a 100-block radius?

She chased the thought away by queuing up her searches for Seychelles' aliases. To her grim delight, she finally got a solid hit. "Henry Lymon" had been confirmed by CCTV facial recognition in Toronto during the past week. Her growing suspicion that he might be trying to enter the US seemed reasonable. The marshals in Buffalo or Rochester could work with border control to anticipate the entry, allow it, and then pick him up on behalf of the Central California District, where his bank fraud warrants had been issued. She'd then let the intelligence agencies know where to find their former asset and under what name and score points for interagency cooperation.

She spent the next hour carefully assembling the information that would allow the district offices involved to confirm the fugitive's identity and writing up her official confirmation that

"Henry Lymon" was a fugitive of heightened interest with multiple aliases. A scanned passport with any of those known aliases would set off the right alarm bells.

Her summary finished to her satisfaction, she forwarded it to Gustavo for his review. She hoped Seychelles did enter the US—it would be deeply satisfying to have him in custody and put an end to his dabbling in misery.

What wasn't satisfying was how quickly her brain, freed from the Zen bliss of assembling pieces of the Seychelles' puzzle, returned to scanning through memories of Kesa and motels. She didn't like having personal secrets, and that's what her history with Kesa was. If Paz and Josie continued to date, that secret could well turn toxic.

That would be bad, wouldn't it? Of course it would. She and Kesa should have a private talk to discuss their affair. Not affair, their…thing.

Her evening bus ride was crowded and hot, so she waited until she was home to look Kesa up on social media. A Twitter account popped up for Kesa Sapiro, "*Couturière*, Designs for Women, Loves Movies."

Shannon tapped open a direct message screen, chose her words carefully, and pressed Send.

CHAPTER SIXTEEN

"Got it? My hand is slipping." Kesa couldn't keep the panic out of her voice.

"I can hold it." Paz flashed her a confident smile. "Long enough for you to adjust."

Josie dodged around them on the stairs. "I'll get the door open."

Kesa quickly wound the thick blanket they were using as a sling around her arm and shoulder again. The sewing machine wasn't heavy for two people, but it was awkward. Getting them both out of the apartment hadn't been hard—a rolling cart and elevator had done the trick. But the elevator in her new workspace had chosen to break down midafternoon. Paz's suggestion of a sling was a good one, that is, until it had slipped off her shoulder.

The second machine went up the stairs more easily, and the three of them sprawled on the folding chairs Kesa had bought earlier at the discount office supply outlet.

"Thanks, really, I mean it. I couldn't have done that without you." She dug her phone out of her pocket. It was already low on battery and had been buzzing off and on for the last few minutes. "Dinner's on me. That is, if you want pizza."

"I have to get home," Paz said. "Shannon is expecting me for dinner."

Kesa stared at the message from ShannonD. She realized Paz had said something and glanced up. "I'm sorry. Shannon...?"

"She's expecting me for dinner."

"Another time then," Kesa said vaguely. She looked at her phone again.

Shannon had written, "I think we have things to talk about. I'd prefer to do it privately. Could we meet some evening this week?"

Josie's shadow fell over the display. "Is something wrong?"

Kesa hurriedly shoved the phone back into her pocket. "No. No, the battery is really low is all."

"I'm going to walk Paz to his car. I'll be back in a few. Maybe instead of pizza we could pick up Chinese on the way home?"

"Sure." Kesa had known she and Shannon would see each other again, but not alone. Though the request made sense, she supposed. Wherever they met, though, it needed to be as far away from a motel as possible. "Fine."

Josie gave her an odd look but followed Paz out the door. She could hear their voices rising and falling as they went down the stairs, light and happy. They had no history to weigh down their words. What was it about them that made it so easy?

She took a deep breath as she surveyed her new surroundings. Two projects were jumbled together on the folding table. Both had a deadline of this Friday. Bolts of fabric were stacked haphazardly in several piles on the floor. Now that she had space she could haunt remainder sales and build up a good stock of quality accessories at bargain prices, but first it all had to be organized. She'd make one more trip tonight for the last of the boxes and some supplies to make the kitchen useful, but she also needed to buy a coffeemaker and ice cube trays and something for clients to sit on that wasn't a bargain basement folding chair.

Money was going out the door every minute and it was up to her to bring some in. It wasn't as if any of this was optional. She'd become a workaholic because the other choice had been losing Josie to Child Services.

She was going to lose Josie to Paz. Or someone like him. That was the way of life, wasn't it?

Kesa didn't realize she was crying until a wide-eyed Josie asked her what was wrong.

"Nothing, Jo-Jo." She wiped at her eyes. "I'm overwhelmed. Really tired."

To her surprise, Josie knelt on the floor next to her chair to give her a bracing hug. "This is huge. You have a workshop, at last. Maybe we can skip dinner and go right to ice cream."

Kesa laughed and agreed. Her phone was like a lead weight in her pocket. She would answer Shannon later. Right now ice cream took precedence.

CHAPTER SEVENTEEN

Nom Nom Pocha in Koreatown was about as prosaic as a meeting place could be. The chatter of other patrons, clang of pots and pans, and the hissing spatter of an espresso machine combined to make romance hard to contemplate. Kesa hoped Shannon wasn't late. She'd deliberately picked the half hour before the Mahjong game so that she would have to leave. There would be no prolonged contact. No finding themselves in front of another motel.

She knew she'd made the right decision when she saw Shannon framed in the doorway. Her light gray suit jacket and slacks accentuated her long, lean frame, and the pale peach tint of her Oxford shirt brought out hints of red in her hair. Competent, professional, cool—it was as if she'd taken lessons from the marshals on how not to be noticed while instantly conveying authority.

Shannon tucked her sunglasses into a pocket inside her jacket and her gaze swept the eatery to settle almost immediately on Kesa. The lines in her face eased and her lips curved in a smile

Kesa helplessly returned. Just like that, Kesa's heart fluttered in her throat. Her ears singed the side of her head. The reaction was purely physical, and it didn't mean anything. It didn't *have* to mean anything, she told herself staunchly. Their tryst had been completely consensual, and her feeling that she ought to be guilty about it was puritanical social conditioning, and that was all.

She saw her attempt to school her reaction mirrored in Shannon's shifting expression: caution, distance, but nothing that could be called nonchalance.

There would be no repeats, Kesa told herself as her eyes devoured every detail of Shannon's walk, and she really didn't want anyone else to know about four years ago, let alone Friday night. She pushed away the voice that asked, if there was nothing to be ashamed of, then why did she want to keep it a secret?

Her last thought before Shannon slid into the chair on the other side of the small table was, "I don't have to make sense if I don't want to!"

"Hi." Shannon glanced at Kesa's coffee cup. "Is it good here?"

"It's coffee. Hot brown liquid in a cup."

"Sounds great. I don't get the trend toward burnt and full of sediment. I'll be right back."

Kesa pretended to check her phone while she used her peripheral vision to watch Shannon navigate the line. Though she chided herself for being ridiculous, she even feigned not immediately noticing when Shannon approached the table again. She wasn't aware of Shannon's every move, no, not her. She reminded herself that this woman had put her into a tailspin that had left her an emotional zombie. It wasn't going to happen again. Absolutely not.

The silence was, of course, awkward. Like it could be anything else, Kesa thought. Shannon was stirring her coffee—a favorite pastime it seemed.

Well, there was one thing she could say. "I'm sorry I left. I didn't want to wake you and I wanted to get home before it was too late to explain to Josie."

"I understand." She sipped from her mug. "That's not too bad."

Kesa tore her gaze away from Shannon's hands and retreated to sarcasm. "The coffee is okay. I think we're done here."

"I'm sorry too." Shannon finally looked up from the cup.

Kesa's heart skipped a beat. Those wide brown eyes were tinged with purple, a fact Kesa had once upon a time found beautiful. Not that she did now. "For what exactly?"

"It shouldn't have happened."

Was Shannon talking about Friday night or four years ago? Kesa wasn't brave enough to ask. "Maybe not. But we're consenting adults."

Shannon nodded and went back to stirring her coffee. Kesa quelled the urge to snatch the stir stick out of her hand and stab her with it. Shannon was the one who had thought they should get together to clear the air. Now she seemed to have nothing to say. She hadn't had anything to say four years ago, either, so nothing had changed apparently.

Kesa tried again. "I like Paz. I really do. He helped me finish moving into my workshop. He and Josie are good to each other, at least what I've seen. But that doesn't change how I feel. They're too young. They think...that love fixes everything."

"I don't know that we'll be able to change their minds. So I've been wondering about how we might slow them down. Like until Paz's internships and degree program are all settled. That could be six to nine months from now."

"Josie won't want to wait that long. To her mind microwave popcorn takes *for-ev-er*."

"Does she keep her promises?"

Kesa blinked. "Yes."

"So does Paz. When they come up with their plan, we'll need a bribe that will extract promises from them."

Kesa shook her head. "I don't know. Josie can be inflexible when she's committed to something."

"To tell you the truth, the more you tell me about her, the more I like her."

"Sometimes it's not that easy to live with."

Shannon's lips twisted in a half smile. "I get that."

"So...Paz. He was a foster kid?"

"Yeah. He lived next door and over the years I guess you could say I took him under my wing. We shot hoops at first, then I took him to a Lakers' game for his birthday. Paz taught me how to have fun. Joy was not in my aunt's nature and it took me a while to get out from under that." Shannon swallowed hard.

Kesa remembered stirring in Shannon's arms that magic Sunday afternoon and hearing a thud of a basketball against a backboard and the sound of voices mixed in competition. "So Child Services let him move in with you?"

"No, he lived next door. Gia, his foster mother, was good for him. She was completely suspicious of me at first, but once I convinced her I was gay and there was no hanky-panky with this undeniably attractive teenager, we were cool. I took the boys to the beach a bunch of times. Cheap outing." Shannon blinked and looked away. "It was a lot like having a little brother."

"So when he was released from Child Services he moved in with you?"

Shannon's eyes shuttered and her face stilled. "No, not exactly. He had to move to Portland. I decided to follow him."

Kesa knew her puzzlement showed on her face, even as Shannon's expression sent a chill through her. "Why?"

Shannon took a deep breath as she drummed her fingers on the side of her coffee cup. "A couple years ago he saw something. A very bad crime. He was in the wrong place at the wrong time. I got him into protected custody and he agreed to change his name."

"Oh my god. What—"

"There was nothing official that tied me to him, and I knew the moment he was considered out of danger there he'd be in a new city and his payments for minimal rent would end. He had dreams, practical ones he could make happen. But he was going to pay and pay for being in the wrong place."

Kesa fought down a surge of panic. "Is Josie safe?"

Shannon quickly reached across the table to squeeze Kesa's hand. "I swear to you, she is. She is absolutely safe."

Kesa believed her. Shannon wouldn't lie about Paz's safety, and it wasn't in her nature to care less about Josie's. The warmth of her hand eased the chill of fear. I'd trust this woman with my life, Kesa thought. But not with my heart. I can't do that again.

"I believe you." She withdrew her hand, ostensibly to sip her coffee. "So, you became an unofficial guardian?"

"That about describes it. Gia's love, the tough affection of the older boys, everything that had kept him safe and given him a shot at a level playing field in life was wiped out. And it wasn't his fault. So I moved as soon as I could arrange it. Same job, different location for me. Then he got into UCLA and we came back. I tell myself he's safe and he is. But I'm still me." She gave Kesa a chagrined smile. "There's nothing to worry about, so I worry."

Kesa's fuzzy picture of Shannon's last few years was coming into focus. Her own life had hardly altered its day-to-day demands.

She wished, too, that the sudden departure to Portland could explain why Shannon had ghosted her, but the timing didn't seem to be related at all. She wasn't going to ask why, then. She shouldn't have to, but it was clear that Shannon wasn't going to volunteer the truth either. What did it matter anyway? Her heart was just as shattered. "I can see how he would be truly aware that life isn't guaranteed. Josie feels that way. Maybe because our parents died when she was so little." She struggled to find a smile. "I made a big mistake letting her see *An Inconvenient Truth*. She had nightmares and hounds me about sustainable fabrics."

"Given the weather lately, I'm not sure she's wrong to panic."

"Mad Max Land, she called it. But she's still too young, and I don't think she gets the legal part of marriage. The financial entanglement, for one thing."

"Neither does Paz. Rather, I think he does get it. The problem is that I want him to care about it and he doesn't."

"Josie would probably say that talking about marriage that way is being an assassin of love."

Shannon sighed. "Well, society forced people like us to weigh every unromantic aspect of legal marriage because we couldn't have it until recently."

"True that." Kesa broke the allure of warmth in Shannon's eyes by glancing at her watch. "I really have to get going. An appointment."

"Okay. Um, maybe we could email if we think of a new approach?"

Kesa extracted a business card from her purse as Shannon drew one from her pocket. "I'm guessing you don't want me to email you via the marshals?"

"Right." Shannon took back the card and wrote on the back. "Use this one."

"Okay."

"Yeah, okay."

Get up, Kesa told herself. Time for a graceful exit. Do not think about the way her lips feel and the tenderness in her hands. For heaven's sake, get up.

Shannon was the one who shifted enough to break their eye contact. Kesa struggled to her feet and tucked her purse under her arm. At least she was wearing her boots and her path to the door was steady and quick. She didn't look back.

CHAPTER EIGHTEEN

Shannon watched Kesa's small figure move through the parking lot with such purpose that a sensible person would think twice about getting in her way. Kesa was a packet of unexpected contradictions that was as fascinating as it was unsettling.

Just as she was about to disappear around the adjacent building Kesa turned abruptly and waved toward the street. A young woman, too far away to discern more details than a splash of purple hair, was crossing toward her. Shannon got a good look at Kesa's body, relaxed and unguarded as she bumped shoulders with the newcomer and they continued out of her sight.

Was that the appointment?

She stared into the bottom of her coffee cup and asked herself exactly what she had thought would happen here. Admit it, she told herself. You thought you might end up having dinner, then…

Well, Kesa had closed the door very firmly on that. Shannon didn't even know if Kesa had a girlfriend. She hadn't cared to know and she supposed she ought to feel guilty. Guiltier. Kesa deserved someone younger, more carefree than Shannon would ever be.

Seeing her again had swept away all her common sense. She didn't like herself this way. She preferred a world that connected with clear lines. Puzzles solved. Order established from chaos. She'd thought about Kesa for months and had managed to forget about her—for a while—in Portland. Now Kesa was back in her head, making everything a jumble. She was already wondering how long it would be until she saw Kesa again. This physical thing, this connection, the sizzle and spark. It had been lightning the first time they met. It was lightning now. Brilliant and impermanent. They were meant to have fun together, Shannon told herself. If they could leave it at that it wouldn't feel so dangerous.

She glanced again at the spot where Kesa and the purple-haired woman had gone out of sight. It would be easier if that were a girlfriend, wouldn't it?

CHAPTER NINETEEN

Cami matched her pace with Kesa's as they crossed the street toward Auntie Ivy's. "So who was that?"

"Who was who?"

"In Jason's. Tall, white, definitely handsome?"

Hell, Cami had seen her with Shannon. "A potential client."

Cami let the lie sit for a few paces, then said, "I walked right by you while you two were talking. About clothes, sure."

"Okay, not a client. It concerns Josie."

"She's like a cop or something, right? She was very—like her clothes were deliberately plain. Razor-sharp creases on her slacks. Very *Men in Black*."

Surprised by Cami's keen observation, Kesa explained, "She's an 'or something.'"

"Is Josie okay?"

"Yes. It's not a big deal."

They turned the final corner toward Auntie Ivy's apartment where Kesa usually took a moment to admire the music mural, especially on a bright, sunny day. But she was too unnerved by Cami's knowing about Shannon to care.

"I called out to you while I was in the line. Tried to catch your eye."

"It wasn't an easy conversation."

"You're not…" Cami abruptly stopped walking and glanced in the direction of the apartment, which was not quite yet in view. "If that was a date, I mean, you're not avoiding saying so because it was with a woman, are you?"

Surprised, Kesa asked, "Why would I do that? You know I'm gay."

"It always seemed kind of theoretical."

Ouch. True, but still ouch. "I work, you know how much. Plus, I can be a lesbian, be attracted to women, and not have to have sex with them to prove it."

Cami stared at the stoplight and it struck Kesa how vulnerable she was. "I kind of thought sex was the point."

"It can be. Depends on the people. I only know about me."

"How did you know?"

It was a question no one had ever asked her before. "I guess I realized, like in movies. When Keanu Reeves kisses Carrie-Anne Moss in I forget which Matrix movie, I really wanted to be the one kissing Carrie-Anne Moss. I mean, I didn't want to be Neo, I wanted to be me and kissing Trinity. Like a lot. And that happened all the time. Not even kissing, just being that important to someone. And the someone was always another woman. So, a lesbian."

Cami blurted out, "That's how I feel sometimes," then looked down as if she feared the ground would swallow her whole.

"Cool." Kesa had never had a conversation about the complexity of sexuality with Josie. She probably should have, now that she thought about it. But then Josie's movie star crushes had always been rugged males. Talking about birth control had been the priority. "Thank you for telling me that, and trusting me."

"I don't know how to tell *lola*."

"Auntie Ivy is pretty smart. When you're ready, I bet you can trust her too." What else should she say? Cami looked about to cry. "It's not like you have to make up your mind. There's no deadline."

Cami took a shaky breath. "Everybody says be yourself. Be true to who you are. Well, what if you don't know?"

"Maybe who you are is someone on a journey. Right now." When Cami didn't respond she went on. "Nobody starts out with all the answers. You go along and figure things out. Sometimes you find out the answers you thought you had were false." Her voice trailed away and she looked back toward the deli.

"Everybody at school is bi, or ace, or trans, or queer—they all know."

Kesa brought her gaze back to Cami's face. Her eyes were dark with worry and still shimmered with tears. "I'll let you in on a secret. The people who tell you they have all the answers haven't asked themselves the right questions yet."

"So you don't have all the answers?"

"God, no." I'm a mess, she wanted to admit, but it wasn't something a seventeen-year-old needed to hear. "It took me a while, but now I can tell you the name of any fabric." She touched Cami's shirt at the shoulder. "Cotton knit blend with four percent Lycra. That's experience. I can tell the difference now between damask, jacquard, and matelassé, but I still refer to samples to be sure. The trouble with feelings is that there's no swatch book for them, and we only learn their names as we go along. So a lot of the time, you know you're feeling something but you don't have the words for it. Or you pick the wrong words and it all gets really confusing."

Cami stared at her shoes until the moment the light changed, then bolted across the street, leaving Kesa to trail slightly behind. She understood anger and frustration. Grief and weariness. Anxiety when she'd taken Josie to school for the first time and watched her disappear through the gate. Exhilaration when a client loved the garment Kesa had made for her.

She'd thought she'd had the right word for how she'd felt about Shannon. Resting in Shannon's arms that Sunday afternoon together four years ago, when knowing each other could be measured in hours, she'd been languid and spent. And certain, so certain, she knew the words to describe what she was feeling. The light had softened to gold, and she'd felt brave. Had said softly, into the warm, fuzzy glow of Shannon's drowsy smile, "I love you."

Cami clattered up the stairs to the apartment and Kesa realized she'd forgotten to get lumpia. She called out that she'd be back in five minutes and Cami waved in response.

I love you—the words still echoed in her head. Three beautiful words that became something else entirely when they weren't answered.

CHAPTER TWENTY

As Shannon navigated the welcome distraction of the bus-train links that would get her home, she pictured Kesa's broad smile as she greeted her friend. She hadn't relaxed that way around Shannon. Well, whose fault was that? Who let her go four years ago?

Picking over what she ought to have done didn't solve the present. She had to get Kesa out of her system. Crazed, wild, jungle sex hadn't done it.

Lizard brain suggested they hadn't done it enough and should try again.

She swatted that idea away. She should focus on work, on her running, train for a 10K or something. She even got out her notepad and jotted down an action plan for it: determine reasonable training goals, estimate future readiness, find compatible event as deadline. All the while she relived the soft brush of Kesa's hair on her back and ignored that behind that silken memory were battling emotions, neither of which she wanted to own.

The aroma of Paz's specialty chili greeted her when she reached home. Heavenly, she thought, and then, with a pang, she recognized Josie's laugh. She was going to have to get used to them together, she told herself.

"That smells amazing," she called out as she put her things down on the oak sideboard that had been her aunt's. It was one of the few pieces she'd kept when she'd sold the house in Boyle Heights. Aunt Ryanne had said it had been Shannon's grandmother's. It was literally the only thing Shannon knew for sure her mother had touched. Paz, she thought, didn't even have that. Everything in his world had come to him brand new, yet he was standing in their kitchen hugging a girl he wanted to marry and ready to risk everything to share a future with her.

She honestly did not know where he got his courage.

"All this, and he cooks." Josie was snuggled into Paz as he stirred the chili, and suddenly Shannon could see how her smile resembled her sister's. Lucky Paz to be on the receiving end of the Sapiro charm.

"Gia taught us all how to make eggs, boil pasta, grate cheese, and cook rice and beans. She said anything else was a bonus."

Josie tipped her face into the steam rising from the stove for another appreciative sniff. "I like the sound of Gia."

"She's a good woman," Shannon agreed.

With a glance at Shannon, Paz said, "I was thinking of dropping by to see her sometime soon."

Shannon's gut told her to discourage him. Contact with his past was risky. But she'd told Kesa that Josie wasn't in danger because that was the truth. She had to start believing it herself. "I know she'd like to hear from you. You've turned out well, and she's the biggest reason why."

"Don't I know it." Paz dipped a spoon into the bubbling pot. "Here—taste."

Shannon watched as he blew on the hot beans before offering the spoon to Josie. In her mind's eye she could see him offering the first bite of wedding cake to someone, but what had seemed to be Josie morphed into Kesa and then it wasn't Paz at all. Her voice slightly unsteady, she asked, "When will it be ready?"

"Maybe thirty minutes? Beans are still a little firm."

Josie made deeply appreciative noises. "They are, but it tastes so good."

"You keep stirring. I'll be back in a minute," he added, excusing himself.

Josie took over the slow stir that Paz insisted meant creamier beans. "You did your part too, you know. With him."

Shannon fetched herself a glass of water before easing onto one of the barstools. "Gia undid so much of the harm from his early years. Bouncing around from family to family. He likes stability and Gia was fierce that way."

"It can't have been easy for you, though. You're like a volunteer mom. You didn't have to."

Shannon considered her words carefully. "Nobody *has* to. A shocking number of people have children and don't ever become parents." She thought of Kesa, who had had a choice she hadn't taken and maybe Josie didn't realize that. "They hope someone else will take responsibility while they walk away."

Josie frowned slightly as she stirred. "I don't remember much about my parents. I think we were rich. There are pictures of my mom with these rooms full of shoes and their wedding pictures are lavish. But if there was money when they died Kesa never found it."

"Hard work builds character," Shannon opined. Good lord, she'd just quoted Aunt Ryanne word for word. Cut that out, she reminded herself.

Josie's mouth twisted in half humor. "Then Kesa is quite the character." She glanced toward the hallway and lowered her voice. "I know it's soon, but do you believe we're in love? That we mean it?"

This was turning into an eggshell conversation. "I can't tell you what you feel. I can only decide if I trust your description of it." Well, that sounded terribly clinical, didn't it? "I trust that you are sure of it."

"Well, that's something. I don't think Kesa can understand. She's never been in love. Have you?"

"Yes." Then Shannon realized she'd said it aloud.

"Why didn't it work out?"

"There were lots of reasons." Sure, she chided herself, *now* you can lie. There had only been one reason. She went on lying, hoping that Josie didn't know her well enough to tell. "What you're talking about sounds like love at first sight to me, and I have no proof that love at first sight exists."

She heard a noise behind them and wondered how much Paz had heard. His glance was inquiring, but he resumed stirring the chili without comment.

The conversation was considerably easier over dinner. Josie totally loved the addition of nonfat Greek yogurt spooned atop the chili, along with a sprinkling of grated cheddar cheese.

"It's a diet compromise," Shannon said.

Josie had another bite and made a satisfied sound. "This is so much better than what I'd make for myself. I always cook for myself on Wednesdays."

Shannon tried hard to sound very casual. "Your sister is busy on Wednesdays?"

"She plays Mahjong. Says it's relaxing. The Mahjong gang is fun, but it's not my kind of game." Josie seemed about to roll her eyes but instead added, "It really is the one thing she does every week to take a break from working."

Mahjong? Shannon knew nothing about the game. "She really has to hustle for work, I bet."

"It's endless. She has a couple big name clients, like Jennifer Lamont." Josie clapped a hand to her mouth as Paz whistled. "Please, please don't tell anyone! I'm not supposed to say her name. I saw a picture of her online and recognized the dress from when it was on a dress form in our apartment and that's the only way I even knew. Kesa doesn't say names very much, but I overhear sometimes. There's these agreements she signs."

"Non-disclosure agreements," Shannon said automatically. Her head was spinning a little. "Sounds like a tough business."

"She's really good at it, but she has zero private life time. Work and more work."

Did that mean Kesa didn't have a girlfriend? As much as she wanted to know, Shannon was not about to ask for clarification.

They'd think she was angling for information because she was interested herself. Which was true, but they didn't need to know it.

Paz refilled his bowl. "I looked at some of the stuff she spread out when we moved her into the workshop, so it wouldn't wrinkle. It's engineering with cloth instead of bricks and mortar or solder and silicon. More unpredictable and very fragile." He glanced at his hands. "I'd ruin some of those fabrics."

Josie twined her fingers with his. "Don't sell yourself short. You have a very sensitive touch."

Shannon laughed as his face flamed. "Do you enjoy doing that?" she asked Josie.

"He's so adorable when he blushes. I try not to take advantage of how easy it is."

Paz swatted at her as Josie poked him in the ribs. Though Shannon was still largely filled with unease about their precipitous plans, she was surprised by the unvarnished wave of envy she felt. They were comfortable and fearless.

Exactly what she wasn't.

CHAPTER TWENTY-ONE

Cami seemed more composed when Kesa arrived with lumpia. Auntie Ivy's pinakbet was bubbling on the stovetop and Marisol had brought an apple crisp fresh from her oven. The pungent mix of cinnamon and cardamom in the air made her stomach do a happy dance, and she loaded her plate with extra chunks of squash and eggplant from the stew.

"You all spoil me. I feel bad that I don't make anything from scratch."

Auntie Ivy bit appreciatively into one of the lumpia. "These make up for it."

Kesa savored her first bite of veggies and ground pork from the pinakbet. Ginger filled her nose and cleared her head, which still felt muddled from the conversation in the coffee shop. Truly, this was miracle food. "The truth is, you don't want me cooking for you. I'm not much good at it."

"You always say that, but I'm not sure I buy it," Marisol said. "You follow incredibly complicated directions when you make a garment—a recipe is the same thing. Practice is what you need."

It was hard to argue with that. "Well, me lacking practice, you don't want to eat my food. Josie puts up with my stir fry three nights a week because it's free to her. Tonight I think she's really happy to be having dinner with her new boyfriend. Who apparently cooks."

"She should snap him up right away," Auntie Ivy said. "A man who cooks? They're rare."

"She's snapping him up all right," Kesa muttered. She dipped the end of her lumpia into the pinakbet shrimp sauce and savored the result before continuing with the big news. "They want to get married."

Marisol's eyebrows shot up. "She's still a child!"

"How old is this boy?" Auntie Ivy's face went from intrigued to stormy. "I have never approved of child marriage."

"As Josie forcefully reminds me, she's not a child. She's nineteen. Old enough to vote and join the army and get married in California. Her boyfriend is twenty."

"Was that his mom in Nom Nom Pocha?" Kesa's wide-eyed glare of warning came too late. Cami gulped and had another bite of lumpia.

"Not his mother," Kesa said quickly. "She's a guardian of sorts and concerned, like I am, that they're both too young."

"What will you do?" Marisol began choosing tiles and they all followed suit.

Kesa paused to enjoy the *snick-snick* as the tiles were stacked and aligned. "I'm open to ideas. I mean, they think they fell in love at first sight. That's so ridiculous. They're completely focused on the intensity and not how they'll pay the bills."

"They're too young to know what they want," Auntie Ivy declared. "Who they really are."

Kesa made herself not look at Cami. "They don't think so. He's a very nice young man. I just want…" She swallowed, thinking that what she really wanted was to know that Josie would be safe and okay and happy. As much as she had sometimes out of weariness wished someone would take the burdens of caring for her sister off her shoulders, she didn't want that to happen if Josie wouldn't be safe. And have a chance to make the most of her life that she could. Josie still needed someone to look out for her, guide her. No matter how nice Paz was, he was still a kid too. "I just want her to think through how they're going to live. At least neither of them wants to become parents yet and they seem very aware of the necessary precautions."

"Thank goodness for that." Marisol claimed Auntie Ivy's discarded four-dot and added two fours of her own to create a pong. "Because nature doesn't always go along with our plans."

"Love at first sight, huh?" Cami played chow with Marisol's discarded five-dot. "Sounds romantic."

Kesa stopped herself from remarking that "wasn't Josie lucky to have time for romance." The jealous pang she felt gave her pause. "I'm sure it was."

Auntie Ivy snorted. "Romance is a luxury. It's lovely to have it, and I did with your *lolo*, may he rest in peace. But flowers and chocolate won't get you through the hard times. Then it takes both of you rowing the same direction and a lot of trust."

"Romance isn't only flowers and chocolate," Marisol said. "I think all the romance in the world can fit into a smile hello. It's little things—knowing how much sugar someone takes in their tea."

"I'm afraid that Josie wouldn't take either of our opinions about romance very seriously. She's 'in love' and we're not even dating anyone. We can't possibly understand."

"Youth is wasted on the young," Auntie Ivy said.

Cami spread her hands. "Sitting right here."

"I know, *bata*. Experience is the great teacher."

"So how is Josie supposed to get the great teacher if she doesn't have experiences?"

Kesa frowned at Cami's question. "I don't wish a broken heart on anyone."

Marisol played her second pong, this time red dragons, as she said, "How do you treasure and protect love if you don't know how easily it can be broken?"

Not for the first time Kesa wondered what Marisol's untold story was. There might be a potential beau in Manila, but she'd lost someone to death and rarely brought it up.

Kesa had lost her parents and that still felt like a gaping wound sometimes. Losing Shannon was different but had felt equally deep—and now the pain was fresh all over again. It still ached. She'd put her heart out for Shannon to see and Shannon had looked away.

Cami slowly picked up Kesa's discarded north wind and added it to her hand with a look that Kesa knew too well. If Cami didn't have Mahjong, she was close. "It sounds like you are making a case that broken hearts are an essential experience."

"I don't know about essential," Kesa said. "They may be unavoidable."

Marisol gave way to a fit of giggles. "Like a mammogram or Pap smear."

Auntie Ivy laughed along with Kesa, but Cami took a deep breath and blurted out, "I think I like girls." She tipped her remaining tiles face up onto the table. "Mahjong."

Kesa's heart stopped as Auntie Ivy gasped and said accusingly, "I knew you were hoarding winds!"

"Everybody hoards winds," Cami snapped. "Did you hear what I said?"

"Yes, and I don't want you to get some bug from Kesa's sister—no dating just one girl and thinking you'll get married, not at your age."

"Okay, *lola*. I'll date lots of girls." Cami's smile crumpled and she burst into tears.

The old lady left her seat to wrap her arms around her granddaughter, saying something tenderly in Filipino and adding, "I suspected. Your parents will be fine, you know that."

Kesa battled with her own tears at Cami's courage. "This calls for ice cream," she heard herself saying. "I'll run down to the market."

She was out the door before anyone could point out there was a nice apple crisp warming in the oven. The cooling spring air helped to clear her head a little, but she felt as if she was running ahead of a demon of truth. It chased her into the market where she stewed over the choice of mint chip or caramel toffee.

Cami had been so brave, and Kesa couldn't help but think of the moment she'd said, "I love you" to Shannon. She'd offered up her feelings like a precious crystal and hadn't known Shannon would let it shatter. She'd been sweeping up the pieces for the past four years, and seeing Shannon again had undone all that work.

She wasn't going to break any piece of herself over Shannon, not this time. That they'd gone right back to bed had been catharsis. She needed to hustle some new orders and make her workshop pay for itself. There was no room in her life for heartbreak. Not again.

Her mind was made up about Shannon, which was more than she could say for the ice cream. Mint chip or caramel toffee? She decided to get both and diets be damned.

CHAPTER TWENTY-TWO

Too many nights in a row spent staring at the ceiling. Now it was too many mornings unable to meet her own eyes in the mirror as she brushed her teeth. Shannon would have liked to pretend she didn't know what the problem was. But she did. She'd buried the guilt under worry for Paz, good food and fresh air in Portland, and focus on work.

Coward.

She was schooled by the younger people, who were fearless about their feelings. She wanted to call it reckless, which was an easy out and said in her aunt's voice. The practice of incessant caution made her good at the work she did, which she not only loved but thought helpful in the world.

Other times it quite clearly got in the way.

Kesa had been fearless, once upon a time.

Shannon gripped the sink, unable—unwilling—to hold back the memories. After their skin-searing first night she had arrived home the next day to spin through the living room like Julie Andrews on a mountaintop. She'd felt like sunshine itself.

With a parting breathless kiss, Kesa had agreed to come to Shannon's at six for pizza and a movie. That gave Shannon a few hours to clear away all the telltale signs of Single Woman Living Alone. She tsk'd at her lazy habits: sink full of coffee mugs and spoons, tampon box on the floor in the bathroom, a pile of suits for the dry cleaner, and three containers of science experiments in the refrigerator. Why hadn't she gone ahead with her plan to change the thick living room drapes and replace the thinning carpet? The house still looked as if Aunt Ryanne was alive.

She flung open every window she could, set alight lemongrass-scented candles, and attacked the bathroom with bleach. The antique sideboard's collection of washed but not yet put-away dishes was quickly dealt with, and she revolved through the living room, picking up her aunt's many knickknacks to put in a box buffered by newspaper—a task she'd meant to do on the first anniversary of her aunt's death. Energized, she cleared a small space in the cluttered garage to house the arrangement of pressed flowers in glass frames from the living room. She unearthed a poster print by Clyfford Still she'd bought last year with the intention of finding a better frame before she hung it. The cheap plastic one would have to do. She hung it over the couch where the pressed flower collection had been and was happy to see that the tawny browns and oranges with shocks of blue and black looked as vibrant as she'd hoped.

There was no helping the couch. She pulled a throw of gray and black Drummond tartan out of the hutch. Clan Drummond, her aunt had said, was the source of the Dealans many generations ago. It covered the aging upholstery at least.

The trouble with the sunshine now streaming in through the French doors was how well it showed off all the dust. She could take care of that after she changed the sheets on the bed and put fresh towels in the bathroom. And wiped out the microwave so the movie popcorn wouldn't smell as burnt when she popped it.

The sunshine also showed off the neglected backyard. It was going to be a lovely evening. They could sit outside—if only. Weeds, leaves, cobwebs…

She heard the *thunk-dunk* of the basketball next door and dashed out to the backyard to stand up on a deck chair so she could see over the fence.

Paz and another boy were engaged in one-on-one, but the promise of ten bucks each for a half hour of yard work was tempting enough for their always empty wallets. They made good work of it, too, filling up her yard waste can and two lawn trash bags as well. Then they attacked the fence, patio furniture, and eaves with brooms, whisking away old webs and a first layer of grime from the patio table surface. For good measure they used the seat cushions to whack each other with all the energy and abuse that sixteen-year-olds could dish out, creating clouds of dust in the air.

Amused by their vigor, Shannon made short work of the weeds that obscured the ailing herb garden. Aunt Ryanne had had a green thumb, but Shannon didn't have the time for it. At least the backyard no longer looked like she was prepping for a haunted house event.

As she handed over the cash to the boys, she asked Paz, "Could you run an errand for me, to the corner market?"

"I could," he answered blandly. His housemate had already disappeared next door.

"Smartass. *Would* you run an errand for me?"

"I'd be happy to."

She gave him another twenty. "I need something fresh. Like apples or oranges or both, or flowers. Like I could put them in a bowl or vase and make my dining room table look like I wasn't raised in a cave."

Paz whistled. "You have a date!"

She gave him a narrow look. "A friend is coming over for pizza and a movie."

"Sounds like a date to me." He shoved her money into his pocket. "Want me to text you a photo of stuff before I buy it?"

"Sure."

"Next time I want a ride to the movies…?"

"You got it." It was always easy to strike a bargain with Paz. They shared a finely tuned sense of fairness.

She tackled the bedroom next, filling the laundry bin and pushing it into the closet. Luxurious sheets were a personal indulgence and she had to shake away visions of Kesa—her skin, her hair, the line of her body—against the deep midnight blue cotton she chose. So, so distracting.

After approving a collection of apples and oranges and a small bouquet of harvest-themed flowers Paz sent jpgs of, she cleaned out the fridge and regretted its barren, echoing interior. If Kesa stayed over they'd be having canned soup for breakfast. At least she had cold beer. She quickly texted Paz to buy a lime too, catching him in time. Corona and lime didn't scream "date drink," but it would suit them both. She'd order the pizza after Kesa arrived.

She was a whirlwind after that, running through the house with the old Kirby vacuum and tattered feather duster, wishing she'd paid attention to the commercials promising her the dancing bliss a Swiffer was supposed to bring to her life. All the while a voice inside kept a countdown: "You see her again in 47 minutes… 46 minutes… 45…"

She was out of the shower, dressed in her softest jeans and an untucked slim men's blue-on-white J.Crew button-up, when the doorbell rang. A last look around confirmed big improvements, but there was still far too much of her aunt's aura present. It was a good thing she didn't believe in ghosts, or she'd be picturing Aunt Ryanne's reaction to Shannon's plans. They'd only had one conversation about Shannon's sexuality. It had been extremely uncomfortable and brief and had ended with her aunt's declaration, "It's between you and the Lord. Talk it over with him." Her aunt had retreated to her airless rooms and comforting books.

She definitely would have been full of panicked predictions of mayhem and doom at the thought of Shannon admitting a stranger to the house, let alone one she was hoping to spend the night with again. Her own lack of nerves about it was bizarre and disconcerting, but she would go with the feelings for now. Why not?

She set the bowl of fruit on the sideboard, tweaked the vase of flowers to the center of the dining room table, and tried, unsuccessfully, to keep the heat and desire out of her face.

The nervous smile Kesa gave her was the only reason Shannon didn't grab her and kiss her right there on the porch. The deep animal growl rumbling in the pit of her stomach was more than a little frightening. She managed to say, "You're right on time."

"Your directions were impeccable."

Shannon inhaled the scent of Kesa's rose-and-vanilla perfume as she came into the house. Did anything else smell so delicious? Like she wanted to dive body and soul into it?

"This is a nice place," Kesa said, after putting her purse on the side table Shannon indicated. She turned, holding out the slender bag she'd been carrying under one arm. "I thought a sassy red would go with pizza."

Shannon extracted the bottle to view the label for the casual table wine. "Perfect."

Kesa walked over to the windows to look at the backyard. "It's so green—you have so much light."

It was only then that Shannon appreciated the sleeveless blouse that Kesa was wearing. It looked like watered silk, mottled in dyes from orange to red. It was fitted to Kesa like a second skin, stopping a finger-width short of the waistband of her black jeans. "Would you like to sit outside for a while?"

Kesa glanced down, drawing Shannon's gaze to the high-heeled gold sandals that were a long cry from the black boots of last night. Equally yet differently alluring.

Shannon couldn't help the little purring sound she made. "We'll stick to the patio. No grass stains on those shoes. Too early for a beer?"

"On a day like this, a beer would be perfect."

Their fingertips brushed as Shannon handed her a Corona topped with a lime wedge. She had to give herself a little shake as she led the way to the backyard. There was plenty of time for other activities. Talking in the garden would have its own magic.

Even with all the efforts, Shannon wished the yard was tidier and the cushions not so clearly several seasons sun-faded. At least Kesa didn't know what it had looked like earlier in the day.

"I'm so envious of this." Kesa gazed around the space, taking in the orange tree and garden. "My sister and I share an apartment and there's no balcony or patio in the complex. No place to take dinner outside and relax."

"The house belonged to my aunt for a long time. She lived here with her husband, who died suddenly, and she never remarried. Aunt Ryanne was quite the gardener until she was in her seventies, but I haven't really kept it up. She passed on a couple of years ago."

Shannon pulled out one of the patio chairs for her and they each stretched out with a sigh. They clinked their bottles and bit into their respective lime wedges before having that first refreshing gulp. The dappled sunshine was bright, the breeze light and cool, and they each could put their feet in the sun for warmth. A perfect balance for a fall day, Shannon thought.

"Your aunt sounds like a good woman," Kesa observed.

Good yes, but also cold, Shannon wanted to say. It felt disloyal, though. Aunt Ryanne's paranoia about the wickedness and dangers of the world had grown over the years, but Shannon had been safe and never hungry. "She was twenty years older than my mother. I haven't a clue who my father was, and given her history, my mother probably didn't either. She died from complications after I was born."

She didn't mind telling Kesa a little more. "She was an addict. My hospital admission record shows someone had delivered me, got me breathing, but they hadn't cut the cord. My mother never regained consciousness, and a determined social worker hunted down Aunt Ryanne. Who took me in." It hadn't been perfect, but it was indisputable. "She saved my life. I disrupted hers, but she was a stoic and took care of me because that's what you did."

"She sounds responsible." Kesa quickly added, "And given the way my parents were, that's a compliment, I promise."

"They've passed away?"

"Auto accident." Bitterness clouded Kesa's expression for a moment, but cleared as she raised her face to the breeze and closed her eyes. "They left behind a pile of debts. That was seven-eight years ago."

Shannon wished she had an ounce of artistic talent, because she would have sketched the curving line of Kesa's nose and chin and throat, all in cool brown brushed with golden sunlight. "That must have been hard."

Kesa gave a short nod. "It's heavenly out here." She opened one eye to glance at Shannon, and her lips curved in a smile. "You said something about pizza."

"I did, and I do try to keep my promises. What kind do you like?"

They'd agreed on pancetta and olive and filled in the time waiting for the delivery by curling up together on the sofa. Conversation eased into languid kisses and purposeful explorations until the doorbell rang.

"You should—" Kesa paused to pant into Shannon's ear. "You should answer that." She pushed her fingers further down Shannon's unzipped jeans.

Shannon shifted with a groan. Kesa's touch was so close, and she'd been about to strip off her jeans and beg. "No fair."

Kesa nuzzled at Shannon's nipple, taut and visible through her shirt. "I want my pizza."

Laughing with giddy regret, Shannon managed to get out from under Kesa and tidied her clothes on the way to the door. Payment was quickly managed and she took the steaming, fragrant box into the kitchen and set it on the table. "Let's open that lovely bottle of red. One slice of pizza coming up."

She was on tiptoes at the counter, reaching for the wineglasses, when Kesa's arms went around her waist from behind to undo her jeans again.

"Stay right there," Kesa had whispered. "I'm going to lose my mind if I don't touch you right now."

The pizza had been stone cold by the time they had staggered out of the bedroom wearing old T-shirts. The rest of the night had been heated and languid, quietly intense and filled with talk. They had watched *Galaxy Quest* and then moved to the bedroom.

A loud knock on the bathroom door jolted Shannon out of the memory of Kesa's hands sliding down her hips and the sound of her low, pleased laugh.

"You okay? I can't wait any longer to ask if you've seen my keys." Paz sounded frazzled.

She glanced at the clock next to the shower. She was going to miss her bus if she didn't get her butt in gear. "I thought I saw them on the counter near the bananas."

"Thanks, I'll look." A few moments later he hollered, "Found them! See you later!"

She gave a last pat to her hair and turned away from her now-flushed reflection. Four years ago had been all about sex, hadn't it? A chemistry that still drove them both to distraction, or that motel last Friday never would have happened so easily.

Just sex. Really good sex. Wasn't it brave to claim her sexuality and find no shame in acting on it with another consenting adult? If so, then why did she feel guilty? Why couldn't she look at herself in the mirror? And why did she ache in deep down, dark places?

She arrived at her cubicle without being conscious of the journey, hoping that falling into her usual routine would shake away the numbness that was a byproduct of trying so hard not to think about Kesa. Not thinking about the way her nose twitched when she was about to laugh. Not remembering the way they'd melted into each other to watch TV, cold pizza slices in hand. Waking up in the small hours with a crick in her neck and one hip completely asleep, but not moving for as long as she could stand it because Kesa's head was tucked under her chin and the steady beat of her heart gently pulsed against Shannon's ribs.

Her feelings were a confusion of pain and bliss, as if a broken bone had healed badly, but now was finally set right. That feeling of rightness, of being aligned somehow, had come back the moment she'd seen Kesa in the diner with the kids. It had grown during the night together and reached a radiant glow over a cup of coffee.

Kesa wasn't wound through her again; she'd never left. She'd never not been there, like sunlight on the other side of a curtain Shannon had refused to open, just as her aunt had refused to let any amount of sun into her life.

Four years ago, she reminded herself viciously, you listened to the voices of reason and caution and you let her go. Why would this time be any different than the last? Even if Kesa ever trusted her again, what would keep Shannon from bailing out when feelings got intense? You're worse than Aunt Ryanne. You've kept the curtains closed and bricked up the window for good measure.

She sat at her desk in a fog, idly paging through updates from the overnight chatter. Focus, she told herself. Do something useful. In truth, you hardly know the woman. Aside from the great sex. And the survivor's tenacity. And the drive to succeed. And the artistry. And the fierce protective instinct toward her sister. And that she's easy to talk to, a good listener, laughs from her belly.

Sure. You don't know a thing about her.

She made herself reread all the communiqués again. If her head wasn't in the game it put other people at risk. It was a good thing she did: the third item down, where she'd completely missed it the first time, was a mention of fugitive Seychelles by his Henry Lymon alias. He'd been caught by a CCTV camera outside a police station. A lucky break, perhaps. The report said the person-of-interest had surfaced during a facial recognition scan of an altercation in the station parking lot. Lymon had been standing on the fringe, then quickly walked away when the hubbub began. As a witness, the local police would have liked to question him, but he hadn't turned up.

Now "Henry Lymon" would have to get out of Toronto, Shannon thought. He was smart and paranoid and probably realized he might have been caught by the security camera. Where would he go next? It would be so satisfying to catch him and invite all interested agencies to scrape out every piece of dirt they could on his friends in trafficking.

She couldn't tell the deputy marshal in charge of the "Henry Lymon" warrant the whole story because it was classified, so she worded the update with her usual caution: "Fugitive Lymon has reason to flee Toronto. Trajectory suggests possible US entry out of Ontario. Other agencies may wish to coordinate interrogation." That last sentence was standard code for "This one comes with extra eyes." The deputy would move Lymon up on the watch list, but it would still take a passport scan to trigger an alert. She'd have to have more in order to ask for his face to be part of the already massive daily scanning from vehicle and booth cameras at all border crossings.

Nevertheless, if "Lymon" continued his nonchalant approach to the United States, it would be one less slimeball on the streets maybe. She'd have done something useful for the cause of justice instead of mooning over Kesa.

Kesa. Whom she knew nothing about. Like her favorite color or breakfast or her politics. Show tunes or country? Shakespeare or Shirley Jackson? Atwood or Stephen King? She wanted to know everything and take a long time in the learning. Kesa had been warm—at least at first—in the coffee shop, almost as if she'd forgiven Shannon for four years ago.

Almost. Enough that they could let it slip into the past and make a new beginning?

What they needed was some time spent far, far away from the allure of crisp, cool sheets against their overheated bodies.

She shook herself out of a daze of remembering. As fun as it might be, sex wasn't going to fix anything. They needed to agree to meet, talk, and simply enjoy each other's company.

That's called "dating," the voice of common sense pointed out.

Was she seriously thinking of asking Kesa out on a date? How would she explain that to Paz? A casual desire to get to know his girlfriend's big sister better, right? There was nothing unusual about that.

Did she even have to explain it?

Part of her said a resounding "yes." She didn't like unexplained behavior. People didn't do anything for no reason at all. Including her.

What reason for casually dating Kesa would she give them that they might believe?

Hell, what reason would she give herself that wasn't a lie? Casual? There was nothing casual about it.

CHAPTER TWENTY-THREE

Two more orders for the Suit-Kini by Kesa from different Beverly Hills socialites lightened Kesa's mood considerably. They were new clients and seemed happy to come to her for measurement and fittings. She'd also been able to lure an existing client to her workshop for the final fitting of a custom cocktail dress, pleasing her even more for the time saved.

Instead of driving across LA to the clients, she'd used that time to visit her fellow tenants and discovered most were like her, solitary artisans with clients who dropped in. Several worked with clay and shared in use of a kiln on the first floor. Nearly everyone offered her cucumber water or designer coffee, and she realized she had to take client hospitality seriously. Now she had her eye on a fancy one-cup-at-a-time coffee and tea maker. A pitcher of filtered water was another requirement. While it distracted from the work, having such niceties for her clients and guests made her feel as if her business was maturing.

That had been the whole goal, she reminded herself. If business stayed steady for the next couple of months, she'd be looking for a handwork seamstress to help her out. She would have more time for the fun part: design. She might even be able to take a drawing class, which meant she'd probably land more clients.

The focus on her business kept her from thinking too much about Shannon. They had only promised to get in touch if it was about the kids, and she knew that was for the best. Her head knew it, anyway.

Discovering on Friday morning that her zipper supplies were still under her bed didn't ruin her good mood. She hopped back in the car, cranked up the Beyoncé, and headed home.

She didn't immediately recognize the sound she heard when she opened the door, but as the twining voices sorted themselves out she realized that Josie and Paz had counted on having the place to themselves. Part of her wanted to laugh—seriously, the sounds associated with lovemaking were funny. The rest of her wanted to get in and out of the apartment without them knowing she had been there.

That was not to be. The large flat box of accumulated zippers was stuck on her bed frame. When she finally worked it free she thumped butt-first onto the floor with two broken fingernails. "Damn it!"

Josie's bedroom door flew open and Paz filled the doorway holding the baseball bat Josie kept under her bed. He was, fortunately, partially clothed, though it looked as if he hadn't been wearing the Deadpool boxers a minute ago.

He burst out laughing. "You should see your face!"

Josie, wrapped in her robe, peered out from behind him. "You scared the crap out of me!"

Kesa found his humor infectious. "Believe me, I was hoping you wouldn't know I was here."

"Yeah, we were hoping for some privacy." Josie's cross tone was probably out of embarrassment, Kesa thought.

"I forgot all about moving what was under my bed. I need zippers."

"Not a sentence you hear every day." Paz had pulled a Tamayo *Moon Dog* T-shirt over his head.

"So you're leaving, right?" Josie demanded.

"As soon as I get this in the car." Really, Josie could lighten up. "Next time put a ribbon on the door or something."

"Like that would have disrupted you getting what you wanted when you wanted it."

Even Paz looked puzzled by Josie's biting tone. Well, better he see it now, Kesa thought. "I'm sorry I interrupted—"

"No, you're not. You don't think we should be together."

"I don't think you should get married. But as long as you're safe and you're both agreeable, I don't care what you do in there. I would prefer not to hear it."

Paz blushed. "I am totally in agreement with you on that, *wey.*"

Darn it, she was in danger of really liking the kid.

Josie was having none of their distraction. "Why don't you admit that you'll never support us being together? You don't believe in anything but work. Real human feelings are an annoyance to you. It's not like you know anything about love."

Her flounce back into her bedroom left Kesa and Paz awkwardly not looking at each other. He finally said, "See ya."

"Sure." Kesa wasn't certain what either of them could say. She wasn't going to explain her particular experience of love. Or admit that it hurt for Josie to say—even if she didn't really believe it—that Kesa didn't at least love *her.*

She had to put the fight out of her mind, as she had so many times in the past, but it proved difficult to do. The traffic back to the workshop was horrid. The blue sky had gone gray, and the idea of spending money on a fancy coffeemaker became wastefully risky.

She was used to Josie's passionate outbursts. What she wasn't used to was the persistent image of Shannon that crept around the sides of her hurt. She wanted to relax into Shannon's arms and let the world go away for a while. How stupid was that? Shannon had hurt her worse than any spat with Josie had. Why would she think she could turn to her for safety and comfort? Ridiculous.

The sheer joy of being able to lay out all three projects at once and tack in the zippers via an assembly line helped her get back to a happier mental space. She went ahead and machine-sewed one of the zips into place because the client's measurements were already known. The other two had declared themselves size eights and waved off any need to measure. She had her doubts, not that she would tell a local mover-and-shaker that. Rather than insisting on measurements the client would argue over, she cut too large. Ego pandering came with the territory. One of the aspects she liked most about actor clients was they knew it made no sense to lie to their wardrobe people. Bad measurements meant lumpy clothing and time wasted in extra fittings.

The sunset reflecting on the white walls had all but gone by the time she knew she had to quit or go blind. The three skirts were constructed and one was finished except for final tailoring and hemming. Her phone chirped as she reflected on what had still been a great day's work, all in all, and it topped off a very productive week. In spite of today, she hadn't thought about Shannon…too much.

But it was as if she'd said Beetlejuice too many times. There it was, a message in her inbox from ShannonD.

"I was wondering if you'd like to talk again? We can keep it really casual," it read. "What about The Grog and Game?"

Oh, hell no, Kesa thought. They were not going back to that place with its memories. The strains of "Something" floated out of her brain, along with the dizzying memory of her surrender into Shannon's arms. She glanced around her workshop, much tidier now with accessories sorted into labeled bins and stowed neatly on the shelves. The stacks of patterns that had overflowed the bookshelf at home were now in large, flat envelopes, labeled, and filed in the cabinet by style. The spindles mounted on pegboard held neatly tied off spools of industrial thread that were both useful and colorful. She even knew how she was going to decorate the walls.

This was her place. Finally, everywhere she looked she saw herself.

She was not going back to the woman she was four years ago, and she wasn't going to make the disastrous, still-not-healed mistake of putting her heart on display so Shannon Dealan could decide, all over again, that she didn't want it.

And what the hell did "casual" mean? Casual sex? Not even a real dinner beforehand? Just sex?

Part of her thought that was not what Shannon had meant, and another part thought that was *exactly* what Shannon meant. She was angriest at the part that whispered, "Sounds good, doesn't it?"

Absolutely not. No.

CHAPTER TWENTY-FOUR

"I didn't want to put all of what I was thinking in writing," Kesa said flatly. There was no cup of coffee on the table, and Kesa's hands were clenched around her purse. "What happened was irrational and irresponsible."

Shannon looked down at the cup of coffee in her hand. She'd forgotten to get a wrapper to protect herself from the heat. Her hand was on fire, and the rest of her was frozen to immobility by the coldness in Kesa's eyes. She understood now why Kesa had countered her suggestion of The Grog and Game with a return to the Nom Nom Pocha coffee shop.

They weren't going to be lingering.

She sat down at the minuscule table for two anyway and studied Kesa's rigid posture. She was wrapped tight and not giving Shannon any edges to peel open. Where had the warmer, almost friendly Kesa gone? "Are you talking about recently or four years ago?"

"I don't even want to think about four years ago. Though 'irrational' covers it as well."

Yes, Shannon thought, I'd been irrational, but it was probably not what Kesa was thinking about. Or maybe she was. "Is there any way to..."

All at once she could see Kesa's face four years ago. Her eyes alight with wonder, her mouth soft with desire—no one had ever looked at Shannon as if she was the future. Her ears filled with the tender echo of the earnest words "I don't know how, but I love you, Shannon. I love you." Today she was seeing a completely different Kesa, with sharp corners and flint in her eyes.

Shannon faltered. "I mean, if Josie and Paz keep on the way they're headed, we're going to see each other. I was hoping we could—"

"Make peace? We're not at war. We're not anything." Kesa brushed an imaginary crumb from the table as she stood up. "If you want to talk about the kids let's do it by email. I'm late for an appointment."

"Mahjong?"

"That's Wednesdays." Kesa's mouth snapped closed as if she instantly regretted the words. "A client."

Then she was gone.

Shannon swallowed a large gulp of coffee, but burning the roof of her mouth didn't melt the cold ball in her chest. What had she thought? That her personal charm and their undeniable chemistry would make a sincere "I'm sorry" on her part unnecessary? If Kesa wasn't interested in a long overdue apology there was no way forward, was there?

The next day she dragged herself to work and forced herself to focus. Impatient with the internal whining that robbed her of pleasure in the job, she carefully went through every new communiqué and increased her subscription to more frequent updates, almost doubling her workload. Some intense, extra-hours days wouldn't hurt her at all. It wasn't as if she'd replaced any of the limited socializing she'd given up by moving from Portland or done anything about training for a 10K, let alone looked up her old hiking club to get back on the trails. She ignored the sarcastic inner voice that said shutting out the world was exactly what Aunt Ryanne would tell her to do.

The long afternoon was broken by the usual hubbub of teams coming and going. Her boss Gustavo had once asked the analysts if they wanted to relocate to the quieter admin floor below them, but they'd all said no. Hearing units preparing to go out and the debriefing when a mission was over kept them all aware that the work they did was vital to deputies, their success, and their safety.

She plopped back into her chair after high fiving the deputy-on-point who'd talked the latest team through a combined cooperation arrest with the FBI and LAPD. The high-energy conversation in the wake of a flawlessly executed mission was a welcome upbeat moment in her day. A few taps at the keyboard later and she'd refreshed her queue of status updates and communiqués. It was a long list. With only dinner by herself ahead of her, she decided to work through it all, even if it meant staying late.

It turned out to be a great decision. Halfway down the list she hit personal pay dirt. "Henry Lymon" had been spotted again, and in St. Catharines, south of Toronto. CCTV had picked him up, this time at a screening checkpoint in the Welch Courthouse. Facial recognition had pinged her counterpart in Canada, someone probably in a cubicle much like hers, and he had put the photo and information into the tracking queue.

She consulted a local map and asked herself what Seychelles was doing a mere twenty klicks from the US-Canada border. The intel summary said he'd been registered leaving only a few minutes later. The video didn't show him attempting in any way to hide his face, nor was it apparent he had met with anyone. Could he possibly believe that no one was looking for him anymore?

Criminals got sloppy and Seychelles was a criminal, she reminded herself. She leaned out of her cubicle to see if Gustavo's light was still on. It was, so she quickly wrote up the situation, with the fugitive practically on their border and getting closer, and caught him at his door as he was shrugging into his coat.

She handed him her memo, with Seychelles's dossier information redacted, saying, "I've got a hot one."

He scanned it quickly, a small frown forming. "Bank fraud. Why is this one hot?"

"I think we have a chance of catching him if we promote him to Actively Seeking status. He's capable of using false ID to cross."

Gustavo returned to his tidy desk to log back in to his personal workstation. "You know if I make this request there's always a tech guy who wants to balk because another face adds to the server toll. Plus adding to the active list makes it harder for the agents at the borders to keep all the faces in mind. This guy's not violent."

The last ended on an inquiring note, and Shannon realized she had to give Gustavo something more to explain why Seychelles should be elevated to Actively Seeking. "No, Seychelles isn't violent." She tapped on the redacted block. "There's trafficking under here. Kids."

Gustavo blinked as he took in that information. "That's why you've dogged reports of his whereabouts. I knew there had to be a reason other than financial fraud." He glanced at his watch and wrinkled his nose at it. "It's after six. I'll see if I can get the Marshal to approve it ASAP so he's elevated by tomorrow, but it might not get there until tomorrow afternoon. Unless you have specific urgency?"

She shook her head. "Given his pace from Toronto toward the border, I think he's taking his time. He might try it Saturday, when tourist crossings will make it more chaotic. Fewer people using NEXUS to enter the US means longer lines and more faces."

Glad to think she'd earned her pay and had some worth regardless of how Kesa felt about her, Shannon headed for home feeling more than a little chuffed. If agents on either side of the border caught Seychelles, it would be Cubicle Dwellers 1, Child Trafficker 0. The way it should be.

The bus was not as crowded as it would have been an hour or two earlier and she gratefully took a seat and opened her phone to fetch her personal email. She hadn't expected any communication from Kesa, not after yesterday's thorough dismissal, yet she could feel her spirit deflating. That wasn't good. A can of soup awaited her at home and she was in danger of skipping the soup and heading straight to a Beaujolais. And salted caramel gelato.

Face it, she told herself as she trudged from the bus stop toward the house, life is changing. Paz is a grown man. Even if he didn't get married now, someday he would. He and Josie might live with her for a few years, but her nest would be empty at some point.

Empty.

You're only yearning after Kesa because you're afraid without Paz around you'll turn into your aunt. You love your work, she reminded herself. And you're very good at it. Women aren't incomplete if they don't have a romance in their life, you know that.

You're not feeling incomplete, a small voice whispered. Seeing her again you remembered that you could be more... More, with her.

She distracted the voice by heating up the soup. Why dirty a bowl and waste water washing it out? Sure, caring about the planet was why she ate it directly from the saucepan.

Don't do it, she warned herself, but there she was, looking in her spam folder to make sure she hadn't received any kind of message from Kesa.

The spam folder did have an email with the subject, "Can we meet with you?" It wasn't from Kesa. It was from an exec of a private fraud investigation firm. She'd met the CEO of Integrity last year at the end of a long-term fugitive case where the private investigators, based in Seattle, had surfaced intel that the FBI had referred to their office. Working with a counterpart at their firm, they'd zeroed in on three fugitives living under aliases. Shannon had been the person pulling deep data on their habits, history of weapons, methods, and financial ties. The operation had gone smoothly with three fugitives in custody and a cache of military-grade weapons dug up out of bunkers.

Why would someone from there want to meet with her?

She moved the email to her regular inbox and read it with genuine surprise. Was "the possibility of working with you" a job offer? Huh. She was well aware that private contractors with her skill set made double and triple her public servant rate of pay, but she had no interest in private sector work.

Did she?

She was startled out of her bemusement by Paz's arrival. "Have you eaten? How was your day?"

"Good. That summer internship with Boeing called back and I have an interview. I was really starting to think it wasn't going to pan out."

"That's great news." The internship paid well and she really hoped he would get it. It would open all sorts of doors for his future. "I had a good day myself. Likely one less slime bag walking around free, if all goes well." She couldn't explain more so she gestured at her phone. "And I think I'm being headhunted by some private company. They do fraud investigations, so I don't know what they'd want with me, exactly."

Paz downed half of the glass of orange juice he'd poured for himself before answering. "Your terrific instincts and ability to synthesize wide data? You're good at what you do, and it's something they haven't taught computers to do yet?"

"Thank you." She frowned and added, "Though now I'm wondering if I should be scared of Skynet."

Paz gave her a mock serious gaze. "We should *all* be scared of Skynet."

"I'd have to give a lot of thought to it. Seattle is even colder and wetter than Portland."

"It's in Seattle?" Paz turned to the refrigerator to forage for more food.

"That's where they're headquartered. If it's some kind of job they could want me to move, I guess. But that's a lot of unhatched chickens to be counting. It's been in my spam folder for two days. I'll answer tomorrow."

Paz wandered off to tackle homework and Shannon surfed through her Netflix queue. She couldn't settle on anything, but at least she didn't check her phone again for a message from Kesa that was never going to arrive.

She'd been so cold. So final. "We're not anything," she'd said.

There were enough moving pieces in her life right now. Maybe it was best to accept that Kesa was not one of them. Kesa was fixed in place, and that place didn't include Shannon.

Another night. So many sheep. *1000. 999. 998…*

CHAPTER TWENTY-FIVE

"You're right. The line across here looks irregular compared to the other hip. That's not the look we want." Kesa used the side of her hand to lightly touch the client where her haunch was crossed by a tailoring seam of the coppery silk dress. "I can easily fix that. The drape will be much sleeker."

Aisha Zee frowned at her reflection in the multiple standing mirrors that Kesa had set up to give clients a 360-degree view of themselves. Additional mirrors in pleasing antique frames were so far the most expensive investment in the workshop she'd made to date, but they were proving well worth it. Clients had a better sense of the entire fit than their own home setup often allowed. "I never realized my left hip and right hip are different."

"It's not noticeable," Kesa assured her. Quickly squatting next to her, she used a chalk pencil to dot the fabric. "Only if the clothes accentuate that particular line, and I'll fix that. Let's take it off."

The evening dress was in the first phase of construction and so was difficult to get out of without unraveling the basting. The client was reasonably more concerned with the effect the dress had on her thickly twisted braids as it went over her head than about Kesa's seams. They managed without major mishap, though.

Aisha slipped on the light kimono Kesa handed her and plopped down into the cushioned side chair next to her cooling cup of chai tea. She stretched her legs out onto the plushy ottoman with a sigh. "Can I take a nap here? Nobody knows where I am and it's very peaceful."

"Go right ahead," Kesa said. "The door is locked, and nobody else is due for an hour and a half."

"What is that tree?" Aisha pointed out the window where feathery, pale pink blooms were riffling in the light breeze among soft green fern-like leaves. "Is that the perfume I smell?"

"I think it's a Persian silk, though someone else said it's a Mimosa tree, and someone else said that they're easily confused. I love the smell, but if it bothers you I can close the window."

"Not at all. I get to spend time in a garden instead of having another Cobb salad lunch with the other NFL wives."

The scent was sweet and delicate, like a floral tea with a hint of resin and earth. Honeybees clustered around it at the first-floor level, but Kesa didn't have to worry much about them this high, though occasionally one would wander in through the window, realize its mistake, and wander out again. Hummingbirds loved the tree too and she'd already become used to listening for the buzz of their wings. Their presence felt like a good omen.

With a swipe of the iron, the low-melt thread she'd used for construction ahead of the initial fitting disappeared. Once the garment was perfectly sized she'd go over all the seams with permanent thread and iron away the basting. When she looked up from the board she saw that Aisha had indeed closed her eyes and relaxed.

Her decision to open a workshop had been driven by numbers, but now she saw that numbers had been only one part of the picture. There were intangibles, especially a heightened bond with the clients. Instead of a hired-in seamstress doting on them in their boudoirs, they came to her, which fostered a subtle change in the relationship between them. The time she spent not commuting was time she could spend learning more about them and picking up small cues of likes and dislikes. She could spend time chatting over fabric swatches about whatever was on the client's mind.

Three new referral clients had been so eager to make an appointment and then so effusive about her "studio" that she'd cautiously marked up her rates for them. None of them had blinked an eye as they sipped sparkling water or coffee and relaxed into a comfortable chair, phone charging, shoes off, guard down. She'd finished her decorating this past weekend and so far everyone admired the result. An eclectic range of glassless frames in all sizes and shapes had come from the flea market, and she'd filled them with remnants from bolts of supple vicuña wool, liquid gold muga silks, and a wide range of thickly hand-embroidered, high texture blends.

The fabrics had all been ghastly expensive, and she hadn't been able to part with the odd pieces left from the original commissions even though they were nigh on useless for garments. She was so glad now that she'd hoarded them. The walls burst with rich, opulent, touchable pieces that several clients had already treated like an art exhibit to view while waiting for Kesa to finish a minor adjustment.

Her workshop had become a place of art and air. Raising her rates for new clients had paid for her investments in chairs and the standing mirrors, and all the rest of the small items she'd needed to make her workshop look planned and not the result of yard sales and flea markets and junk dug out from under her bed.

The mirrors reflected back to her the artisan she had always hoped to become, and she was doing her best to believe it was real and permanent. No one was lurking to snatch it all away. Instead of selling her talent with a portfolio book, the entire workshop represented her capability and sense of style. She no longer felt confined by the dim light and tight space of the apartment. The specter of the bill collectors who had followed her and Josie for years after their parents' death was finally starting to fade.

She knew she would face setbacks, but she felt capable of managing them. Her anxiety level was falling. The next rent payment was already in the bank, though she had a lot of work ahead of her to make all the commission deadlines. If these trends stayed true she could look for a handwork helper at the beginning of next month instead of waiting until August or September.

While she was in her workshop she felt like a train running on tracks she'd laid herself, clickety-clacking resolutely toward her goals. If only life with Josie could be so simple. She had hardly spoken to Kesa since that ugly spat in front of Paz.

She would not think about Shannon, she told herself, and just like that, she was thinking about Shannon. She couldn't shake the image of Shannon's eyes wide with disbelief, hurt even, when Kesa had said, "We're not anything."

Well, maybe if Shannon hadn't ghosted her four years ago Kesa wouldn't have been quite so final. So they'd gone right back to bed the moment their paths had crossed again. It was nothing more than a carnal itch. Indignation and regrets ping-ponged across her brain until she pricked her finger and made herself concentrate on the work in her hands.

Seam fixed and rebasted, she made a little clatter at the sink which startled the client awake.

Aisha covered a yawn with her hand. "I feel like a million bucks. What do you put in that tea?"

"Trade secret," Kesa teased.

They worked together to get Aisha back into the gown. The slightly adjusted seam on the left evened out the client's minor irregularity in an otherwise rock-hard booty, making for perfect balance.

"Oh yes," Aisha said. She checked her silhouette in each mirror, her smile broadening. "My husband will love it. This is going to kick some ass. There's supposed to be a media crew covering the event and I'm sure I'll get some camera time."

Kesa could tell Aisha was genuinely pleased. As a first time around, it had gone well, and Aisha was likely to be back. "You were absolutely right about the color. The persimmon wouldn't have popped like this copper does against your skin. It's bringing out all the gold undertones. You're like a summer sunrise."

Aisha waved a hand at her, the braids twisted around her head. "I'm seriously thinking about going all natural with my hair. Let it be big and bold, like this dress. What do you think?"

They discussed hairstyle alternatives, though Kesa knew Aisha would take her stylist's advice far more seriously. Wives of professional athletes were on camera all the time and had a beauty team assembled. "One thing you might consider is giving your manicurist and makeup people a heads-up about the dress color. Let me give you a swatch of the silk so you can start them getting matches. Or have them call me and I'll send one in the mail."

Aisha left all smiles with a couple swatches of fabric and several business cards. Her name in front of the kind of stylist Aisha was likely to have wouldn't hurt. Kesa cleared up the detritus from the fitting and laid out the garment ready for final sewing tomorrow, and she checked messages on her phone. The first she deleted upon hearing "I'm calling from the IRS about updating your bank account for a direct deposit of taxes we owe you." She was no fool. The second was from Scam Likely and she deleted it without listening. She didn't expect more from the third.

"Hi, Kesa, it's Melanie, Jennifer's PA. She's got this New York art opening in three weeks and needs cocktail length that says both modern art and nods a little toward her Fifties detective role. The studio is paying, and it's kind of a rush, so you've got three times the usual budget to work with. She thought the studio designer was too arty. She turned into the background canvas, know what I mean? And not nearly enough smolder. You get her classy, sexy vibe. Send over some sketches, okay? She can do fittings ten to twelve days from now. I know it's last minute, but we'd be okay with you promoting the final on social media too. Otherwise standard NDA."

Hands shaking, she listened to the message again. And squeed. Loudly. Then replayed the message a third time as she danced to the other side of the room and back.

Yes, she did understand how to make the woman inside the outfit the star of the show while the outfit still made everyone go "Oooh." It was terrifyingly exciting, custom creating a high-profile gown for someone like Lamont. Getting to tag it and show it off on Pinterest and Instagram? Priceless!

It was such good news. She wanted to tell *someone*. Shannon flitted across her mind. No, absolutely not. A celebratory drink or two and where would they end up? She pushed away the many suggestive images her memory called up.

No.

She'd share the news at Mahjong tomorrow. Bring along an extra treat to celebrate, even. Maybe Josie could be happy for her, in spite of their current cold war.

She stopped dancing as she considered the issue of sketches. She could do them, but the results wouldn't make her happy. In the past, for really important contracts, she'd asked Josie to touch them up. Maybe if she brought home a tasty dinner Josie might warm up enough to help her out. Heck, with this kind of money involved, she could pay Josie nicely for her time. It might ease the hard chill between them too.

Meanwhile, there was no time for celebrating today, she told herself. A client with a final fitting, and hopefully final payment, was due in twenty minutes, and she could get a lot done before then.

She settled in to work and promptly pricked her finger. The sharp stab reminded her too much of the impasse with Josie. Having a paying gig for her would give them a reason to talk. She didn't know what Paz and Josie were intending to do, or if they were continuing to discuss cohabitating with Shannon. There hadn't been any mention of the plan they'd said they would work on.

She was afraid to ask. It might further destabilize their rocky relationship. Josie could simply defy her outright, knowing that if she did that there was nothing Kesa could or would do about it. How did parents ever wield power when they no longer had any? There was nothing she could withhold or give more of that Josie valued.

Every time she worried about Josie the thought of Shannon was there. The warmth of her touch. The manic way she stirred her coffee. Her voice, low and soft against Kesa's ear. Shannon's hands clenched in her pockets as Kesa told her that their past was irrational and to send future information through email. Kesa knew she'd been rude. It had felt necessary to be final about "them."

Repeating the past was unacceptable. Her heart couldn't take it.

A second happy client sent on her way with a bank transfer payment already in Kesa's account was the frosting on a nearly perfect afternoon. Kesa ended the day by marking and cutting a Little Black Dress for a new client out of a cheap synthetic to practice the tricky structure of the bodice. She wasn't going to waste silk on an experiment.

As the silver of her scissors flashed against the black she found herself reflecting on what Shannon had said last week and she had so brutally dismissed—that they'd have to get used to seeing each other. Paz and Josie dating brought them into each other's orbits. Just because Kesa had taped up old wounds and spread salve over newly bruised feelings didn't mean anything was healing. Every time she saw Shannon the hurts would throb.

What could she do about it? Was desensitizing the answer? If so, she'd have to see Shannon again. And again. And somehow it would get easier. Wouldn't it?

Her head was full of questions when she finally switched off the workshop lights and locked the door. After stopping for the luxury of takeout dim sum, she headed for home. Dim sum was Josie's favorite, and she'd gotten bean paste and barbecued pork baos because Josie liked both. She could make peace with Josie. So maybe it wasn't so bizarre to think she could find some sort of peace with Shannon.

Her stomach growled as the car filled with the tantalizing, warm blend of ginger and garlic. At a long stoplight she had to actively resist the urge to pry open the container of har gow and pop one of the melting-good shrimp dumplings into her mouth. She turned up the radio as if it would drown out the smell and sang along with Janet Jackson because she did feel so g-g-g-good.

Why, then, did her happy heart make her think about Shannon? She had to keep it hardened, she warned herself. She had to get to a place she could tolerate, where meeting up with Shannon would be uneventful.

She ignored the gut reaction to that idea. Uneventful? When the sight of her hurt expression had made Kesa want to pull her close and say she didn't mean it?

They needed ground rules. No angling to be alone. No long looks full of memories. Maybe a drink and snacks at a prosaic chain restaurant, nothing charming or memorable that she would think about afterward, the way she did The Grog and Game. If those were the rules, she could invite Shannon out for a casual dinner.

That was probably what Shannon had meant all along. It was her own lustful heart that had decided Shannon meant something else. They could have a future that didn't include the past, couldn't they?

The savory, umami aroma of sui mai was calming. She inhaled it all the way up in the elevator. She was happy to see Paz and thanked him as he took one of the bags of takeout and closed the apartment door behind her. "Hungry? If I make rice there's plenty for three."

His handsome face was a comic mixture of I-should-politely-refuse and I'm-starving emotions. "Uh—"

"Tell him to stay," she said to Josie as she eased her purse and the other bag of takeout onto the kitchen table where they had both spread out textbooks. They had taken the time to open the curtains now that dress forms and tall bolts of fabric no longer blocked access to them. Josie's watercolors helped brighten the dingy walls. Spring sunshine poured across the table, giving the worn pine highlights of gold. It almost, very nearly, felt like a home where they lived and not a cave where they got by.

Josie prodded the bag closest to her with a pencil. "Is there bao?"

"Of course. Pork and some bean paste too. I know you like both." Kesa wasn't forgetting that Josie was the one who'd gone off the deep end in that fight, but just because it hadn't been her fault didn't mean Kesa couldn't start mending the breach in the hopes that Josie would make the effort too.

Paz's eyes were very large and puppy-like as one hand inched toward the bag nearest him. "I will happily eat any that you don't want."

Josie slapped his hand away. "Nuh-uh. I love you, but I love bao too."

He tried to look wounded but failed. "Okay, I know where I stand now."

Kesa actively kept herself from asking about Shannon. She quickly measured rice and water into the rice cooker and tossed in some salt and a cube of frozen ginger. "I'm having a good week so far. Tell me about yours."

"I got a ninety-three on my last Infinite Series quiz," Josie volunteered.

Paz offered, "I think my interview for a summer internship at Boeing went well. I'm hoping to hear any day." A light shadow of worry crossed his face. "I'd be able to pay off the last I owe Shannon for my car and still have a bunch left if I get it. For... other expenses."

"Anything new and exciting in the world of the US Marshals?" Kesa hoped her voice sounded casual.

"Not that she could tell me," Paz said. "Well, she did get a job offer out of the blue. Some private company in Seattle. They have a headhunter meeting with her." He rubbed the tips of his fingers against his thumb in the universal money gesture. "*Muy dinero.*"

Paz's voice was lost behind a roar in Kesa's ears. She gathered plates, checked the timer on the rice, wiped the counter, got out the soy sauce, all the while smiling and nodding as if she could hear what he and Josie were saying. Shannon was free to move away, of course. As she'd said, they weren't anything to each other now. Shannon really meant nothing to her, but her brain was screaming the truth at her heart: You've lost her. You've lost her forever.

Josie and Paz went back to their studies and Kesa pretended to focus on her phone and calendar book. Why did she feel as if she'd lost Shannon? She'd never had Shannon to begin with, not then and not now.

The feeling of loss turned the delicious dinner into lead in her stomach. She'd served up her heart in a giddy schoolgirl, totally lesbian U-Haul move, saying "I love you" after two nights together. Shannon had had every reason to run for the hills, Kesa told herself. For all that she felt finally in charge of her life, and about to rise above the years of struggle to keep it together, was she still a stupid little fool about Shannon? Was she still that dumb?

The question was easy to answer and she didn't like the answer one bit. And then kicked herself because Josie and Paz finished up their work and took off for a rally before Kesa remembered to ask Josie about the sketches.

One mention of Shannon and all her other priorities go out the door? No, she swore to herself. This wasn't happening and wasn't going to happen. She hadn't fought her way to financial stability and peace of mind only to be upended by her foolish heart all over again.

CHAPTER TWENTY-SIX

I am dog tired. Shannon wondered idly where that expression came from as she slogged home from the bus. An eyestrain headache had been following her for most of the week and she felt as if her bones were screaming, "Oil can!" with every step. She had spent far too many hours at her desk without moving.

She ought to do some yoga. Stretch out some kinks.

All she really wanted to do was cover her eyes with a cold cloth and stay prone. Her brain was numb from the workload she herself had chosen to increase. Frustrating, too, was that her advice to elevate the capture of fugitive Seychelles hadn't born any fruit. There had been no more sightings. The path felt cold now.

The only break in the long days of poring over briefings had been lunch with the headhunter from Integrity Investigations. It hadn't been so much a job interview as a sounding out. How did she feel about the private sector? What was her personal philosophy of justice? What had been some of her more tense cases, to the extent that she could discuss them?

Shannon hadn't felt so much put on the spot as mostly unpracticed at answering such probing, thoughtful questions about her chosen field of work. When they'd parted the headhunter had simply said, "You'll be hearing from us," and expressed his thanks for a pleasant hour.

It had been pleasant—and unnerving. She went back to work feeling disloyal and unsettled. The feeling had gone away as she refreshed her reading queue. She sifted through the endless details of surveillance from multiple agencies, always looking for the data points relevant to her portfolio of fugitives. The Marshals Service would someday catch every last one of them, she told herself.

There were so many words on the screen and so little time. She really, really wanted a nap and a cold compress on her eyes. Her back was telling her all about making too many promises to exercise and not keeping any of them. The bus ride home sent her headache into jackhammer status.

Paz and Josie were enjoying the sunshine in the backyard, their ubiquitous textbooks spread out on the picnic table. Rocks kept handy for the purpose were holding down papers in the light breeze. She thought about joining them after she changed her clothes, but the dappled sunlight would probably make her eyes water.

They had changed positions when Shannon padded back to the kitchen in her comfy sweats. Josie was snuggled on Paz's lap, her face buried in his hair.

"I know, Jo-Jo, but it's not what we said we'd do."

Shannon was about to call out a hello when Josie's answer rooted her to the spot.

"We can go to Vegas and be done. Kesa is never going to give us her permission and we don't need it anyway. No more stress or arguments."

Holy beeswax! Were they thinking of eloping? She ducked out of sight behind the curtains, even as she told herself that eavesdropping was wrong.

"She was really cheerful last night." Paz laughed a little, adding, "She brought you your favorite bao, after all. And you said she wants to pay you to do sketches."

"It's a bribe. Anything to keep me dependent."

"Are you sure about that?" Paz sighed. "You realize that your sister could have dumped you into foster care, right?"

"I know."

"But she didn't."

"Well, it wasn't because she loves me. I became work she had to do."

"Hey," he said softly. "You don't really believe that."

There was a loud snuffle, and Josie muttered, "I don't. It's so hard sometimes. I feel like she never sees me."

"Maybe," he said, just as quietly, "you're mad because you owe her, like, a lot. And you may never be able to repay her."

There was a long silence and then Josie's voice was muffled as if Paz were holding her close. "I never thought of that."

"It's complicated, *cariña* Jo-Jo. You and me, we owe people or we wouldn't be here. We would have never met."

"I don't want to pay the price Kesa wants, which is to be like her. We're different people."

"I don't know her like you do. But all I've heard her say is that she wants you to have a wide open future."

"You're right, you don't know her like I do." A shift in volume suggested that Josie had moved back to her chair. "I want to get married, Paz. Waiting for permission we don't need will take too long."

"I don't want Shannon to worry."

"You're an adult. So am I."

"*Sí*, but I don't want to make a family by breaking our families. We lose, they lose."

Head spinning and heart aching, Shannon had to make herself duck into the living room where she could no longer hear them. She thought about her aunt, who had taken in an infant because blood looked after blood but who had had no love or warmth to spare. It wasn't blood that had drawn her to Paz or made him accept her overtures of friendship at face value. She'd always felt like the lucky one. He had enriched her life, and that had begun before the horrible night he'd been in the wrong place at the wrong time. He was the brother she'd have loved to have had growing up. They were family.

What would a loving mother or sister do in this situation? She didn't want him to run away to get married. She wanted to be there, wearing a dainty hat and sobbing into a lacy handkerchief. She wanted to know Josie better and to be sure she was good enough for Paz. She seemed to be, but how could Shannon be sure? How was anyone ever sure?

Her head wanted to run a full background check on Josie, as if that would settle anything. Trust your gut, she told herself. You know she's exactly what she seems: a passionate, forthright young woman out to shape her world to her liking. All qualities you admire in people.

All qualities you admire in her sister too. The problem was that Kesa didn't want to have a thing to do with her now. Why should she? She'd offered her heart and Shannon had reacted like it was radioactive. The only way she had known—still knew—how to deal with big emotions was to deny they existed. Head down, work hard. Don't waste time on daft ideas. Don't make yourself a target. Rainbows are illusions, dreams never come true. Those had been the solid, steady lessons her aunt had relentlessly drilled into her.

Why would she want to visit that kind of smothering on Paz when the fact was she envied him? They were considering eloping, that was the urgent part of the conversation she'd overheard. She wasn't supposed to know, and the kids were adults. Could she keep it to herself and let life run its course? They wanted to take the risk and face the future together. Why shouldn't she let them?

There might be a good job offer coming from the Integrity people. She should take it, maybe. Paz didn't need her. Kesa didn't want her. Run away because, sure, that would solve everything.

She wrapped a blue-ice pack in a tea towel and nearly cried with relief as she stretched out prone on the sofa and set it across her eyes. The cool quickly subdued the fire and calmed the throb in her skull. After a few minutes she transferred the pack to her right shoulder, which was barking loudly about all the mousing she'd been doing.

Who knew nonstop reading could be a contact sport? It happens so fast, she thought. All of a sudden you're staring at forty and lying to yourself that a good night's sleep will fix it all.

"Hey, are you okay?" Paz's voice made her open her eyes.

"Yeah, bad headache."

Josie's face appeared around Paz's shoulder. "Would you like some herbal tea? I keep tea bags in my backpack, I mean, who can afford two bucks a bag at S-bux? It's a calming blend, with orange zest and a little ginger, and it's great for headaches. No caffeine."

"Thank you," Shannon said as she struggled to sit up. "That sounds good. I've had too much caffeine today."

Josie was back within minutes with a fragrant mug. The aroma alone made Shannon feel better. She also noticed how at home Josie seemed in their kitchen. She was going to have to get used to that.

For a moment she was tempted to ask them about their plans. To try to get them to admit they were thinking about eloping. But before she could do more than thank Josie for the tea, Josie was packing up her backpack.

"I'll be back in a while," Paz said, keys in hand.

She drank the rest of the tea as the house went completely dark. The sliding glass door was open, letting in cool night air through the screen. The next thing Shannon knew the clock said it was two a.m., and Paz had covered her with the blanket she kept in the hutch for cold nights. She thought about moving to her bed and while she was still worrying that it would wake her up too much to get back to sleep she was out again. There was time to worry tomorrow.

CHAPTER TWENTY-SEVEN

Kesa thrust a green bottle at Cami as she opened Auntie Ivy's door. "I brought bubbly!"

"I can't drink—oh! Sparkling apple juice. Thank you, I like this stuff." She peered at the bag in Kesa's other hand.

"Samosas. I'm celebrating a big deal at work."

Cami's eyes widened with anticipation. With her hair in two pigtails she looked twelve. "What kind?"

"Paneer with carrot, and I also got sweet with mango. They should be great with Marisol's fruit bowl when we take a break."

"She's not here yet, but I heard her front door a few minutes ago, so I think she just got home."

"*Kumusta*, Auntie Ivy," Kesa called as they moved into the small hallway where she shed her shoes and deposited her purse on the floor next to them. "The pinakbet smells terrific."

"It is terrific," came the answer, then Kesa was in the kitchen to collect a hug. "You look well."

"Thank you." She tweaked the sleeve of Auntie Ivy's housecoat. "I like this one. Rose is a good color for you."

"Did I hear you say you brought sweet samosas? What's the occasion?"

"A big commission that will have good publicity if I can pull it off. My sister agreed to help out with a part of it this morning, which will make a big difference." She wanted to add that Shannon was leaving town, but how could she do that when she'd never told them about Shannon to begin with? It was ridiculous, wanting comfort over something that never was or would be. "And in general, my workshop is going great."

"I knew you would be successful. You are very talented, and you know how to work hard." Auntie Ivy gave the stew a last stir.

The three of them did their usual dance of negotiation in the small space. Cami set out plates and cutlery, which entailed ducking around Auntie Ivy, who was rummaging in the refrigerator. Kesa scooted between the other two women on the way to the far end of the kitchen counter.

She upended the bag of samosas onto a small cookie sheet, slid them into the toaster oven, and set the temperature to warm. "That'll keep them until we're ready. Brown, fried, yummy goodness." She was slightly breathless from the walk to get here and turned to the sink for a glass of water. "It's a beautiful day out. Not a cloud in the sky. And the sky is actually blue. Traffic is—"

She whirled around at the sound of a strangled gasp. Auntie Ivy staggered toward her, hands flailing as her knees buckled. By some miracle she missed the stove as Kesa caught her and was able to slow her fall. They both landed with a thud.

Cami dropped to her knees, patting the old lady's ashen face while chanting, "No, no, no."

"I'll get Marisol," Kesa exclaimed. "Call 911!"

Marisol was still buttoning her blouse as she opened her door in response to Kesa's frantic knocking.

"Auntie Ivy—something's wrong."

With a muttered exclamation, Marisol retreated into her apartment and returned in moments with a first aid kit. "Did you call 911?"

"Cami was going to." They hurried along the walkway back to the door Kesa had left open.

Kesa got out of Marisol's way and stood ready to do anything if needed. She'd never seen this side of Marisol, though she'd known it had to exist—calm and commanding.

"Ivy, did you take your pills this morning? Can you squeeze my hand?"

Auntie Ivy was trying to answer Marisol's questions, but she couldn't seem to catch her breath. Pain deepened the lines on her face.

Cami was frantically repeating the nearest cross street for the dispatcher. "The apartment is on the second floor. If they take the middle set of stairs our door is right at the top."

Marisol flipped open the first aid kit and settled the ends of a stethoscope into her ears. "Ivy, I know it's hard, but try to breathe as normally as possible." She listened intently to several places on Auntie Ivy's chest, then pulled a slim flashlight out of the kit, flicking light into each eye. She grunted to herself and reached for Cami's phone.

The string of medical terms meant little to Kesa, though she understood, "Sluggish response" and "Equal reaction in each eye." Marisol listened for a moment and said tersely, "I'll be here when the ambulance arrives."

She handed the phone back to Cami. "Stay on the line with the dispatcher. Did Ivy say anything about not feeling well?"

"She had a headache earlier, but said it went away."

"Ivy, did you take anything for your headache?" Marisol's hands moved to take Auntie Ivy's pulse at her wrist, then she scrabbled a small bottle out of her kit.

Auntie Ivy gave a minimal shake of the head.

"Okay. I'm not sure this is a heart attack. It doesn't sound right. I don't see signs of stroke, but I can't rule it out either. You are getting enough oxygen, though the pain is making it hard to breathe. I really need you to swallow this aspirin, Ivy. You can chew it."

Auntie Ivy was doing her best to nod, and she let Marisol slip the tablet between her lips.

Kesa lightly touched Marisol's shoulder. "Water?"

"Only if needed. But she's swallowed it." Marisol smiled broadly as she peered down at Auntie Ivy. "Good girl. Really, what you'll do to avoid losing at Mahjong."

Auntie Ivy tried to smile. Kesa could tell Cami was trying not to cry. They spent the next several minutes in a holding pattern until Kesa heard the siren and ran out to the stairway railing to wave.

The two paramedics worked seamlessly with Marisol to get Auntie Ivy strapped onto their stretcher for the journey down the stairs. Marisol turned to Cami as they navigated through the doorway. "I'll go in the ambulance and make sure they take her to Kaiser, where she was before. You get her ID and insurance card and all her medications and follow as soon as you can."

The no-nonsense tone steadied Cami a little, but she was shaking and still close to tears.

Though she felt a little wobbly too, Kesa adopted Marisol's aura of calm. "I'll drive you. I can get a Lyft home from there. No big deal. Gather up the stuff Marisol asked for. I'll take care of things in here."

She covered the pinakbet still bubbling on the stove. After making sure all the stove burners were now off, she pulled the samosas out of the toaster oven and clicked it off as well. She put a half dozen of the paneer samosas back into the bag they'd been in, thinking it would probably be a good idea to get Cami to eat one or two. Marisol was likely also hungry. The rest she covered with a tea towel to keep them moist as they cooled.

Cami bustled back into the kitchen and held out a narrow shoebox. "These are her pills. I also got her hairbrush and the lotion she puts on her hands before bed. She likes the lavender smell." Cami looked at a loss, as if she wasn't sure why she was holding these items.

"How about her insurance information and her ID?"

"Oh yeah." Cami rifled through Auntie Ivy's purse and came up with a slim wallet. "In here, I think."

Kesa peered over her shoulder as Cami went through the contents. "There's her Medi-Cal card and her Kaiser card. Why don't you bring the whole wallet, in case there's something else."

"Sure."

"Get your keys, and how about a sweater? Your phone and a charger?"

They were about five minutes behind the ambulance by the time they were underway. Traffic wasn't parting for them the way it would for emergency lights and sirens. It felt like forever getting across the 101, and Kesa was extra cautious because she wasn't used to Cami's little Nissan. The last thing they needed was a fender bender.

By the time they reached the admissions desk, Marisol was waiting for them. "They've taken her up for the usual series of tests. She was already feeling a little bit better by the time we got here. As attacks go, it seems minor, but we'll know more after the tests."

"Let's go sit down," Kesa suggested. She waved the now-cool bag with the samosas. "And have a bite to eat."

Marisol gave a gusty sigh of relief. "I'm famished."

Cami did as they suggested, and once she'd nibbled on some food and sipped water the color began to come back into her face.

"I know Ivy is a pain about it, but she does take her pills." Marisol patted Cami's hand. "And she's worked on her diet and moving around more. I think you'll be home in a few hours."

Cami wiped away a stray tear of tension. "I'm not ready to lose her. I'm never going to be ready." She cleared her throat. "I don't know how you did it, Kesa. You lost both your parents at the same time and you weren't much older than I am, were you? That must have been so hard."

"It was." But not for all the reasons Cami thought. Kesa wasn't going to tell her that the worst part of it had been the anger that went with it and the self-disgust for being angry—and resentful. She'd been on the verge of escaping her parents' chaos. No more sudden relocations and never answering the door because bill collectors were the most frequent visitor. She had enrolled at the community college and had even lined up a bed in a three-way share of a dorm-style apartment. Finally the money she earned taking in alterations would be hers to keep. If she worked hard enough she might be able to give Josie a place to escape to when she was old enough.

The future had been within her grasp. It wasn't as if they'd been big dreams that tilted at fate. They all went kaboom anyway.

Now Josie wanted to leave her too. And Shannon…Shannon was a chance she couldn't take again. Not that she was going to get that chance. A fancy job was going to take Shannon away. Or she'd stop answering her phone the way she had four years ago.

Kesa shook off the memories. "I think I'll get a soda. Do either of you want one?"

Cami asked for a diet anything. Kesa found the vending area and tapped her phone against the Coke machine. Strange world, strange life. On the outside, she had a phone and credit cards and a career that was getting better every day. On the inside, she was a great big maw of emptiness that no amount of ice cream would ever fill.

There were no answers in the soda, but the doctor's short visit and a longer visit from a nurse who knew Marisol did a lot to ease her worry about Auntie Ivy. She was low on potassium and her blood thinner was working a little too well, causing the "event." Cami was all smiles when they allowed her to go back to see her grandmother, who would be released tomorrow pending good test results in the morning. Cami could even stay with her overnight in the same room if she wanted to. Which she did.

Kesa and Marisol shared a ride back to the apartment complex, and then Kesa walked home the way she usually would have, though a little later. The orange sunset deepened to indigo, which reflected her mood. The music from the spontaneous street parties and colors of the bright murals felt as if they were behind a thick veil of scratchy gauze. The dark velvet of the sky was mottled with moving red and white lights. Some people's lives were unbound from gravity. She could stretch toward heaven, but she still didn't know if her fingers would ever touch the sky.

At the last streetlight before home her phone chirped and she stared dumbfounded at the message.

"We have to talk. Soon please, it's urgent."

It was probably about Josie and Paz, Kesa thought. Without thinking it through, she sent back, "I'll stay late at my workshop tomorrow night," and included the address.

The import of what she'd done hit her as she crossed the street. She would have memories of Shannon in her workshop now. She should change it to a coffee shop or parking lot, anywhere but the place that had absolutely no associations with heartbreak. Would that seem as if she were a coward, afraid to be alone with Shannon?

She stared at her phone and couldn't make up her mind what to do. An onslaught of bone-jarring vibration from a passing car jolted her into moving again. Sketches, she thought. You have to do Jennifer Lamont's sketches. Focus on the work, and you'll get through this.

It would have helped if she'd had a clue what "this" actually was.

CHAPTER TWENTY-EIGHT

Kesa's workshop wasn't hard to find. The neighborhood was a mix of houses and small commercial buildings, ranging along wide streets that slowly pitched upward toward Elysian Park and Dodger Stadium. Shannon might have even passed by the building years ago on her way to a meeting of intelligence analyst counterparts hosted at the LAPD academy.

All day she had toyed with the idea of running away to Seattle, even though there had been no follow-up yet from Integrity Investigations. There were too many knots in her world now. It would be simplest to cut them all and blame it on a new job. Yet here she was. She wished she were certain that she was acting out of concern for Paz and Josie and not because she wanted to see Kesa again.

She supposed it was a mixture of the two, not that that made anything better. She ought to be talking to Paz, not Josie's sister. She was powerless to turn the car around, though.

A warm blanket of early evening settled on Shannon as she parked and got out of the car. The sun was hot enough to welcome the shady parking spot. A startled pigeon flew into the nearby bushes, its outrage fading into the persistent surf-like roar of traffic on Glendale Boulevard. The mouthwatering aroma of hot, fresh bread wafted over her from the bakery on the corner.

She told herself to relax into it, but how could she with one foot in the past and no certainty about the future? She'd met Kesa on a Friday night that was still blistering hot in her memory. They'd spent Saturday night proving that the magic hadn't been a one-time thing.

Then Sunday. Sunday had been full of golden sunshine and easy laughter, softness and tangled sheets, all eclipsed by the bright light in Kesa's eyes.

Then ashes. Now acid. And all her fault, for being a coward.

If you want forgiveness, an inner sarcastic voice pointed out, you could apologize. That never made anything worse, you know.

The past has nothing to do with the very urgent present, she argued back. If Paz and Josie were planning to elope, she and Kesa needed to find a way to move forward. They couldn't stop the nuptials, not if the two young people remained committed to it. As far as Shannon was concerned their choice was not really a choice at all: support them or lose them. She didn't want to lose Paz in her life, but the idea of open warfare with Kesa over it was untenable as well.

Thanks for this, Universe.

The building was quiet, though hardly deserted. The walls were a soft white and the carpet a deep gray, and individual doors were decorated to reflect the tenant beyond. A potter's workshop occupied half of the first floor. There was a sweet tang of sandalwood outside the office of Wonder Aestheticists. She didn't know what an aesthetician did, but it sounded very LA and very expensive. She took the stairs and negotiated her way around a tall, exceedingly fit woman carrying a hefty dress bag with one of Kesa's business cards taped to it. Shannon felt as if she ought to recognize her but a name didn't come to mind. A satisfied customer, hopefully.

The feeling of approaching an executioner increased with every step toward the door marked "Designs by Kesa." Was there any way through that didn't include breaking to pieces?

There was no bell, so she knocked and strove for calm, or at least the appearance of it.

It lasted the three seconds it took for Kesa to open the door. One look and Shannon's breath tightened in her chest. Her heart pounded at the insides of her ribs, and she had to stuff her hands into her jacket pockets to hide that her fingers were curled as if to shape Kesa's face in her hands.

They shared awkward hellos as Kesa stood way back to allow Shannon to enter. She didn't know quite what she had expected. She'd never been in a space Kesa called hers, and she sought the studio for clues. Dressmaker dummies, of course. She remembered those from the car. Tables with fabric in neat rolls, yes. A drafting table with a pad of paper clipped to it, that made sense too. A good portion of the space was set aside with mirrors and a changing screen, plus some very comfy-looking chairs. The kitchen area was a bonus, Shannon thought. Like the rest of the space, it was exceedingly tidy. Everything had a place and everything was in it.

Most surprising were the picture frames showing off not standard photographs of finished garments but instead sumptuous samples of rich fabrics. She wanted to take her time to look at them and ask why their reds and golds and greens were like nothing she'd seen in the places she usually shopped. She felt decidedly dowdy in her off-the-rack suit jacket. If anything didn't fit in this crisp, tightly perfect space, it was her.

Kesa fit it, though. She was so flawlessly dressed and manicured that it looked as if she hadn't even tried. Black slacks brushed the tops of low-heeled silver sandals. Her sleeveless blouse was two shades darker than her eyes, with a hint of green that made those eyes all the bluer. Long gold and silver earrings twined with the heavy, silky hair that Shannon adored against her body. Every bit of Kesa was as powerfully attractive as she'd been in that Olvera Street bar. And more so—this was her turf, and she controlled every inch of it with a leashed power that made Shannon's head swim.

Kesa had closed the door behind Shannon. She said something, but Shannon didn't catch it.

"I'm sorry?"

Kesa's lips twitched. "Would you like some coffee, tea, or sparkling water?"

"No. No, uh, thanks. Thank you." Off to a swimming start. "I know this is a bad thing to confess to, but I overheard something that I wasn't supposed to. The kids are considering eloping."

The skin around Kesa's eyes paled and thinned, like tissue paper in a mist. "They can't be serious."

"I think they are. And we can't stop them." She took a deep breath to control her voice, which suddenly threatened to break.

"I'll talk to Josie," Kesa said through stiff lips. She seemed rooted to the spot just inside the door.

"Do you really think she'll change her mind?"

"No." She swallowed hard.

"I realized that I can talk all I want to Paz, but ultimately, if I deliver any ultimatums about getting married, I become unwelcome in his life. There'll always be a shadow of my distrust and doubt about his judgment. I don't want—" Her voice cracked in spite of her attempts to keep it even. "I don't want to find out how optional I am."

"You're not—he loves and respects you," Kesa blurted out. "Not like Josie and me. The only reason I'm not optional is that I pay the bills." She gulped in air and turned her back, her head bowed.

What do I do now? Shannon wondered. She wanted to hold her, and her mind elaborately, moment-by-moment, suggested what would happen after that. There was a lot of space on the floor. The tables, the counter.

She'd had no idea that her libido could be so completely inappropriate. This situation was serious, she told herself. She doesn't want you. She's not yours.

Sounding cautious, Kesa asked, "Has something changed the situation? I thought they were going to make a plan. Talk to you about renting from you. Is that not going to happen for... for some reason?"

"They haven't brought it up. I kept expecting them to, but it wasn't as if I wanted to hurry them along by reminding Paz."

"So nothing happened?"

Kesa almost sounded as if she thought something had. "Not that I'm aware of. Did something happen with Josie?"

"No more than the usual." With a little shake, Kesa finally moved. She gave Shannon a wide berth as she headed toward the nearest window, but it didn't keep the delicate scent of her deeply remembered cologne from tickling at Shannon's nose. "I wish I kept booze in the cupboard," she muttered, mostly to herself.

"We could go for a drink." A spectacularly stupid idea, she scolded herself. Alcohol wasn't going to put out any of these flames, let alone that it wasn't known for helping anyone's common sense.

Kesa was already shaking her head as she closed and locked the open windows and pulled down the blinds. "I have to visit someone who got out of the hospital today."

"I'm sorry. Is it serious?"

"Auntie Ivy has a heart condition."

Shannon had had the impression that Kesa and Josie had no family in the area. "Auntie?"

"You play enough Mahjong, everyone becomes family and the problems of the world are solved." Kesa wiped at the already pristine counter next to the sink. "She taught me how to play. Wants me to be more in touch with my Filipino roots."

"Do you want to be?"

"Yes, though it's hard to find any time for it. My parents actively avoided...our roots." Kesa started to add something else, then fell silent.

"I'm sorry. I don't mean to pry."

"Thank you for telling me about their plans."

Okay, back to the original subject, Shannon thought. A good idea. "I don't really know what to do. Other than make it clear that if they're going ahead I would like to be there." She cleared her abruptly aching throat. "Paz... The way life worked out, I'm his family. And he's mine."

Kesa was standing at the small sink, her back rigid and hands gripping the counter. "When Josie is passionate about something, she finds a way to get what she wants. She'd leave school to make it work. It would be such a mistake. The kind you don't ever come back from."

Before Shannon could possibly think of an appropriate response, Kesa snatched a sheet of paper towel from the roll and pressed it to her eyes. Through a muffled sob she said, "I have to go or Auntie Ivy will be asleep."

Shannon did her best to quell responsive tears of her own. "Is there—can I help?"

"You can't." Kesa ran water on the paper towel and mopped at her face. "I get a grip on one thing and everything else slips through my fingers."

Unable to stand the distance between them any longer, Shannon took a cautious step toward her. "Kesa—"

"Don't." She finally faced Shannon again, her eyes red and mouth trembling. "There's no fix for it."

At a complete loss, Shannon finally said, "I hope your friend will be okay."

Kesa blinked. After a pause she shook her head and jangled a ring of keys. "Fine. I need to lock up."

They went down the stairs in silence broken only by Kesa's occasional sniffle. Shannon ruthlessly shoved back the voice in her head that was chanting, "Hold her, hold her." Kesa was angry and afraid, that was clear, but Shannon felt as if it were all directed at her. Was that her reward for bringing unwelcome news?

The spring sunset was in full glorious progress, painting the sky with peach and lemon. Shannon turned to say goodbye to Kesa and was stunned silent by the sight of her face washed with gold, like it had been that Sunday afternoon four years ago.

She was back in that moment of magic. Connected to this woman by sunlight, desire, and the unexpected something more. She wanted to say the words that rattled against the back of her teeth, to give life to her feelings. Name them so they could be real.

But as she had four years ago, Kesa spoke first. This time, though, the words were not about impossible feelings. Instead, they cut at her, powered by eyes of burning sapphire. "And you stand there like a block of stone. Go ahead and leave. What was I thinking?"

Shannon remained frozen in place until Kesa's hatchback turned out of the parking lot. The words she'd wanted to say then and now would not reach the light.

Disbelief and fear had kept her silent then.

And now? What was the point?

CHAPTER TWENTY-NINE

"How are those coming along?" Josie locked the apartment door behind her as she kicked off her shoes.

Kesa wanted to demand every detail about an impending elopement but managed to hold herself back. Like Shannon, she was afraid of confirming how optional she was to her sister. What a crazy pendulum—she wanted Josie to be independent, and then she wanted Josie to be safe at home. On top of that she was desperately trying to shake off the encounter with Shannon. Her heart ached, and nothing she did helped.

Focusing on work had succeeded in the past, but it wasn't going well now. The one bright spot was that Auntie Ivy had been her usual self and Marisol very pleased with all of the test results. "I have a good idea. It doesn't look right on paper. I don't have your talent for it."

Josie gave her an all-knowing look. "I've had classes, you know, including one on drawing figures. You of all people know how much practice matters."

"It's so frustrating that what I can see in my head won't come out of this pencil." She sighed so gustily that the sheet closest to her fluttered against the table.

"That's what practice is for. I can draw beautiful pottery, but if I wanted to make it for real I'd have to practice with real clay and a wheel and the paints. You're the one who told me that art is magic but making it real is work."

"I know." She supposed she ought to be gratified that Josie had actually been listening. "I really intend to take classes, honest. I appreciate you being willing to help."

Josie leaned over Kesa's shoulder to tap the handkerchief-sized square of fabric on the table. "So that's what you're using? What an awesome shade of blue. Is that cerulean?"

Kesa was pleased that Josie hadn't bolted for her bedroom and shut the door. Instead, they were having a conversation like adults. She would bring up Paz, but for now she was content with signs of a truce. "Cerulean with white and phthalo blue. Do you think it matches this?" She picked up her phone to show Josie the image of Van Gogh's *Almond Blossoms*.

"Yes, the color is close to the painting, that is, if that image is displaying accurately on your phone. Colors can be tricky."

"I know. But I think it's close enough. The fabric is a silk and hemp blend. I thought the slubs in it—" She held it up for Josie's closer inspection. "I thought the roughness was suggestive of a painter's canvas. It's a Fifties retro swing dress, and there'll be a pillbox hat with lacy fascinators and a veil, similar to what the actress wears in her series."

"The 'Detective Della Field Mysteries'? Not the one where she's a zombie hunter?"

"I'm not confirming that's who the dress is for, you know." Kesa tapped the pencil against the tip of her nose. "However, I will say this is not for a zombie hunter, though that would be a cool party dress. No, they want it to sort of feel like a Fifties detective but not be expressly in character." She traced her finger over the sketch she liked best, though there was something not right about the proportions. "The circle swing skirt with all those gores is the sweetheart look of the Fifties. But instead of the usual halter or squared-off neckline for the bodice, I'm going off-the-shoulder. Putting some Marilyn Monroe cleavage into a Doris Day dress. The demure bombshell." Kesa doodled another series of triangles and circles that made up the bodice and skirt as she described it.

Josie made a hmm sound. "It's for an art opening, you said."

"Yes, and I want to remind people of Van Gogh. This color is quite distinctive, for one thing. I'll use ecru and white cording blended for branches and white gauze clusters with hint of pink centers to suggest the blossoms." She started a new drawing to represent the back. "Beginning here at the shoulder blade, I'll create a dramatic line of branches and flowers that cascades around the right hip and down to the hem. Show off all the curves." She made solid dots to indicate the beginning and transition points.

"That's a lot of handwork."

"She's paying me a lot of money. Three times what I've ever been paid for a project."

Josie took a deep breath. "I'm pleased for you."

"Thank you." Why did courtesy and support come so hard to both of them? When had they become enemies? Had it always been that way, from the moment that Kesa had had to make all the hard, painful decisions and little, bereft Josie hadn't understood any of the necessity? Or had she naturally gotten all the caution and worry and Josie all the wings and fire?

She cleared her throat. "I can pull this off with the fabrics and embellishments available at the textile mart right now. There's no time to special order."

Josie tucked her backpack under the table and drew up a chair next to Kesa. Taking a fresh piece of paper she re-created the general outline Kesa had drawn. Her strokes were confident and precise, and her pencil filled in details quickly. Josie might credit the classes, but there was an inherent skill as well. Neither of their parents had spent time in artistic pursuits. Did it stem from Josie's ease with complex math and geometry?

She leaned into Josie to look at the drawing from the same perspective. "More flowers, less branch. And elongate—fashion drawings always make the model look ten feet tall."

"Gotcha. I don't have a lot of time tonight, but I could do a line drawing and a pastel tomorrow. Anything special about the back underneath the embellishments?"

"It's solid, with the built-in, off-the-shoulder wrap at the top. A zip from base of spine to the top. And tea length—a few inches below the knee. The waist is natural."

Josie moved the waistline down with a heavy line. "There?"

"That's better, yes." Kesa looked at the Van Gogh painting again. It wasn't Lamont's signature blue, but the shade would still be very flattering to her coloring. "I'll rough out where I think the flowers ought to go specifically."

Josie hummed exactly the way she had as an eight-year-old with a coloring book and box of crayons. "How was Auntie Ivy?"

"Almost back to her old self. That was so scary, all of it."

"I get that."

"Doing this dress is scary too, but it feels like we've got it under control." Kesa took a deep breath. "So that means the scariest thing in my life is you."

Josie's gaze was focused on her pencil moving across the paper. "Huh?"

"I'm scared for you, Jo-Jo."

Her gaze left the paper to meet Kesa's. "That's because you don't trust me."

"Do you trust you?"

"Yes and no. But I'm responsible for me now." Her voice increasingly tighter with frustration, Josie added, "I will own my mistakes, Key. You don't have to be like Mom and Dad anymore."

"I'm nothing like them." The words were out before she could stop them. She felt Josie startle slightly and would not look at her.

"What does that mean?" There was more puzzlement than hostility in the question.

Josie wanted to be treated like an adult. Kesa was so tired of quelling the anger that was always there when she thought of her parents. So, maybe the way forward was to treat Josie like the adult she claimed she was.

Where to start? "What do you remember about life when they were alive?"

Josie pursed her lips. "We lived in big houses. There was a lady who came in to make dinner every night for a while. Mom was so pretty. I remember one night she and Dad were dressed super fancy. He had a tuxedo and she was wearing a long dress, with jewels, and I remember her jacket was soft and furry, I loved it. I suppose it was animal fur, but I didn't know that then. It felt wonderful."

"Do you wonder why we didn't live like that after they died?"

"You've said there were bills." It wasn't exactly a question.

"A lot of them. They'd been dodging collectors for years, that's why we moved a lot. The art on the walls and the furs Mom wore were all rented. The house was a rental too and they'd already received an eviction notice. I had barely a week to find us a new place to live. People were showing up at all times of the day and night demanding money." Her voice thickened with remembered anxiety and so many tears, and she reminded herself that those days were long over.

Josie toyed with the pencil as she slowly said, "That must have been frightening."

"It gets worse. The car was a lease. They had no insurance. So I had to pay the towing company for the wreck and the county for the emergency vehicles. And the ambulance to take them to a hospital to declare them dead and then transport from there to the funeral parlor. All more bills, none of which I could pay so they became my debt. On the only credit card I had at that age. I was in bankruptcy by the time I turned twenty-one—it was the only way out. That's followed me around all these years."

"I didn't know," Josie whispered. Clearing her throat, she went on, "You always seemed mad at them. I thought it was because they died. But they left you in a bad place. Financially."

"You think I'm all about the money? That's all I care about?" She tried to take the anger out of her tone. "I could have been like them and kept running. Pulling you out of schools, back and forth across district lines. Evaded Child Services, I suppose, and lied my way through credit card applications."

Josie actually laughed a little. "That is *so* not you."

Kesa blinked back more tears. "The only reason I was going to college was that I'd found a few sources of sewing on my own and I did it at school during lunch so Mom never knew. I was afraid she'd take it."

"I didn't know you were going to college."

Kesa pushed away the image of a path not taken. The one she was on was finally hopeful and steadier every day. "I was going to take real design classes. I might have learned how to sketch. There's still time. We'll see."

Josie took a tissue while Kesa studied the faded woodgrain of the table. After a sniff, Josie asked, "Is that why sometimes it seemed like you hated me?"

Pierced by Josie's words, Kesa buried her face in her hands, unable to hold back the flood. "I'm so sorry," she managed to gasp. "I never, ever hated you. I was trying to do the best I could."

Josie put her arm around Kesa and they rocked for a while. Kesa finally was able to add, "I resented you sometimes. I'm not a saint. I've been so angry at them, for so long. Because you and I were afterthoughts, every day. Especially you. I could stand on my own two feet, but you were a child. I didn't want to leave you, but I thought if I made good I could be there for you too. Something solid you could count on."

"I'm so sorry."

"None of it was your fault. Not one bit."

"If it wasn't my fault, it wasn't yours either, Key. But you got stuck with it."

"Life isn't fair."

Kesa felt a half-laugh ripple through Josie's chest before Josie let go of her. "So you have often told me. I really didn't know any of this."

"I didn't want you to know. Only that life wasn't easy for us and anything we had we'd have to work for. Any advantage we could get we'd have to take, short of stealing it."

Josie suddenly went rigid. "Oh!"

"What?"

"I remember something. One of the social worker people had dropped by and I remember you getting out that box you used to keep money in and showing a book to her. You said something about how when the box was getting low you knew you had to get even more work in. I hadn't realized that before. After that I would peek in the box sometimes, to make sure there was money. But I remember after the woman had left, you kicked over the chair she'd been sitting in."

Oh, *that* one. "I remember. Vividly. It scared you and I felt terrible."

"Why did you do that? General frustration?"

"No. She thought I was a hooker—that's where the cash came from. Said it out loud, that I was a young Asian girl with fancy clothes and makeup, like there couldn't be any other reason I might want to dress and look nice. Men would pay, she said, the implication being that of course I'd let them. That I was letting them. If she had any proof, she said, she'd take you away."

Josie stiffened with outrage. "And that she had no proof couldn't be because there was no proof?"

"I know. Seriously, right?" I could have told her some of this sooner, Kesa thought. It's not as if a light had gone off telling her that Josie was ready to hear the truth. "That was even after I explained that my appearance was a walking billboard for taking in more and more complicated projects that paid better. She smirked and agreed I was a walking 'something.' I was wearing careful copies I'd made myself of clothes that rich white girls were wearing in TV shows. And she told me I looked like a prostitute. Only she said 'geisha' like I was Japanese and she understood what the word meant."

Josie let out a harsh, believing/not-believing laugh. "That's some racist shit."

"There were plenty of them—and other people too—who didn't say it, but I knew they were thinking it. I know the social workers must have dealt with really terrible situations and saw all kinds of parents who did horrible things to their kids. But that wasn't me. I felt like they were blind to how hard I was trying. It felt like—" She paused to wipe her nose with a tissue. "It felt like nobody saw or appreciated anything I did, ever."

Josie held her tissue against her eyes. "You hid a lot of it from me."

"You were a kid, Jo-Jo, and that was my job. When you got into UCLA it was because of your hard work, I know that. But for me it was as if the universe finally told me I'd done good. That's why I'm so scared now, I guess."

"My life is not about you."

It sounded like Josie's usual defiance, but there was a plea in it that made Kesa's heart ache. "I know. But it is. So that's one thing, and I promise I will work hard at letting go."

Josie sighed. "So what's the 'but' I know you're going to say?"

"But, but, but." Kesa couldn't help the flash of childishness. "I know that you believe you fell in love at first sight or something. But you want to base your entire future on that always being true. Crap happens—and I don't mean you or Paz stop being in love," she added quickly as Josie bristled. "I mean that bad things happen. You could find yourself the sole wage earner, supporting both of you. Sometimes kids happen whether you mean them to or not. And then you're a woman whose skin isn't white supporting an entire family. If that happens and you didn't finish school your options will be much, much harder."

"School isn't a guarantee life will be any easier or fairer, and besides—"

"Without it you're guaranteed the hard road, all the way."

"And besides, I'm going to finish school." Josie pushed back from the table, but she didn't immediately get up. "You can stop worrying about that. It's as important to him as it is to me."

Kesa thought about all the women she'd heard of who had agreed to take a break from their college plans so that the man could finish his degree first and then were left with neither when he got the degree and decided he loved someone or something else. Paz didn't seem like that at all, but how could she be sure? The anxiety in her brain wouldn't let go. What if Paz got killed at a traffic stop? What if one of them was maimed in a shooting at school or a concert or just walking around? Or killed in a car accident like their parents?

"We both know that accidents happen. That's all I'm trying to say. Please don't think it can't happen to you."

"I know it can. I'm choosing to live like it won't. Because I don't want to live like—" Josie bit back what she was going to say.

Kesa finally looked at Josie. Her eyes were puffy and nose red. She looked so young. "You don't want to live like me." Good lord, what would Josie ever make of her boring, careful sister saying "I love you" to Shannon after knowing her less than two days? Part of her still couldn't believe she'd said it. It had been true, though. The way she'd felt had been real.

She pushed away the little voice asking why she was using past tense. "You won't have responsibilities like mine, you know."

"Not at first. I understand better than I did. What you—what you managed to do. Against some heavy odds. I'm grateful," she hurried on. "I really am. I'm sorry if it seems like I'm not. Paz says that gratitude is complicated. I think…" Josie took a deep breath. "I'll think about that."

With a gulp of fear, Kesa pleaded, "Please don't elope."

The chair clattered backward as Josie shot to her feet. "How did you know? Shannon?"

"She accidentally overheard you. We're both just trying to help. If you're determined to go ahead, you don't have to run away to do it. Okay?"

Josie turned her back but otherwise didn't move. Kesa could tell Josie wanted to storm into her room and slam the door to end this confrontation like so many others. But she didn't.

As calmly and carefully as she could manage, with her heart pounding and throat so tight she almost couldn't breathe, Kesa said, "If you guys came up with a plan we could talk about how to help. Not take over. Help, when you need us to."

"When did you two get so chummy?"

A searing memory of her knees between Shannon's thighs stole her voice for a moment. That was one secret she wasn't going to let go of—not right now, at least. "We just want to help," she repeated.

Without looking back Josie went into her room. She didn't slam the door, and Kesa would take what hope she could from that.

She had no clue what Josie was going to do next. She wanted to tell Shannon what had happened, but what could that possibly change?

Nothing, she thought. Except it would likely make her feel better to talk to Shannon. She wanted a hug in the worst way. Her brain quickly migrated from hugs to kisses to the sound of her clothes falling to the floor.

She smacked the side of her head like a TV that wouldn't tune a station, but the ultra-high-definition images went right on playing, complete with Dolby surround sound.

CHAPTER THIRTY

"*You stand there like a block of stone.*"
Kesa's bitter words wouldn't stop echoing in Shannon's head. She was more than halfway down a large glass of pinot noir when Paz stumbled out of his bedroom looking as numb as Shannon felt. She thought she knew the look—too much reading, thinking, screen time, typing. But this time she was wrong.

He squared his shoulders and pointed an accusing finger. "You told Kesa that Josie and I were going to elope?"

Whoa! Shannon thought. That came around way faster than she had thought it would. "I overheard you and I quite literally didn't know what to do."

He bounced on his toes. "How about talking to me, *metiche*?"

The lad asked good questions, darn it. She ought to have gone right to his room and apologized. Instead she was a little tipsy and ridiculously close to tears. She set aside the files she hadn't been reading anyway. "I really need some ice cream."

"Shit, Shannon."

"Language," she warned.

"Josie is really upset. Her sister told her all this stuff about their parents Josie never knew, and it totally explains a lot. But mostly she's upset that you eavesdropped when it's not your life. And I am too."

"She's right. You're both right, and I apologize to you. And I will apologize to her." Shannon pulled the salted caramel gelato out of the freezer. "Want some?"

"Stop acting like this isn't a big deal." He glanced at the container and his shoulders relaxed. "And yes."

"It is a big deal." She swallowed down the lump in her throat as she busied herself with the scoop and two bowls. "I was embarrassed that I'd eavesdropped. It was unintentional, but I should have let you know I was there or walked away. I'm really sorry." She tossed the empty carton into the compostables bin and handed him his generously filled bowl. "Please don't elope."

"I don't want to, not really."

They both had a large spoonful of ice cream and shared very similar sighs of relief. Shannon let another spoonful melt in her mouth as she returned to her corner of the sofa while Paz hovered near the sliding glass door, looking out at the backyard.

"Why do you think you have to?"

"Lots of things, but one is it'll be easier to rent an apartment if we're married."

She felt the beginnings of brain freeze and slowed down the deep gelato dive. "What happened to the plan of maybe renting from me?"

He looked puzzled that she'd ask. "Well, if you're moving to Seattle—"

Shannon shook her head in surprise. "Who said I was moving to Seattle?"

"Job offer?"

"Which I don't even have yet. And I'm not likely to take."

His gaze unfocused as if he was searching the logic path that had made him draw a wrong conclusion. "But it would be a lot of money. You sounded like you were pleased about it."

Damn, she hadn't realized what the possibility would do to Paz's outlook on his own plans. "I'm flattered by it, sure. But I like living in LA. Being near you has been important to me. It still is."

"Okay." His gleaming eyes focused on her again. "But you didn't seem all that open to us renting from you."

"That's because I'm not." She pointed her spoon at him in response to his "See?" expression. "Not if it enables you rushing into something you haven't thought through. Paying the bills is not the only reason to be patient."

He began his usual process of stirring the gelato into an even softer texture. "So what are the other reasons?"

She considered how much she should admit to insecurities and issues that were not his problem. "At first, when I met Josie, in the coffee shop, I didn't know if she was who she said she was."

Clearly exasperated, Paz rolled his eyes. "Did you run a background check on her?"

"No. But I wanted to." She had another bite of gelato and added sullenly, "I didn't know her last name at first."

"Why would you want to? You keep telling me I'm safe."

"You are. I'm suspicious and afraid of my own shadow. So sue me."

"So that's the way you are. What are you going to do about it?"

She narrowed her eyes to let him know she didn't appreciate having words she'd said to him thrown back at her. The little shit, he was too smart for his own good. "I'm going to drink my wine and finish my ice cream."

His smug expression suggested that he knew he had the upper hand, at least for now. "I went to see Gia the other day."

His foster mother? Surprised, though she acknowledged that she shouldn't be, Shannon asked, "How was she?"

"Fine. Not much has changed. She was really glad to see me and appreciated knowing that I'd been okay after that night."

"She deserved to know." Her heart went into overtime even as she told herself he was safe, everything was fine.

"She said that at no point has anyone ever come asking about me."

"That's a relief."

"Kind of. It does mean my family really never did look for me."

Some friend she was. She'd forgotten that he could still be hurt by the way he'd been abandoned. "I am sorry about that."

"I know you are. I thought I was over it."

"Funny how the past can reach up and slap you. Stuff that wasn't your fault. Decisions other people made." She stared into her bowl, wondering how it had become so empty and so quickly. "And mistakes you made."

He flopped into the overstuffed chair opposite her. "I don't think I made any mistakes with my family. They dumped me at a church when I was four."

"No you didn't, and yes they did. Sorry. I wasn't talking about you."

"You've made mistakes that have come back to slap you?"

He sounded ironic enough to earn another narrow gaze. She set down her bowl and had another swallow of wine, which she instantly regretted. The lingering taste of the gelato did not lend itself to a plummy bouquet with notes of oak and peach. "Yes, I have made mistakes, some shitty ones."

"Language!"

She stuck her tongue out at him.

"You didn't answer my question. What are the other reasons for us to wait to get married, now that you know Josie isn't looking to pop a cap in my head?"

"What if you fall out of love as fast as you fell into it?"

"Does love work that way?"

"I don't know about love at first sight." She heard the lie and this time she couldn't ignore it. "Look, I fell hard and fast for someone once. It was scary and I couldn't keep it together."

"Well, that explains a lot. That's you, not me."

"I know." She thought of Kesa's rejection. *You stand there like a block of stone. Go ahead and leave.* "People do fall out of love. Marriage makes falling out of love very messy. You're both thinking about it as the ultimate expression of love, but it's also a contract with legally binding aspects. You thought about the contract UCLA offered you. You went over all of it, really carefully. Have you done that for marriage? Car insurance, cell phone plans, health care decisions, responsibility for her actions and debts, joint bank accounts—"

"I get it, okay?" Paz sat up straight. "I did think about it before I proposed. I have a lot riding on the next couple of years. Well, so does she. We're both hanging on, hoping that life will let us have a shot and make a difference before the planet melts. I am stronger with her. And I feel like a hero when I have her back."

Shannon let out a breath as if he'd punched her. "Where did you learn that?"

"What?"

"How to be so fucking brave?"

He threw back his head and laughed. "Language!"

"Shit."

He laughed harder and she found herself helplessly joining him. Later, staring at the ceiling in the dark for what felt like the umpteenth night in a row, his words came back to her the way that truth does, and she couldn't shake them out of her head. Another idea had occurred to her, too, and she wished she'd thought of it before going to bed.

She finally turned the light back on and considered reading. Instead, she went to her dresser and pulled open the drawer with bras and underwear. Searching by touch all the way to the back, behind even the bra with the sprung wire she ought to have thrown away, her fingers finally touched the small box.

Back in bed she set the box on her chest and thought about opening it. She'd seen it twice in the past four years. Once when moving to Portland and once when moving back. She had told herself it was a useful reminder of how crazy she had been. Crazy in love.

Because when Kesa said "I love you" she had been about to say it herself. The idea that what she felt might truly be real was incomprehensible. It was daft. Certifiable. Truly crazy in love. All at once her aunt's lifetime of predicting nothing good could ever come out of dreams had stopped the words in her throat.

Kesa was the one reckless enough to put it into words first. Even now, Shannon wondered if she'd said it first, would it have scared her less?

The leather-covered box felt as if it had a heartbeat of its own, taking hers over. Finally, she opened it and looked at the ring she had bought for Kesa four years ago. The simple gold band was inset with sapphire chips that matched Kesa's eyes.

The guilt she felt at ghosting Kesa had layers, and this was the heaviest. Swinging wildly back and forth between an uncharted, unforeseen future she didn't know how to trust and the familiar shores of an entire life spent clinging to safety, she'd woken up that Monday morning paralyzed with fear. How could she be in love? Love at first sight was a fool's dream, and it would be crushed.

By lunchtime she was euphorically sure their feelings were forever and had rushed out to buy the ring to add to her apology for not saying "I love you" back. By dinner the heavy, insistent voice of her aunt had kept her from returning Kesa's first call, though her finger had hovered over the phone icon repeatedly.

By nightfall several text messages were unanswered. She couldn't answer them at night, she told herself. It would seem like a booty call, that she'd waited so they could have phone sex or something. Kesa's sister would be back from her school trip anyway. Kesa would soon realize that she couldn't fit a relationship into her busy, responsibility-laden life and all this hope she felt would be wasted.

Love was real.

Love was madness. It wasn't safe to feel this way.

The messages and voice mails stacked up like a wall, leaving Shannon on her side with fear and embarrassment as her best friends.

Kesa's words had only been a moment of wild abandon, Shannon told herself again. Or so she had been able to think, until today. The woman whose workshop she'd seen this afternoon was not reckless. Careful and precise. Tenacious. A builder, step-by-step.

Which made that impetuous declaration of love an anomaly and therefore not something to be trusted.

That or Shannon was an expert at rationalizing away what she didn't want to confront—her own fears. She'd hoped by leaving love untended it would die and she would be safe from the risk of the truth.

It hadn't worked.

Did it ever pay off to bet against love?

Idiot. She was absolutely, without doubt, the biggest chicken in the room. She'd chopped off an arm to make sure she never got a hangnail. Four years without the woman she'd fallen so hard for in her life, and now she looked back on lonely hours, lost conversations, a thousand kisses never shared. The ache she'd hidden in deep, dark places throbbed inside her bones and she snapped the ring box shut again.

You chose to feel this way, she reminded herself, and you didn't give Kesa a choice. Was it any wonder Kesa had pushed her away with such finality?

Calling it impossibly insane hadn't fixed anything. Her heart was still not her own. She was still crazy and even more so because somehow she had thought Kesa would forgive her and that somehow they would find a fresh start.

She heard Paz's footsteps heading toward the kitchen. She wrapped herself in her robe and followed the sound of rummaging.

Mouth full of Cheerios, he asked, "Did I wake you?"

"No, I'm having trouble sleeping is all. Say, did you tell Josie I was moving to Seattle?"

"Yeah. I didn't think it was a secret. That's what scared her into wanting to elope. That and fighting with her sister."

"Does her sister know?"

"Josie may have told her." He popped another fistful of circular oaty goodness into his mouth. "Actually, I think I mentioned it in passing."

You stand there like a block of stone. Go ahead and leave.

Shannon ignored his puzzled expression and took herself back to bed.

1000. Maybe... *999.* Maybe not... *998.* Maybe...

CHAPTER THIRTY-ONE

Josie was gone to school the next morning by the time Kesa was making her own breakfast and noticed that two dress sketches, front and back, were on the table, complete in pastel pencils. Had Josie even slept if she'd finished these already? There was nothing hurried about them.

She'd caught the line of the dress, the complex bodice, and the suggestion of the branches and flowers against the rich, lustrous blue. She'd even added a general outline of a tall, curvaceous brunette with long curls of hair pulled over one shoulder.

Meaning every word, she texted Josie, "Beautiful, perfect, you did great. Thank you!" She followed it up by sending her the money she'd promised. She didn't add, "Please don't run away and get married," but she held her phone against her forehead for a moment and prayed.

She had enough skill with a pen to add an artful rendition of her logo and a copyright mark alongside the sketch. At her workshop she took careful, well-lit photos of the sketches and sent them to Jennifer's assistant. Life with Josie might be at its rockiest point ever, but Friday at work was looking good. *I get a grip on one thing and everything else slips through my fingers.*

Unfortunately, the simple final embellishments and hemming for her latest suit-kini order left her brain free to think about Shannon. She tried to be philosophical. Nothing had really changed, had it? *If you hadn't met up with her again she would still be out of your life, right?* She had to start counting the days all over again until it didn't hurt, that's all.

Sure, that's all.

Lunch was a warm, delectable and highly comforting meat pie from the bakery. It helped settle the too many cups of coffee and anxious nerves she felt every time her phone chimed and she thought, "This is it, a photo of Josie and Paz in Vegas."

One more fitting for a suit-kini completed and cash in the bank, she checked her messages after she closed the door behind the departing client. Jennifer's P.A. had written back.

Kesa whooped as she read, "JL LOVES LOVES LOVES this. Scheduling details back to you in a few."

She had enough time to text Josie that her sketches had sold the deal, and then the promised follow-up to schedule Jennifer Lamont's fittings arrived.

She plunked down so hard onto her work chair that she reflexively rubbed her butt. "Travel plans upended. Is there any way at all she can do a prelim fitting on Monday? Final ten days later? We know this is a big ask."

Monday? She wanted to say it was impossible. One did not say that word to clients, though, and certainly not to this client. Her gaze fell on her existing store of the cheap polyester fabric she stocked up for experiments and first drafts. Lamont and her people were reasonable to work with and they understood that garments were built in multiple stages. She already knew Lamont's measurements to a certainty. Using a fabric she didn't care got ruined by the inevitable mistakes, she could have the component pieces ready if she worked all weekend. Stitching them together into a prototype garment Lamont could try on was possibly achievable by late Monday. There would be no embellishments, but she could make a few of the flowers to get them the way she envisioned and mark the prototype with the line she was going to follow. That part *would* be easier with Lamont in the dress.

She sent the gist of her thoughts to the assistant and got back a promise for a five thirty p.m. fitting on Monday. Recognizing that Kesa was pulling off a minor miracle, Lamont agreed to come to Kesa, saving Kesa another hour.

Small blessings—there would be no time to maunder over Shannon, she thought. She sent Josie another text, telling her not to expect her for most of the weekend and why.

To her relief she finally got an answer back. "Got it. Congrats."

She would have to be content with that. Whatever Josie and Paz decided to do, it was out of her hands.

The gentle scent from the mimosa tree seemed to wrap around her as she steadied herself against her worktable. Was this seeping sense of loss, like a tide going out, what it felt like to let go?

Glad she had already eaten enough to get her through the rest of the day and long through the evening, she unfurled the roll of pattern paper across her drafting table, got out her master ruler and sharp 4H pencils, and settled down to work.

CHAPTER THIRTY-TWO

When Paz didn't come home Friday night and didn't send a text letting her know his whereabouts, Shannon fully expected to hear about a wedding in Vegas. She'd messed up big time by eavesdropping and then telling Kesa about it.

To her relief, he breezed in Saturday afternoon as she was unsuccessfully trying to focus on the case reading she'd brought home.

"I spent the night at Josie's. I probably will tonight too." He didn't seem upset, only distracted as he disappeared into his room. "I'm looking all over for one of my textbooks. I owe it back to Lucio."

"Look in the laundry room," Shannon called. "There's a stack of something on the dryer. It's been there since Wednesday."

"Really?" There was a slight pause, then, "There it is! And the other one too. And my notes from Comp Stat."

"That's right, my two X chromosomes combine to make a tracking device," she said, not loud enough for him to hear.

He reappeared, books under one arm and phone in the other. His mouth was literally hanging open.

"What's up?"

He peered more closely at his phone. "I got the internship! Letter will be in the mail."

Shannon bounded to her feet with a shout of victory. "You did it!"

They met in the middle of the room for a rib-cracking hug.

"I don't believe it! I have to tell Josie."

He spun away in a vortex of happiness, his voice several tones higher than usual as he delivered the great news. Josie's excited voice was audible even from a distance.

"Can I take you guys out to dinner?" she called after him. "To celebrate?"

He gave her a thumbs-up and she tried very hard not to listen in on his side of a rapidly shmoopy-goopy conversation full of "No, you are," and "I'll hang up if you'll hang up."

Her legs felt a little wobbly and she settled into the sofa again to sort out the flood of emotions. A corporate internship meant a probable sponsorship to do his master's degree in return for a commitment to work for them after graduation. The next four or five years of his life could be safely settled, and he'd be doing something he really enjoyed. Between the money for the summer and part-time jobs when school resumed, the kids might be able to come up with enough bank to make rent as a couple.

Another life-changing moment, she thought. That horrible night, in the wrong place at the wrong time, had nearly destroyed this future, but now the scales had balanced. It felt like a little bit of justice.

She was startled by Paz's return. He was still bouncing up and down on his toes. "Josie's at campus, but she can meet us at the Korean barbecue off Olympic in about an hour."

"Sounds great. You drive and I'll catch a bus back."

Today we'll celebrate, she told herself as he drove them through the clogged weekend streets. It was a bright, hot day that promised summer would be there any minute, and he turned on the air conditioning as the sun warmed his little hatchback. As they bounced around ideas about how the internship might proceed, she decided her best plan for Paz and Josie going forward would be to shut up and listen to them talk about the future. She wasn't sure there had ever been another option—she'd just wanted to think so.

Josie was waiting for them in the parking lot. She flung her arms around Paz, exclaiming, "I'm so proud of you!"

He lifted her off her feet in a bear hug. "It changes everything."

She let them smooch in private while she went inside to ask for a table. She felt hungry for the first time all day. The heavy, delicious scents of orange and pepper and roasted garlic sent her stomach into one long growl. When the two of them joined her at the table, they quickly agreed on a starter of gyeran mari while they decided on their entrees.

"So we're here to celebrate, but I also truly want to apologize for eavesdropping. I'm ashamed of myself, and as I told Paz, I really did not know what to do. I hope you'll accept my apology, both of you." There, that wasn't so hard, she thought. You can say something to someone instead of thinking it and wondering why nothing gets better.

Josie took a philosophical tone. "It's not as if we are super serious. I mean we were kind of serious but not *super* serious. I talked about some stuff with my sister and maybe that helped."

"Nevertheless, I won't make a habit of it."

"Thank you." Paz nodded along with Josie and Shannon relaxed. All might not be forgotten, but it was mostly forgiven. "Have whatever you want," Shannon told Josie. "Enough for some leftovers later."

"That's so awesome. Kesa is working at her shop all weekend—a really huge deal commission that's a big rush. So I'm on my own."

Paz bestowed a look of pure adoration on Josie. "Your sketches turned out? That's great!"

"They did, and I already got the paycheck. Here." Josie fished out her phone and turned it toward Paz next to her. "I took pictures of them, see?"

Paz duly admired them, then she tipped the display toward Shannon.

The tall figure and blue dress were beautifully rendered. Shannon hadn't realized how talented Josie was. And the dress itself was stylish and fun—a piece of walking art. "Is this for that actress whose name I swear I've completely forgotten?"

"That's the one." Josie tucked the phone away. "Whose name I don't know, nope."

"I don't know what you're talking about," Paz deadpanned.

"Kesa makes that kind of dress? No wonder she's a successful *couturière.*"

"You know, I think she's just getting started." Josie took a last look at the phone. "I'm proud of her."

Something Kesa might like to hear, Shannon thought, but give it time.

The omelet roulade was delivered and they all tucked in. Shannon's favorite thing was dipping the edge of a slice in a little bit of sweet chili sauce. Bell peppers, carrots, and eggs were meant to be together, she thought. Her stomach definitely agreed and the growling went away. She was equally pleased with her heaping bibimbap that arrived shortly thereafter. The bowl of savory seasoned rice, heaped with veggies, chicken, and egg, was usually more than she could finish, but today she scraped the bottom. Josie and Paz shared halfsies of their two choices, a fragrant seafood pancake and sizzling, barbecue bulgogi.

The bus journey was convoluted on a weekend, but she reached home without incident. She decided to take her work outside to enjoy the late afternoon sun before the warmth left the backyard.

All the while the knowledge that Kesa was at her workshop played in the back of her mind, and an imp of distraction constructed any number of stupid excuses to drop by. Maybe sit in the parking lot for a while. As if that wouldn't be a hundred percent childish move. Stalker, much? Not to mention there was no proof Kesa wanted to hear anything she had to say. Certainly not now, with a lot riding on a big commission.

When the loss of sunlight drove her back inside, she indulged in a very loud viewing of *Wonder Woman* and then returned to the reading she'd brought home. She'd reached the bottom of the stack of unclassified printouts and realized she'd finally made her way into genuine backlog from the government shutdown at the beginning of the year. A quick glance indicated it was probably inconsequential chatter that had not been anyone's priority when they'd returned from furlough.

She was glad she took the time to read it, because it was a fairly amusing summary of a fugitive trying to get himself captured, quite literally, because he thought custody was safer than what would happen if his angry ex-confederates in bank robbery found him first. The analyst who'd written it up had done so with a dry, ironic flair that such summaries rarely had. Standing in banks hoping to be questioned, running out on his tab at cop bars, even walking back and forth in front of ATMs. Finally, he'd joked at an airport about having a bomb and was now happily behind bars.

It might have been the second glass of wine that made falling asleep so easy for once. But when she snapped awake at five a.m., heart pounding, she knew instantly why.

That summary—a fugitive who *wanted* to get caught.

She made coffee and sat down to think while the sun rose.

CHAPTER THIRTY-THREE

Parking was simple on a Sunday, and Shannon found a space near the marshals' office. There was no line for the security screening, but the elevator was being worked on. The journey up the stairs made her glad she'd worn sneakers instead of her usual business heels.

From chatter on the second-floor landing she gathered there had been an incident at the courthouse late Friday, easily contained. The third and fourth floors seemed deserted, but they were mostly occupied by administrative workers who kept the usual M-F 9-5 schedule.

The fifth floor was quieter than on a weekday, but there were deputies at desks and a group gathered in the small conference room where street maps were up on the television display.

Tau, the usual keymaster, wasn't at work on a Sunday, and she hunted down the person listed for weekend coverage. Once her desk and computer were unlocked she opened up her summary of the known movements of Seychelles, a.k.a. "Henry Lymon" and several other aliases, along with the raw intel behind each sighting.

Hanging around a police station. Walking through security in a courthouse. Caught in Toronto by CCTV cameras that he had to know were there.

People did not do anything for no reason at all.

Seychelles had been a playboy miscreant brother of an Eastern European head of state, then turned asset for the CIA. What if he wanted back into the CIA's good graces? Even more worrisome, what if he wasn't rogue at all and was trying to signal that he needed discreet contact? Had she missed anything that would have claimed him as an active asset?

If he was an active asset, then it was very possible her elevating his profile had jeopardized a long-term operation. At the very least, if he was trying to come back into the fold, that meant he had intel he thought was valuable and she'd jeopardized the capture of it. But if all he wanted was to come in, he could have contacted his previous handler and arranged it. Instead, almost as if he was hissing "Psst! Over here!," he'd shown his face to cameras connected to active facial recognition scans that quickly made their way through the intelligence network. She'd assumed it was stupidity and bad luck. What if it wasn't?

She went back to the beginning, read every communiqué and update, read between the lines, even scraped through the complete classified Seychelles dossier again. There was nothing to find that she hadn't already known. Officially, Seychelles was a rogue asset who had dropped out of sight, until a month ago.

Still… Her gut told her something wasn't right even if her head had no concrete proof to support the feeling. It wasn't something she could take to her boss, not yet. She was going to have to blind-call into the CIA, and she couldn't even tell her boss the details. Protocol and common sense made her dash off a note to warn him that she was making extra-channel contact and, of course, she'd let him know the outcome. He wouldn't be blindsided if someone at the CIA decided to take umbrage and complain up the chain.

The dossier had the agent number for Seychelles's last handler before he was reported as having dropped out of contact. She dialed into the secure portal and gave the pleasant, bland voice on the other end the number and her own contact ID details, the dossier number she was calling about, and waited. A few minutes later, she was told that her "desire for contact" would be relayed and the voice disconnected. It was all very CIA. She of course understood protocols existed for everyone's protection. Nevertheless she couldn't help but hear cloak-and-dagger noir music playing in her head as she logged the result of her call into her file.

Even as she wondered if she ought to linger next to her phone for the rest of the day in hopes of a callback, the phone rang. She quickly tapped her headset to answer it.

A gravelly masculine voice asked, "Shannon Dealan?"

"Speaking."

He rattled off his credentials, which matched up to her files, and then she did the same. He said, "Hang on," and she knew he was verifying her clearance level. About ninety seconds later, he said, "Go ahead."

"I'm the analyst in support of an arrest warrant for bank fraud out of the Central California District. Henry Lymon is an alias in this particular dossier."

"Yes?"

"Henry Lymon has been captured by three separate CCTV facial recognitions from our counterparts in Canada. A provincial revenue office, a courthouse, and a police station." She gave him the dates and cities. "We initiated our protocol anticipating entry into the US with plans to pick Lymon up after he left Canadian jurisdiction. A clean, documented capture of Henry Lymon. Then I would alert several agencies that they have interests—"

"I see." He put her on hold.

Sheesh. She drummed her fingers on her desk and finally heard the faint pop that meant the line was live again.

"We would appreciate it if Lymon was removed from elevated scrutiny at border points of entry."

"Because?"

"That's need to know."

"I have clearance and I need to know." She could match him gruff for gruff. "Is he trying to phone home?"

The slight hint of background noise told her he hadn't hung up in the long silence that followed her question. "Those locations and the timing suggest that is the case. We are eager for him to do so."

"Thank you. I'll make heavy recommendation to reduce Lymon's scrutiny at border points of entry unless something official comes through from your agency to countermand that."

There was only the slightest easing in tone as the agent said, "Thank you," and disconnected.

Damn. She had been so hoping to see Seychelles at last in custody. He might end up with yet another alias, and it was entirely possible she would never know.

It was unsatisfying, to say the least.

She wrote up a detailed description of her logic, the steps she had taken to confirm, and the pertinent identification numbers from the CIA dossier and agent. That filed, she sent a redacted version to her boss with the promised recommendation.

That was exactly what Gustavo was waving at her when she got to work on Monday morning. "Good work, Dealan!"

"It doesn't feel like it. Lots of slimeballs get shelter because they might be useful to someone else." She lowered her voice. "I want the guy in handcuffs. With a very public perp walk and the words 'child trafficking' under his picture."

"That would be very satisfying, I agree." He sighed as he turned back to his office. "We have to trust that if he turns out useless they'll kick him down the food chain."

Gustavo didn't know that Seychelles was related to someone with a lot of power in a murky part of the world. For all Shannon knew, their being called off an active hunt was a favor to a CIA source in that other country. An "I'll let this guy go if you give me intel on that other guy" arrangement. Meanwhile, it was possible kids were getting hurt. Of course, it was possible he was ratting out other traffickers.

The not knowing irked her, and it was hard to settle down in a good frame of mind. She was cheered in the afternoon, a little, by the copy she received of a note to her file from the Marshal himself, praising her "extensive research capabilities, stellar instincts in data interpretation, and commitment to interagency cooperation."

Let it go, she told herself. Seychelles had been a persistent puzzle, but it was time to clear her mind of him. The lack of justice bruised her outlook, though. Justice shouldn't be invisible. Who could believe in truth and fairness when you couldn't see them? Every time they brought a fugitive in to face justice she felt rewarded for her faith in it. Such foolish faith, her aunt had always insisted, would always be disappointed.

Hush up, Aunt Ryanne, Shannon thought irritably. If she ever told her aunt it was sunny out, she'd answer back that there'd be rain by morning. Shannon would not believe her faith in justice was misplaced. One setback didn't break the world.

One bad guy gets away, she told herself, but many other bad guys would not be so fortunate. Maya Angelou was right—justice was like air. Their luck would run out.

She took up other case files. There was never a shortage of puzzles and pieces waiting for her attention. It was important to keep working because if she stopped she would think about Kesa. Kesa, who had not seen fairness or truth from Shannon and had no reason to believe that she ever would.

The point of her pencil snapped against her notepaper. She stared at the jagged edge of the lead and confronted the fact that she couldn't bury herself in work forever to hide from problems of her own making. It was possible that Kesa thought Shannon was about to leave town and that was why she'd been so angry and final in spite of the magnetic chemistry between them. What if Kesa learned that a job offer hadn't materialized? Even more to the point, that even if it did, Shannon wasn't taking it? She wouldn't even consider it, not if there was any hope of a second chance with Kesa.

But what if Kesa doesn't want you in her life—aye, there's the rub. She doesn't know anything that really matters, Shannon reminded herself. *You were hoping she'd forgive the past without you ever having to do the perp walk and allocute. Without knowing that you have tried to change.*

She sharpened the pencil, tore a page from her notebook, and started writing.

CHAPTER THIRTY-FOUR

Kesa glanced at the clock again, even as she told herself she was wasting time doing so. Five-twenty. Jennifer Lamont would be here in ten minutes or less and the final stitching that attached the off-the-shoulder collar to the main bodice of the dress wasn't finished. She needed every single second.

Her back hurt, her fingers hurt, her eyes hurt, her knees hurt.

She whipped in the final stitch, tied it off, and then threw herself at the piles of discarded fabric and pattern paper that she'd let accumulate on chairs and the floor. Bundling it into a great wad, she shoved it into the narrow broom closet. Accumulated dishes and takeout containers were set willy-nilly into the dishwasher. She'd sort it all out later, after sleeping for more than a three-hour stretch.

After checking her hair in the mirror and tucking her blouse into her slacks, she checked the clock. Thankfully, Lamont was late.

Even as Kesa thought she could perhaps add some of the embellishments to the prototype she heard swift, decisive footsteps in the hall coming toward her door, which she'd left propped open. A moment later Lamont poked her head in. "Hey there, I found you."

Kesa tamped down her usual flustered response to Lamont's limitless magnetism. "Please come in."

The star's luminous eyes were hidden behind dark glasses, and a gold-black Strikers cap covered her casually pulled back hair. If they were an attempt to disguise Jennifer Lamont from fans, they failed. There was no mistaking the expressive mouth and long legs. The sleeveless sundress and ankle-wrapping Gucci sandals were worn with utmost confidence.

Tucking her sunglasses into her Kate Spade handbag, Lamont went directly to the dressmaker dummy where the prototype was waiting. "This is it?"

"It doesn't look like much," Kesa began.

"On the contrary." Lamont ran a finger along the neckline with an evaluative expression. "This should be really flattering."

"The final will have a tuck right here, where the faux wrap overlap ends." She pointed out the spot she meant, which would settle about three inches off center of Lamont's cleavage. "And then a fold for emphasis. I'm sorry I didn't have time to make this perfect."

"That you did this in a couple of days is amazing. Is it ready to try on?"

"Yes." She gestured toward the privacy screen. "Please let me know if you need anything."

"I'm fine for now, thanks."

Kesa indulged herself for a moment as she watched Lamont cross the room, then she told her inner pervert to knock it off. Disgusted with herself, she went to lock the door and nearly fell over her own feet. Get a grip, idiot!

"That open window," Lamont called from behind the screen. "Is it line of sight to another building? On the other side of the trees?"

Kesa hadn't thought about it. "I don't know. I'll close the blinds, just in case."

"I appreciate it. I've had too many run-ins with determined paparazzi." Lamont's dress was now flung over the screen. "Sorry I didn't wear a strapless bra. I will of course at the event. Those things are torture traps," she said as she came out from around the screen.

It was Lamont's impersonal professionalism, even wearing only her underwear, that brought Kesa fully back to the business at hand. A welcome calm settled over her as she lifted the dress from the form. "The stitching is really loose so we'll have to do this slow. This is a knit and it isn't lined, either, so it's going to droop a little. The final dress will have structure, trust me on that."

"Gotcha." Lamont slipped off her rings and bracelets, dropped them into the ball cap, which joined her purse on a chair. Turning her arms so that her palms were out, she guided the dress over her head, then let Kesa do the work of settling it into place.

"The waist is too loose. I will definitely fix that."

"I'm back at the training gym for the next season of zombie slaughtering. Nice to know it's working."

"Let me get the back." Kesa hooked a stool with her foot and stepped up to draw the zip all the way up and fasten the hidden hook at the top. "There."

Lamont's head was tipped as she considered her reflection in several of the standing mirrors. "It seems long."

"It's unhemmed and lack of lining is making it hang long. And this flat black polyester looks overall bigger than it is because you can't see the drape of it." She retrieved the roll of the beautiful blue silk-hemp blend she was actually going to make the dress from. "This is the color and fabric, with a light blue cotton voile lining."

"Oh…" Lamont breathed out with pleasure. She gathered it to her waist as Kesa draped it around her. "That's stunning. Supple and yet crisp, which was very big in the Fifties. Tell me about the embellishments. Flowers and branches?"

Kesa quickly walked Lamont through the illusion of a flowering almond tree she was hoping to create across the back and then sweeping around to the front. As she described it she used a silver Sharpie to illustrate the lines that would be created. With Lamont actually in the dress it was easy to pick exactly the right places for emphasis and avoid all the wrong ones.

"It won't look lopsided, all the embellishment on one side?"

"I don't think so," Kesa said, "but I'll keep that in mind. The skirt does need to drape symmetrically. I can scale it back if need be."

With a wide smile, Lamont relinquished the fabric back into Kesa's care. "This is exactly what I wanted. Can I take a fabric sample to look through my shoes?"

"Certainly. What do you think of a pillbox hat to finish it?"

"Veil?"

"And a fascinator with the same gauze I'm using for the flowers."

"I am loving this." Lamont ran her hands over her hips. "Even in this fabric the dress is wonderful."

"It was the era of Chanel and Dior and Jacques Fath, before anyone had ever heard of Twiggy." Kesa let go of the tight knot of tension in her chest. Lamont loved the dress. The style was a perfect foil for her charm and stature. Yes, there was a lot of work ahead of her, but now there would be time to do it and do it right.

Investing in herself had paid off. Maybe, just maybe, nothing bad was going to take it all away again.

They spent a few minutes discussing the hem and overall fit. Lamont walked back and forth in front of the mirrors, watching the sweep of the circle skirt as she turned. Kesa was captivated by the way the star tested the set of her shoulders, trying out a range of minute shifts that conveyed everything from demure reticence to outright vamp. Then, with her sandals on, she did a runway approach to one mirror, pirouetted, and walked away at a normal gait. Pausing, she glanced quickly over her shoulder at her reflection. "I don't want to tell you your business, but if the silver line you drew is where you're going to add embellishment, I think it should be closer to my spine."

"I see what you mean," Kesa said quickly. "The line will crumple if it's that close to the side and you move freely."

Jennifer turned to face her. "Why are you such a professional?"

"Um..."

"You collaborate. No tantrums because I have an idea or two."

"Well, I know I can learn from you. You ruled the runway as a model, and you're endlessly stylish."

Kesa wailed inwardly that she sounded like a gauche sycophant, but Lamont's eyes sparkled. "I think you really mean that."

"I do!"

"Then it's possibly the nicest thing anyone not married to me has said to me in a while."

"You must work with a lot of idiots," Kesa muttered before thinking better of it.

Lamont's throaty laugh seemed to fill every corner of the room. "Not idiots. Just people so used to lavishing praise that it's impossible to tell what's sincere and what's patter." She glanced at the clock.

"Time to get out of that?"

"Yes, my wife is expecting me for dinner. Date night."

As they worked together to slide the dress up and over Lamont's head, Kesa asked casually, "What kind of things do you do for date night?"

"Take-out and bingeing *Jeopardy!*"

"Sounds fun."

"Every minute."

With a last gentle tug, the dress seemed to come free in Kesa's hands, but Lamont gave a yelp of surprise. "I'm caught!"

"Oh, it must be a pin. I'm sorry!" She quickly followed the taut line of fabric to the lace on the waistband of Lamont's bikini briefs. "I thought I got them all."

She was on one knee trying to remove the pin without jabbing the client further when she heard the worst possible noise: the sound of the workshop door opening.

She'd locked it, she knew she had. The pin came free as she whirled to her feet to face the intruder.

For a very long moment Shannon stood stock-still with her mouth open in shock. Her gaze was frozen on Lamont, then with a gasp she clasped her hands over her eyes. "I'm sorry, oh my god, oh my god, I'm so sorry!"

"Shannon, what the hell! Get out!"

Shannon backed away, one hand still over her eyes while the other groped for the door. "I'm sorry, I wrote you a letter, I'm so sorry. I was going to put it under the door, but you were here, and that would have been another coward move along with all the others I put you through, I'm so sor—"

"Go," Kesa ordered. She snatched up her notebook and threw it at Shannon to make her point. "Go now."

It missed by a mile, but the flapping and subsequent thud as it hit the wall propelled Shannon into full flight. The door slammed behind her.

Kesa raced to the door and checked the lock. The damn thing *was* locked, but the knob still turned easily. How long had it been that way? How could she have not noticed? "It's broken. Ms. Lamont, I am so embarrassed."

She slowly turned to face her client's ire. This was it, she was going to lose the commission and the client. Disaster, just like always.

Lamont had already whisked on her sundress. The easy smiles were gone. "Usually someone has to buy a movie ticket to see that much of me."

"I promise you, there was no camera. Shannon works for the US Marshals Service and she would never, ever do anything sleazy or gossip." Near tears, Kesa added shakily, "I can get her to sign an NDA if—"

"It's okay. It was an accident," Lamont added tersely as she pushed bracelets onto her arm. "I trust you and I'm sure your girlfriend is trustworthy too."

"She's not my girlfriend."

Lamont paused in looking through her handbag. "Really?"

Not sure why it mattered so much to set the record straight, Kesa rushed on. "We had a thing, but we're not even dating. We blew it the first time around."

Lamont was quickly brushing out her hair. "That was a lot of 'I'm sorry' for not even dating."

"There's no point in repeating history." *Shut up*, Kesa shouted in her head. Jennifer Lamont does not want to know your drama. As if the woman had nothing better to listen to, especially after a stranger got an eyeful of her in her undies. "I'm really sorry about the door."

"I know a little about history," Lamont said as if Kesa hadn't spoken. Her expression turned pensive as she slipped her glittering rose diamond and sapphire wedding ring back onto her finger. "As we say in the business, when the past gets too messy, reboot it. The past is still there. It's still real and that story is still true. But your life doesn't have to be anchored to it anymore. You're free to write new history going forward."

Kesa swallowed and managed to say, "Thank you. I'll think about it."

"Promise me one thing at a minimum, though."

"Okay," Kesa agreed, unsettled by the amused mischief in Lamont's eyes.

"Get that lock fixed."

CHAPTER THIRTY-FIVE

What else was there to do but run, and run fast? Shannon had backed out of her parking space and turned out onto the street before she had any thought other than putting as much distance as possible between her and Kesa and a celebrity she should have never seen in her underwear.

She was running away but where to? Oh dear lord, could it have gone any worse? The letter she'd written was still in her pocket. She'd realized Kesa was there, screwed up all her courage to open the door, and never once told herself maybe Kesa was working. That perhaps dropping in on Kesa's place of business for personal reasons wasn't smart.

She pulled over to the curb to try to decide what to do. Love was supposed to be some kind of lofty, expansive, uplifting experience. It brought out the best in you, helped you be all you can be.

No, that was the Army.

"You need to make a plan, soldier," she told her reflection in the rearview mirror. The sight of her wide, wild eyes nearly set off a bout of hysterical laughter, but she quelled it with the sobering thought that she might have cost Kesa her most famous client. Another crime to put on her list.

She tapped up Kesa's email and wrote, "I will never tell another soul about what I saw. It was an accident. If I brag about it that makes me a pervert. I have never aspired to be a pervert and I'm not starting now." She tapped Send, then groaned. That had sounded really stupid, and besides, there was more she'd meant to say.

Her second email said, "I'm not trying to be funny. I'm really very sorry. I hope that your client forgives me and doesn't hold my stupidity against you. The door didn't seem to be locked, just a little stiff." She clicked Send and then realized that her email program had helpfully added to the message a list of locksmiths in the area.

She said a really bad word, could hear Paz in her head shouting, "Language!" and gave up punching out words and fighting autocorrect on her tiny screen. She pressed the microphone button so she could dictate the message. "I'm incredibly sorry. Please can't we have a beer and talk? I promise sex is off the table, not going to happen even if you begged me. Okay I'm lying, I'd be your sex poodle any time you made that request."

She laughed at herself and clicked the microphone off. She deleted the entire draft and started over. "I hate my phone right now. Please let me say I'm sorry in person. I want to say so many other things. I hope you'll let me. I'm going to get a drink at The Grog and Game. I'll be there for at least an hour. Maybe more. No motels. Just talk."

Sent.

When she realized the phone had added a helpful map to the bar with nearby motels pinned she nearly threw it out the window.

CHAPTER THIRTY-SIX

Jennifer Lamont was gone and absolutely pleased with the dress, which was all good. The incident with Shannon was all bad. Kesa felt pummeled and it didn't help that she was exhausted in every fiber of her body.

She found that lying prone on the floor cooled her back and helped get it into alignment again. She nearly fell asleep, but the quiet *ping* of her phone persisted and she made herself sit up.

By the time she got to Shannon's second email she was caught between amusement and annoyance. She did need a locksmith, but she was perfectly capable of finding one on her own. The third email made her shake her head. Shannon was offering a drink when all Kesa wanted to do was sleep? She'd sent a map with motels marked on it? What was Shannon thinking? Kesa was only going to a motel if it involved sleeping and breakfast in bed followed by a nap.

She gazed up at Lamont's dress, thinking of the hours of labor ahead of her. That should be her focus, as well as the other projects she had deadlines for.

Looking back at her phone, she couldn't deny the pull. Shannon had reached out. She'd said she was sorry earlier. Sorry about what exactly, Kesa didn't know. But it mattered. If she blew this chance, would there ever be another? Would it hurt more to listen than to give up for good? Maybe, finally, Shannon's actions would make some sense.

It was hard to get to her feet. The most important thing to do was to text the building manager about the lock. That done, she bolted the window and fiddled with the door lock until the knob finally latched. After pulling the door closed she tested it and it didn't move.

The car was pointed toward The Grog and Game before she realized she'd made up her mind. All the stoplights were green and there was very little traffic. That could be an omen a la *L.A. Story*, she thought. As she turned into the parking lot she could see that there were plenty of spaces open. It was not an omen, she told herself. Monday nights were bound to be slow.

I will not believe that the universe is doing something magic again. Look where it got us the first time.

The quirky rhythm of "When I'm Sixty-Four" greeted her as she went inside. She didn't look for Shannon at first. Instead she took the bartender's advice about a cream ale and enjoyed a hearty swallow of the cold, sweet brew before looking around. The game tables were half empty, but nearby there was a rousing conflict involving dice, cards, and declarations of "I drink and I know things!" with unison callbacks of "It's what I do!" She hid a smile in her beer when one guy leaped to his feet and shouted, "I am the Mother of Dragons!"

Feeling slightly more relaxed than when she'd walked in the door, she decided since Shannon was not in sight, it meant she was upstairs. Promise yourself, she bargained, not to take one look at her and forget what happened four years ago. If she's sorry, she needs to be *damned* sorry.

Of course Shannon was at the same table they'd occupied back then. Kesa drank in the outline of her profile as she fought the familiar mixing of searing memories from the past and all the present uncertainties. The pilsner glass in front of Shannon was nearly empty and she was checking her watch.

Two other tables were occupied, but otherwise they had the space to themselves. Kesa had taken only a step or two when Shannon caught sight of her. She shot to her feet with a nervous smile. "I wasn't sure."

"Neither was I." She sat down at the small table and watched Shannon retake her seat.

Shannon's gaze hadn't left her face. "Did it—how was your client? After I left? I'm really very sorry."

"The lock is broken. She understood it was an accident." She had another sip of the ale and told herself to relax. "Thanks for the list of locksmiths."

Shannon groaned. "The phone did that. It's like having some unctuous concierge always trying to help when really, you just want it to go away. The map—same thing. I meant what I said."

Kesa lifted an eyebrow because it was a bit satisfying to see Shannon squirm.

"Anyway, I'm glad Jen—the client was okay. That's a relief." Shannon picked up her empty glass, frowned at it, and set it down again. "I'm really hungry. I skipped dinner. How about you?"

"I think I had lunch. I'm not sure."

"I smell something chickeny and fried. Why don't I get us some? I want another beer too."

Food couldn't hurt. If she drank all of the beer on her empty stomach she'd be unfit to drive for a while, not to mention the possibility of making really bad decisions involving Shannon and the motel map. "Okay."

She watched Shannon walk away, remembering the strength in her legs and the power in her hands. With a helpless groan she folded her arms on the table and rested her head on them. Shannon's open, easy smile was painted on the back of her eyelids.

A hand on her shoulder shook her gently awake.

She rubbed her eyes. "I can't believe I did that."

"I didn't want to wake you, but some of the food's here."

Please let me not have drooled all over the table. She swiped at it with her napkin just in case. "I've had a really, really long weekend."

"Josie told me."

"Oh lord, don't tell me they eloped."

"No—no. Eat something. Paz had really good news so we celebrated."

Kesa dug into the chicken fingers as Shannon explained about the internship and how it put him at the front of the line for sponsorship of his graduate degree and perhaps a post-degree job.

Another server with a tray of food paused next to their table. He lifted a huge order of golden brown onion rings but froze as Shannon waved a hand.

"Those can't be for us," Shannon corrected before he could set the plate down. "She can't eat them. We're the sweet potato tater tots."

Kesa was touched that Shannon remembered about the onion rings, but it was also unsettling. Why would she have remembered something so trivial about a woman she didn't intend to ever see again? "Thanks. Tater tots—childhood in a crunchy cylinder of goodness."

"That's what I was thinking. And hey, vegetable."

"Sure. That color orange occurs in nature."

"Spoilsport."

They ate in silence for a few minutes and Kesa felt a little bit of life creep back into her bones. "So we're finally having a casual dinner. I'm sorry I was—that I said no before. We have to get used to seeing each other."

"Yes." Shannon wiped her fingers on her napkin before having a hearty swallow of her beer. She started to say something, then covered her mouth to delicately burp. "Excuse me."

"The joy of beer."

Shannon tucked her hair behind her ear and Kesa had to actively push away the memory of her lips on the soft, tender skin of Shannon's neck. "Anyway, I understand why you pushed me away. Yes, we have to get used to seeing each other, but it was a cover excuse I hoped you'd accept. I wanted to see you again and hoped the past would just...just fade out."

Kesa discovered it was impossible to summon a serious frown while licking the ketchup off a tater tot. Well played, Shannon, well played. "It doesn't work that way, does it? We would go fifty years without ever talking about that crappy thing you did?"

Shannon spread her hands helplessly. "I'm not excusing it. But I should tell you the context. If you want to hear it."

The vulnerability in Shannon's eyes made up her mind. It was an unexpected, new moment of intimacy, a kind they'd not shared before. "I'll listen."

Shannon took a deep breath. "I grew up in a very, very quiet house. My aunt was in her sixties when I was a teenager. She had been disappointed in life and she made sure I knew that disappointment was all there would ever be for me too. She was a pessimist on steroids, nothing but doom and gloom. She kept the curtains closed all the time. Then 9-11 broke her for good. She wouldn't listen to the news. She read the same three books over and over. Only one thing I ever did truly pleased her, and that was working for the Marshals. I could stop another 9-11 from happening. No pressure there."

Kesa let Shannon be silent for a moment, even though she didn't understand where Shannon was going with it.

After absentmindedly eating another tater tot, Shannon seemed to find her way out of memories. "My mother was an addict. I told you that, I think." At Kesa's nod she went on, "My aunt told me my mother was given to wild dreams and outrageous ideas, and they killed her. I know almost nothing else about her except what's in a string of arrest records for petty theft, possession, prostitution. Intellectually I knew that addiction is what killed her, but emotionally? I was afraid of turning into her. So I believed my aunt when she said things like 'Keep your head down or someone will cut it off.' That was her philosophy, and I heard it from the time I was a baby."

"That's awful," Kesa exclaimed.

"Especially since it sank in. My mother was proof that my aunt's way was better. I didn't realize until after she was gone that she was suffering a kind of mental illness and that it had affected me too. I had kept my dreams small, achievable, unremarkable. After she died that frame of mind started to change. Like, I decided to push for a higher security clearance because I wasn't going to be afraid of bad guys I couldn't see or that the powers-that-be would hold me back because I was gay." A smile softened her intensity. "And Paz—I've only just realized how much he brought into my life, bit by bit. That you don't always have to test the water before you jump in. And—and I met an amazing woman in a bar and invited her to spend the night."

"I never thought that was something you did all the time. But I didn't realize that I was..."

"Unique," Shannon supplied. "Nothing like you had ever happened to me before."

The shifting image of Shannon in her mind was unnerving. To realize that for all her strength and assurance—especially in bed—she'd been hiding an almost crippling fear and insecurity. It unfortunately sounded far too familiar. The demons of the parents were powerful long after they gone, Kesa thought. "You'd have told me this eventually."

"If we'd had time, but I made sure we didn't. I crawled into a hole and shut out the light you brought. Head down. I might have come back up for air, but then the thing with Paz—we were in Portland and I was so very embarrassed."

Kesa took a deep breath. "So that's the context? I scared you."

"Big time." Shannon was blinking back tears even though she was also smiling. "Have you ever held a hot slice of pizza in one hand and an ice-cold soda in the other? And there's no way to even that out—one hand burning and the other going numb?"

"I hope to god I was the pizza."

Shannon sniffed as she chuckled. "Yeah, you were the pizza. I threw away the heat and kept the ice. I didn't know how else to feel safe."

"So when I left on Sunday and I thought we were cool, we weren't. You were really freaked out because I said that I loved you."

"Not quite." Shannon sipped nervously from her beer and took a shaky breath. "You said 'I love you' and it sounded utterly, completely batshit crazy to me."

It hurt to hear her own fears said aloud. It *had* been a positively insane thing to say. If she'd kept it to herself they would have seen each other again, very likely. "I can understand that, but you couldn't even text me and say 'it's been fun' or something like that?"

"I didn't want to do that."

"So you did nothing." Kesa rolled her shoulders to shake off some tension. "Nothing at all."

Shannon had another nervous sip of beer. "By day I'm a crime-fighting data superhero. By night I'm a lovelorn loser who can't find a way to say 'I love you.' I was going to say it. Back then."

"Wait. What?" She couldn't possibly have heard that right. "You were going to say it back to me?"

"No, I had wanted to say it before you did. I was undone by you. That afternoon was…"

"Magic," Kesa said softly.

"Magic. You were looking at me like everything that could be beautiful to you was all in me. I opened my mouth to say it and you said it first."

"I don't understand, then. Why—"

"It sounded absolutely batshit crazy. Utterly daft. I mean, there was no way you could fall for me in two days. I realized if I said it to you then you'd know I was insane and you'd run for the hills."

Kesa spread her hands in disbelief. "That doesn't make any sense."

The stony cop face was back as Shannon snapped, "I'm well aware of that." She held up a hand. "I'm sorry. I wasn't afraid of your crazy, I was afraid of *mine*. What I felt completely upended my entire life to that moment. All of it. I'm not impulsive. I don't jump out of planes."

"Neither do I. But I don't make things up. I don't lie about how I feel." She lowered her gaze because there was too much truth in her eyes. "Why couldn't we have been batshit crazy together?"

"I thought about it. I bought this."

Shannon had set a small box on the table between them. Kesa recoiled as if it were radioactive. "What is that?"

"It's a ring. I bought a ring. Because I was batshit crazy in love, even though I knew it was impossible. And at the time I couldn't think of anything more powerful to shut off all the fear. It worked—for an hour. Then instead of magic it felt like The One Ring…"

Kesa stabbed a finger at it. "Put that away! You did not want to get married. That's crazy."

Shannon spread her hands in a gesture of acceptance. "See?"

Kesa opened and closed her mouth. A sip of beer helped her gather her wits as all the things she'd said to Josie floated back to her. Oh the irony. Only funny when it happens to other people. "I knew there had to be a reason."

"It's not a very good one for all the pain I know it caused you. And for what we lost. What might have been."

Where do we go from here? Kesa wondered. "Traveling down roads not taken—I don't have time for that. What I do know is that what you *almost* did and *nearly* said doesn't change what happened. You're not making some grand gesture with a ring from Mordor and suddenly bygones are bygones. I cried for a month."

"I know. That was completely unjust of me, to punish you because I was afraid of the truth. That I'd fallen in love with a girl I'd just met. Because she was stunning and powerful and driven and wasn't afraid to have dreams."

Shannon's eyes shimmered with tears and they were just like a sad puppy dog's—stop that, Kesa warned herself. "So you didn't return my texts or calls not because I'd freaked you out, but because you were in love with me too?"

"I know that's messed up." She forestalled Kesa's agreement with a gesture. "I was trying to have Schrödinger's relationship. Together because I never broke it off but not together because, well…"

"Because you were a loser?"

Shannon gave a mock philosophical nod. "We'll go with that."

"So we run into each other again and you can't say you're sorry at least? And don't give me any of that 'love means never having to say you're sorry' nonsense."

Shannon held up a warning finger. "I did try. I was going to that second time at the coffee shop, but you were not happy to see me."

Annoyed, Kesa asked, "Can you blame me? It seemed like all you wanted to do was repeat the past. It was already too late."

"The past was a huge mistake. My mistake."

Kesa suddenly couldn't breathe. Did Shannon mean the sex and the love? "What mistake?"

Shannon reached across the table to grasp Kesa's hands. "I didn't grab onto you like this and hold on. I didn't believe in the impossible thing right in front of my eyes."

Kesa was losing what hold she had left on her heart as the warmth of Shannon's hands unraveled her. "I cried for a month and hated you for the rest of a year. What do you want from me, Shannon? You're moving to Seattle and—"

"I'm not going anywhere. Paz misunderstood." Her voice soft and low, she said, "If there is any chance we can start over I will stay right here forever."

Chin quivering, Kesa said, "You don't understand how many dreams I've had that got taken away. Loving you was one of them. I can't let that go over a beer. Because of some nice words."

Shannon blinked rapidly. "I know I hurt you, hurt you a lot. I hurt myself but that doesn't make it better. This will take time. That's all I'm asking for right now. A chance."

"Every day I'm afraid some random thing will ruin everything I tried to build up." She found a hint of a smile. "And now I realize I sound like your aunt."

"Oh, you really don't. You didn't let being afraid stop you from living. You took a chance on love. You've also taken chances on yourself."

Wasn't it always a choice in a reboot whether to reference the past or ignore it completely? Kesa felt as if her life was holding its breath, waiting for her to choose.

Shannon was saying, "It's hard to trust the world to ever be fair. I believe that it can be, but we have to help. And when it mattered I didn't help us. I've been letting life run me instead of the other way around." She swallowed several times before adding, "If it really is too late, I understand."

"You have to hold on tight." Kesa raised Shannon's hands to her face. Well, nearly. Their elbows were in their plates.

Shannon moved first, sliding out of her chair and pulling Kesa to her feet as well. They folded each other close and Kesa breathed in the deeply remembered scent of Shannon's skin. "You touch me and the world fades away."

"Then the right thing to do is to never let go."

She laughed into Shannon's shirt. "Next you'll be saying that you're just a girl, standing in front of a girl—"

Shannon's shoulders shook as she chuckled. "You had me at hello."

"Stop that." The warmth of Shannon's body was threatening to melt her on the spot. She wasn't ready to laugh off the past—it was too real. "I can't pretend it didn't happen."

"I don't expect you to." Her arms tightened around Kesa for a moment. "Neither can I. If I don't forget it, I won't repeat it. At least I think that's how it's supposed to work."

So, Kesa thought, their reboot would have all the messy baggage, but at least they both owned it now.

George Harrison's "Something" wafted out of the sound system like it had four years ago and they swayed in each other's arms.

"I'm going to fall asleep on my feet," Kesa admitted. "And the other half of my brain has a bullhorn out and is chanting 'motel, motel, motel.'"

Shannon brushed Kesa's hair back and cupped her face. "I would really, really like to sleep with you. I mean sleep. Though I've fantasized plenty about other things, holding you close and just breathing is high on the list."

"Right now I can't think of anything more perfect." She gazed up into Shannon's face. "We can take this slow, can't we?"

"We need time, so I think slow is the only way forward."

"Yes. That's wise." She tucked herself back into Shannon's arms. Stress rolled off her shoulders in a tidal wave of release. This was home, though a part of her still didn't want to trust the feeling. They would be wise. Take it slow. "Shannon?"

"Mm-hmm?"

"I really do want to sleep with you."

"I like this plan."

Sometimes, being cautious and wise was stupid. "And I really want you to put me to sleep."

Shannon stiffened against her and Kesa could suddenly hear the pounding of her heart.

In a shaky voice, Shannon said, "It would be my pleasure."

Neither of them made a move to stop the slow swaying until the song ended. When Shannon let her go Kesa realized her knees were weak with fatigue and desire. "It's not going to take long."

"I don't care." Shannon pulled her close for a breathless, warm kiss that left Kesa faint. "I do have one question. How are we going to tell the kids?"

CHAPTER THIRTY-SEVEN

"You guys are dating? But you just met!" Josie put her hands on her hips, milking the moment for all it was worth. "How can you be so irresponsible?"

Paz wasn't above gloating either, to Shannon's dismay. He wagged his finger at them both. "Are you safe? I mean—kids. That would be bad."

"Love at first sight never lasts."

"It'll be over as fast as it began—"

Josie elbowed Paz. "And to think we set them up."

"Worked like a charm." They shared a smug fist bump.

"Enough," Shannon said, one hand upraised. "Before you break your arms patting yourselves on the back, we'd met before."

Paz's eyebrows shot up. "You didn't act like you had."

"Oh." Josie's voice was thick with suggestive intent. "You had *met* before."

Kesa was staring at the floor. "I'm taking the Fifth."

Josie gave a little laugh. "We'll talk about this later, missy."

Shannon didn't know if it was better for them to think they'd had a no-strings one-night stand or to know the truth. She and Kesa hadn't been able to agree on how much to share. Winging it wasn't really working out either. "Meeting up again has made us realize that we have feelings, and yes, I get the irony." Now to throw them a distraction. "We've come up with a plan."

"For the summer," Kesa chimed in. "Then we'll reevaluate. The apartment is easier for Paz's commute to his internship. If I add Josie's name to the lease it stays rent-controlled even if I'm not living there—as long as she is. Which is affordable for you guys for now. But you have to pay the rent or we'll lose the rent cap."

"And that would make you very, very unhappy, am I right?" Josie had taken a seat at the table, and everyone followed suit.

"Oh, you are so right," Kesa said.

"I have ice cream," Shannon announced. It seemed a good time for it.

"Salted caramel gelato?"

Josie swatted Paz. "You are so easy."

"We're working things out, and I get ice cream. Tell me how this is bad?"

Shannon paused in the act of getting down bowls. "Want some, Josie?"

"Yes, of course. I'm not a fool," and she laughed as Paz tickled her.

The indulgent smile on Kesa's face momentarily took Shannon's breath away. Relaxed and full of hope, the curve of her lips was beguiling and oh-so-kissable. Kisses had been in short supply, though. Kesa was loaded with work and there was no end in sight.

She scooped out gelato and enjoyed a playback of the motel they'd gone to after The Grog and Game. She didn't remember a thing about the place except the bed. Kesa had fallen asleep very easily and Shannon had joined her. They'd overslept, though. Their shared shower had had its moments, but it hadn't been entirely satisfying.

Neither of them had liked the week apart that followed. An hour stolen for dinner together and hungry kisses in the car was simply not going to do. Other than hiding their chagrin, secrecy had no purpose. Kesa had been the one to suggest their proposal of musical house chairs.

"And then I would move into the house with Shannon," she was saying. "No foot in each place. Like we mean it to be forever." Her gaze met Shannon's. "Because we hope that it will be."

"Moving in so fast?" Josie's tone grew even more teasing. "I've heard that about lesbians."

Kesa glowered at her. "Shut it."

"This is a great plan," Paz said after he accepted the bowl of ice cream with thanks. "We could turn Kesa's bedroom into a study room."

"So one of us could game without disturbing the other." Josie gave an excited wiggle.

"I wouldn't want you in another room all the time, *cariña* Jo-Jo."

"Well, that didn't take much persuading," Shannon whispered to Kesa as the conversation got predictably and still adorably goopy.

Kesa offered her a spoonful of gelato from her own bowl. "A token of my affection."

"You must really love me." She slowly and deliberately licked the ice cream off Kesa's spoon and was rewarded by a flare of desire in Kesa's eyes. "I suppose now you want some of mine?"

A low half-growl of agreement sent tingles down Shannon's spine.

"And we'll get married in the fall," Josie exclaimed.

Kesa's head came up. "Say what what, huh?"

"Married. We still want to get married."

"No," Kesa said before she could stop herself.

Josie went rigid with ire. "Why?"

"Because I said so."

Josie was so outraged she was momentarily silenced.

Paz, however, sucked in a surprised breath and belly laughed. "You are hilarious."

Kesa sighed. "At least someone gets my sense of humor."

"I didn't know you had one," Josie muttered.

They stuck their tongues out at each other because some things would never change.

They discussed the logistics of moving and picked the following Saturday. "I still have to pass scrutiny of the Mahjong gang," Shannon said. "It could not go my way."

"This is true." Kesa nodded sagely. "They're a tough bunch."

Shannon collected the empty bowls and put them in the sink. After she'd rinsed her hands, she returned to the table with her wallet. "And now I'm going to give you twenty bucks to go the movies."

Josie threw back her head and howled while Paz, ever the bargainer, said, "Twenty bucks won't get us both into a movie. It's prime time right now."

"Then it's twenty bucks to leave, and you can do whatever you want with it."

"Fine. C'mon, *cariña* Jo-Jo, let's go to your place. I mean," he corrected with a huge smile. "I mean *our* place."

"That was a subtle bribe," Kesa said as the door closed behind them. She had moved to look out the kitchen window into the side yard. "I like the house. I mean, I can probably live anywhere with you, but this is full of sunshine. And it's not too big."

"Bungalow-sized, the realtor said. Would you like to sit outside for a while? The backyard is small, but the neighbor's jacaranda gives afternoon shade."

"Maybe later." She gave Shannon a smoldering look through her lashes. "Show me the rest of the house first."

The trembling in the pit of her stomach was not helped by lizard brain shouting in her ear, "Start with the bedroom!"

"This is the pantry," she said, opening the door. "And over here is the door to the garage. Here is the coffeemaker."

"Idiot," Kesa said fondly, slipping her hand into Shannon's.

"Eejit," Shannon corrected. "It's pretty much the only Irish I know."

"Would you like sometime to go to Ireland?"

"Who doesn't? Do you want to go to the Philippines?"

"Someday, yes. I don't know if there are Sapiros there who'd be happy to see me, but I have catching up to do. If I had enough money and she were well enough, I'd take Auntie Ivy."

"Oh," Shannon said in a small voice.

"And you, silly."

She beamed at her. "I was worried there for a moment. If we saved up and you make lots more dresses, it could all happen."

Kesa tugged on Shannon's hand. "The rest of the house?"

"Do you mean the bedroom?"

Kesa began unbuttoning her blouse. "What gives you that idea?"

"You're ruining my fun," Shannon said. "I like undressing you."

"Then what are you waiting for?"

"An invitation."

Kesa stepped very close but didn't touch her. "I want to be naked and in your arms." Her blue eyes flashed with intent. "How's that?"

"Perfect." The silk of Kesa's blouse was warm against her fingers as she finished unbuttoning it. "I love your skin. More than I love gelato."

"I should hope so." Kesa closed her eyes with a pleased moan as Shannon's fingers traced along her ribs. "How do you do that to me so quickly?"

"Trade secret," Shannon murmured. A sharp pulse pounded in her ears at the thought of kissing her way along Kesa's spine.

"Then don't tell me." Kesa brushed a finger over Shannon's lips, her eyes cloudy with desire. "I believe it's magic."

"It is. Because of you."

Shannon felt Kesa's laughter through her fingertips. "We're as besotted as Josie and Paz."

She slid her arms all the way around and lifted Kesa off her feet with a whoop. "It's impossible, isn't it?"

"Impossible," Kesa echoed and then her lips were on Shannon's, firm and warm as she wrapped her legs around Shannon's hips. "Bedroom. Now."

The edge of command thrilled her. They were on the bed, though Shannon didn't know how. Kisses blended with laughter as their arms tangled trying to twist out of their clothes. Kesa had a head start and her bare breasts against Shannon's stomach sent a molten wave of pleasure bone deep.

She arched against the lean muscle of Kesa's thigh and felt Kesa's hand already there. Urgency took over and she opened her legs with a breathless hiss of yes.

Kesa went inside her with a long groan of need. "I can feel how much you want this."

She tried to say yes again, but there were no words in her for a long while after that. Kesa's fingers were strong and sensitive, and for a while Shannon tried to push back, but she was dissolving into the heat of Kesa's touch. When Kesa's tongue glided alongside her fingers and found every soft place that yearned for her, Shannon let go of her tears while one hand wound in Kesa's hair. She was flying so high, jumping out of a plane, and there was no parachute, only trust that Kesa would not let her fall.

Not falling, rising. Rising to her touch, again. Again. Hold on tight, she thought. Hold on. She felt Kesa shift positions and then the scent and taste of her was shared in a brief, almost bruising kiss.

Kesa's other hand was behind her neck now as they strained against each other. The sapphire eyes were looking all the way into Shannon's heart, reading every reaction, knowing every thought. Kesa's fingers went deeper, gently, then harder.

Finally she found the words she'd held back and they burst out in a gasp as she reached the edge of abandon. "I love you," ragged, desperate.

"Darling," she thought Kesa said, "I love you too."

She came back to herself when she finally caught her breath. Kesa was snuggled against her side, head resting on Shannon's shoulder. "You haven't left me any strength."

"I'm sure you'll get some back." She scooted up onto one elbow to look into Shannon's eyes. "Thank you."

"It's the other way around, isn't it?"

"You make me feel strong." A fingertip lazily caressed one of Shannon's nipples and she smiled wickedly when Shannon gasped. "And powerful."

Two could play that game. She slid her knee between Kesa's leg and flipped her onto her back. "Maybe a little weak as well?"

"More than a little." That look was there again in Kesa's eyes as she gazed up at Shannon, as if Shannon was the future. "You make surrender so easy. I meant what I said about wanting this to be forever. Does that scare you?"

"No," Shannon said honestly. "If it's impossible or crazy, then let's be that together."

CHAPTER THIRTY-EIGHT

"I wanted you all to meet her, and I wanted her to know where I go every Wednesday." Kesa made shy introductions. "This is Marisol. And Cami. And Auntie Ivy."

Shannon shook hands all around and cocked her head at Cami for a minute, with a look Kesa was learning meant she'd connected two-and-two. She'd have to ask later.

"I don't know what that is cooking, but it smells delicious."

"You will come with me." Auntie Ivy hooked her arm with Shannon's. "I'll explain what everything is."

"I like her," Marisol whispered. "She's very tall and handsome."

Kesa felt her face burn and the hot flush spread to her ears when Auntie Ivy turned back to say, "She's very strong," as she gave Shannon's arm a squeeze.

"Goodness, *lola*," Cami scolded. "Are you going to check her teeth?"

"I already did. She's got a nice smile."

Kesa made a helpless gesture at Shannon.

Shannon gave her a wicked glance and said to Auntie Ivy, "Tell me all about Kesa."

"She's a good girl. A hard worker. Not very good at Mahjong, but we like her."

Kesa couldn't hear any more, especially when Cami nudged her and said, "I knew you two were on a date when I saw you at Nom Nom Pocha."

"It really wasn't. I mean, if it was, neither of us knows what dating is."

"Do you know now?" Marisol tipped the box of tiles onto the table.

"We're definitely getting better at it."

Cami rolled her eyes. "Stop talking about sex."

"We weren't," Kesa protested.

"But we could," Marisol teased.

Cami would have snarked back, but the sight of Shannon emerging from the kitchen with a laden plate sent her dashing to get her own.

"Want to share?" Shannon lifted the plate toward her with a suggestive waggle of her eyebrows.

"Absolutely not. Are you kidding? Pinakbet is one of my favorite things. What you don't want I'll eat." She pulled another chair up to the card table next to her usual place. "Sit over here. We can squeeze in together."

"I'll see if I can pick up how to play this game."

Auntie Ivy joined them and gave Shannon a speculative look. "Do you want to learn?"

"I'd love to. If you should ever need a fourth, it could be handy."

"Marisol," Auntie Ivy called. "She wants to learn."

Marisol emerged from the kitchen, plate in hand. "Does she now?"

"You're in for it, fresh meat." Talking out of the side of her mouth like a gangster, Kesa asked, "Did you bring cash, folding green stuff, some do-re-mi?"

Shannon looked alarmed. "Um, no."

"Well, these sharks don't give credit. I'll stake you, but you'll have to owe me."

"Okay. Sure." Slyly she added, "I'll pay interest."

Kesa giggled. "We play for pennies, but I'm going to charge you a thousand percent. You'll have to work it off."

"Gross." Cami slid into her seat across from Kesa. "You *are* talking about sex."

"Okay, we were. We'll stop." Kesa sighed happily as she savored her first bite of lumpia slathered with Auntie Ivy's tamarind-orange marmalade.

Watching her, Shannon followed suit and made a fervent, appreciative noise. "That is delicious. And I've never had eggplant in a stew before."

"It'll be too hot next week to make it. We'll have chicken adobo."

Cami wiggled happily. "I like summer."

Marisol began flipping tiles face down and they all followed suit. In a matter of seconds the four walls were built.

"That was impressive," Shannon said.

"Four women playing Mahjong can fix the world." Auntie Ivy tipped her head toward Marisol. "Your turn to be East."

It took Marisol only a moment to discard an eight-bamboo.

"Chow." Kesa picked up the discard and laid down her run of three. She discarded a four-dot and watched Auntie Ivy draw from her wall. Cami didn't have a play and stuck her tongue out when Marisol played a pong of nines with Cami's discard. The pace of play picked up and Kesa quickly had to decide if her pair would be winds or dragons. She knew Cami was hoarding dragons, so she chose to discard the North Wind.

Auntie Ivy pounced on it and called Mahjong.

"Damn," Kesa muttered.

"You lost, right?" Shannon asked.

"I usually do. They're sharks, I tell you."

"I completely missed the strategy of that. It was like you were all talking to each other in silence."

Marisol got up to take her plate to the kitchen. "It was a good hand."

"I needed that eight-bamboo you snapped up." Cami scraped the last of her pinakbet off her plate.

"Little good it did me. I finally had to choose between winds and dragons."

"She chose poorly," Auntie Ivy said cheerily. "And that's how I got Mahjong."

Shannon gave Auntie Ivy a narrow gaze. "I'm starting to see the fins."

"Wait until the shark teeth come out." Kesa pointed at herself. "Voice of experience. It's not pretty."

Auntie Ivy pulled all the tiles toward her to begin dealing the next hand. "Let's play a hand with our tiles showing, no scoring, and go slow so Shannon can follow."

Kesa enjoyed Shannon's warmth against her as she leaned in to look at the tiles and ask about the rules. By the third hand Shannon had the basic principles. All the while she answered a barrage of not-so-subtle questions with good grace. Yes, she knew a lot of secrets she couldn't talk about, not even to Kesa. Yes, she had grown up in LA. No, she had never arrested anyone. Yes, she was vested in the Federal Employees pension plan.

They took a break to have generous helpings of the scrumptious mango float Marisol had made. Though it was a little sweeter than Kesa generally liked, there was nothing better than the crunch of the graham cracker and all that whipped cream and slices of mango in every bite.

"I remember way, way back this was something my mother made for us," Kesa said. "What do you think?"

"It's simple and really good."

Kesa glanced sidelong toward the other three women who were chatting over their plates. "And? What do you think?"

"When you said they were like your family, I get that now. They care about you a lot." Shannon juggled her plate as she pulled her phone out of her pocket.

"They like you. I can tell." Kesa didn't know what to make of the odd expression that crept over Shannon's face. She finally asked, "What is it?"

In answer Shannon held the phone out so Kesa could see an email. "Please see attachment?"

Shannon tapped and the PDF opened. It was a letter from Integrity Investigations in Seattle. Her heart gave a painful thump as she took in the first sentence. "A job offer? I thought you weren't—"

"I'm not. I wasn't—I mean, I got a letter last week with an opening in Seattle and I told them I wouldn't relocate. I thought that was that. Your work is here, so I'm here too."

Auntie Ivy and Marisol sensed that it was a good time to take more dishes to the kitchen. Cami watched their exchange as if it were a tennis match.

Kesa asked, "Why didn't you tell me?"

"I didn't want you to worry." Shannon gulped. "Which is what you're doing now. Okay, I see the error of my ways. I'm still getting used to not being secretive."

Kesa made a mental note to bring that up when they didn't have an audience. "So what is this about?"

"Scroll down."

The flutter in her heart got worse. "That is a boatload of money. Two boatloads." She felt faint.

"Scroll down some more," Shannon urged her.

The tiny print wavered in her vision. "They're opening an office in Los Angeles this fall?"

"Yes. And it's a boatload of money."

"But you love the Marshals Service."

"I really do."

Kesa's heartbeat steadied. For a moment it had felt as if every happy dream of the last few weeks was about to be snatched away. She would do better at trusting in their future. Shannon wanted to be with her.

Her voice shook slightly as she asked, "So what are you going to do?"

"I think," Shannon said slowly, "I think we should play another hand and talk over what *we're* going to do."

Bella Books, Inc.

Women. Books. Even Better Together.

P.O. Box 10543
Tallahassee, FL 32302

Phone: 800-729-4992
www.bellabooks.com